RESCUED *by the* WOLF

BLOOD MOON BROTHERHOOD

RESCUED *by the* WOLF

BLOOD MOON BROTHERHOOD

USA TODAY BESTSELLING AUTHOR

SASHA A. SUMMERS

This book is a work of fiction. Names, characters, places, and incidents are the product of the author's imagination or are used fictitiously. Any resemblance to actual events, locales, or persons, living or dead, is coincidental.

Entangled Publishing, LLC
644 Shrewsbury Commons Ave
STE 181
Shrewsbury, PA 17361
rights@entangledpublishing.com

Amara is an imprint of Entangled Publishing, LLC.

Edited by Candace Havens
Cover design by Kelly Martin
Cover photography by pio3 and Elena Schweitzer/Shutterstock
deagreez1/DepositPhotos

Manufactured in the United States of America

First Edition August 2017

Previously released on Entangled's Covet imprint

Chapter One

"Fuck," Mal growled as they slammed him against the stone wall, making every shredded muscle and broken bone throb with pain. His wolf paced, wanting to fight—to make Mal fight. But now, in human form, it wouldn't be much of one.

"You look like shit, Mal," Dickhead was laughing.

"Yeah, get some sleep man," Numb Nuts added.

"Can't. Got a date." He spit the blood from his mouth.

"Date?" Dickhead glared.

"You think you're funny?" Numb Nuts asked, sighing.

"Depends. Is it your sister or your mate that's bringing me dinner? Didn't notice it takes her a while?" He smiled at Numb Nuts.

"Shut the fuck up." Numb Nuts slammed his fist into his face.

Mal shook his head, still smiling, ignoring the pop of cartilage. His nose was broken. Again. Not that it mattered. The blade buried in his shoulder was the problem. He needed to dig it out. The silver was already weakening him. But, damn, he couldn't resist taunting the stupid sons of bitches when he had the chance. His wolf needed it, too. They wanted to break him. But they needed to know that was never going to happen.

"Leave him." Dickhead pushed Numb Nuts back.

Mal kept on grinning, knowing that baited the other more than anything. "You wouldn't want to upset the man in charge." Mal nodded, even though the motion radiated pain down his spine until he saw stars.

Numb Nuts was growling, his pupils dilated, his jaw locked. He shook off the hands Dickhead placed on his arm, fastened the thick silver collar around Mal's neck, and stormed out of the cell. Dickhead followed, pulling the cage door shut behind him. "Have fun digging that out," he said.

Mal flipped him off, still grinning.

He waited until the fluorescent lights cut off, glaring at the single bulb in the corner. He'd almost rather it was dark. His wolf could see better in total darkness. And that's why Cyrus and his pack of wannabe badasses kept the light on. Anything to get under his skin, anything to weaken his resolve, or make his loyalty to Finn and his pack waver.

"Fucker," he mumbled, shoving thoughts of Finn and the others aside. He didn't want to be loyal to them, not anymore. They'd left him for dead, left him with the enemy—made every day since a pain-filled torture-fest courtesy of Cyrus's sick-as-fuck wolves. But one of the joys of being a werewolf: no choices. A pack was a pack, and Finn was his Alpha. Even if Mal wanted to rip his throat out and challenge that right.

The faint burn of the silver collar around his neck was nothing compared to the fire in his shoulder. The blade had to come out, now. He probed the wound along the ball of the joint, sucked in a deep breath, gritted his jaw, and slid his forefinger and thumb into the severed muscle. The blade had slid deep before they'd broken it off. Now the jagged edge sliced through his fingertips, making it harder to grip the metal and almost impossible to hold.

It helped to imagine sliding the blade into one of the Others. It didn't matter which. But if he could pick, it'd be their motherfucking Alpha, Cyrus. Not his chest. No way that asshole had a heart. Maybe his neck. Or his eye. His eyes were soulless—evil. They haunted Mal when he was sleeping. His eye would be good.

He dropped the blade on the floor and sagged against the stone wall, swallowing back the bile that choked him.

The stairwell lights flipped on then, bright and relentless after Mal had lived in the gloom so long. He had no idea how long he'd been here, only that he had to get out or he'd lose his mind. Mal braced himself, trying not to react. He wouldn't give them the satisfaction.

There had to be cameras here, somewhere. They'd be watching him. And now that the silver was out, they'd want to do something else to keep him weak. His gaze wandered around the small room. No sign of any wires or camera, just the damn light in the corner. One room, two large cages. He occupied one. The other had housed four different occupants so far, but none had stayed for long. He was the special one. When they killed him, and he knew they all wanted to, it wasn't going to be quick and easy. He'd wish he'd bled out hanging upside down in that damn tree—wish the Others had left him there to burn up. Instead, his pack, his *brothers*, had left him behind. With the enemy.

"Stop kicking," a voice echoed. "Now, dammit."

Mal heard another voice, a woman's voice—garbled and desperate.

He sighed, resting his head. Looks like he had a new roommate. Sucks to be them.

The Big Guy, a wall of a man with a piss-poor attitude and brick punch, appeared. A woman hung under his arm, kicking and flailing and trying her best to scream past the rag shoved in her mouth.

The Big Guy kicked open the stall next to Mal, tossed the woman in, and slammed it shut.

The woman lay there, no doubt stunned from the impact. She was human, he and his wolf could tell that much. A woman that smelled good. Clean.

She tugged the rag from her mouth. "Jerk!"

The Big Guy snorted and headed back up the stairs.

Mal laughed then. Jerk? She had no idea what the hell was about to happen to her. Unlike the other four… Three. One had been a plant—an attempt to stir some sort of inner hero-complex. It had almost worked. He closed his eyes, shutting out everything else. Healing was all the mattered. The silver was out, but the goddamn collar would still slow things down. And he didn't know how much time he had until they came back for him. He had to get his shit together before then.

The lights flipped off, the door shut, and there was silence.

"Hello?" she asked.

He didn't say a thing.

"I saw you, so I know you're there." She sat up, hissing and covering her leg with both hands.

He glanced her way, the waver of her breath and unsteady beat of her heart too real to be a ploy. She was in pain. And scared. And not his problem.

"No chance you're a doctor?" she asked.

He was no doctor. He shut his eyes again, but his wolf… His wolf refused to shut her out. Dammit.

"My leg's bleeding." She tried to move and cried out, the sound echoing off the walls. "Bad."

His wolf paced, wanting him to do something. He ignored the wolf and the girl, his only focus on healing his nose. Then the gouge in his shoulder. The muscles along his side had been pummeled repeatedly, bruising the tissue fibers and crushing the nerve endings. It would be easier if he could change—his wolf form would heal quickly—and come back stronger. But if he could shift, he wouldn't be here, stuck in a cage. It wasn't the cage or the chain holding him, it was the silver. If he could be silver-free, he could get out. His wolf was too strong to be held. And Cyrus knew as much.

"Fine. Okay. I'm bleeding, and I have no idea where I am." Her voice dropped, the words spilling out of her like a stream of consciousness. She slid into the light, her breathing accelerating. She sagged against the bars, sucking air deep into her lungs before lifting her hands off her leg. "This is bad." Panic edged her voice. "Too much blood."

The wolf prodded him until he gave up. His eyes popped open, assessing the woman. The effect she had on his wolf was too potent. Maybe he'd been in the dark too long, away from women and life and soap… But her scent grabbed him and his wolf by the throat and shook his senses awake. It had been a long time since he'd felt something other than fury or pain. Too long. She didn't fit here, didn't belong. The others had an air of futility about them, a loss of fight or hope. But she wasn't broken yet, even if she was bleeding out all over the floor. Even with a bruised face, she was something to look at.

He sniffed, the scent of her blood flooding him. "Your thigh?" he asked.

She jumped, sniffing, pressing her hand over her thigh then hissing. "Y-yes."

A tourniquet. She needed something to stop the bleeding. Soon. "Are you wearing a belt?" he asked.

"What?" She blinked, trying to see him.

He was glad of the shadows then. Naked, chained, and scarred to hell, he'd only upset her more. "A belt?" he repeated.

She shook her head. "No."

His gaze traveled over her. Boots. Jeans. A T-shirt. A cotton hoodie. "You need to stop the bleeding."

She stilled, her gaze meeting his. She nodded slowly. "Okay." But she didn't move. Clearly, she saw enough of him to react. The picture he presented was hardly reassuring. Her breathing grew thready, her heart kicked into overdrive… Which wouldn't help the bleeding problem.

"Now," he snapped, which pissed off his wolf.

She jumped, lifting her hands from the wound. Her palms were wet with blood.

"Lose the shirt," he said. "Tie it tight, above the wound."

She blinked, sitting forward to shrug out of her hoodie. She moved quickly, her gaze returning to him again and again. "Are you…are you okay?" she asked.

He ran a hand over his shaggy head. "I'm fucking great, lady."

She glared at him then, her posture going rigid and her eyes narrowing. She tugged her shirt over her head, seemingly oblivious to her now half-naked state.

Mal, however, was not. Neither was his wolf. He went from disinterested to fully aware of every single damn breath she took and every freaking move she made. Her skin was creamy, the curve of her breasts spilling in abundance over her bra downright breathtaking. What he wouldn't give to lose himself, face between those gorgeous boobs, the rest of him buried deep inside. His wolf agreed, focusing so intently that Mal was unable to see or hear or think about anything but the woman in the cage.

She twisted her T-shirt and wrapped it around her thigh, crying out as she tugged the fabric tight. She sobbed, falling to her side.

The wolf growled, forgetting about the collar that trapped them. Mal felt it, too—the urge to go to her, even if it didn't make one damn bit of sense. But the tourniquet wasn't tight enough. Her blood was still dripping. "Tighter," he barked.

She did as he said, her movements short and jerky.

"Put on your hoodie," he growled. She was pure temptation, even laying there gasping on the floor. He didn't want to think about Cyrus or The Big Guy looking at her. Hell, it was better for himself and his wolf if she covered up. Because right now, even chained to the fucking wall, his wolf was barely under control.

...

Olivia lay still, her eyes pressed shut. Maybe this was all some sort of nightmare. Maybe Chase had put something into her drink. Her brother had done it before—he had a weird sense of humor. But this didn't feel like that. This felt real. And it hurt more than anything had ever hurt.

Still, opening her eyes meant acknowledging where she was.

In a cage. In some basement, tunnel, or underground.

She had no idea where, or what was happening, or why it was happening to her. Only that she was completely alone and scared. No, not scared. Terrified.

She didn't know what to fear more: the guy in the cage beside her her, or what could come through the door next. She glanced at the man, mostly hidden in shadows. The top of his head and face were visible enough. His eyes remained fixed on her, unnerving, unwavering. The bridge of his nose was swollen, and the skin on his cheek was discolored.

"Do you know where we are?" she asked, hating the silence of the room and the screaming in her brain. She had to calm down, had to figure this out…

"No," he answered. "Bleeding's slowed."

She frowned. "How do you know?" There was no possible way he could know that.

The corners of his eyes crinkled. "I know. Stay still."

"Not like I can go anywhere," she muttered, bristling at

his tone. She placed her hand on the floor, preparing to push up.

"Stay still," he repeated. "You move, you'll start bleeding again."

She lay still. "So, you are a doctor?"

"No."

"But I should listen to you?" she asked, her control slipping. "Some guy in a spooky cage with a chip on his shoulder?"

His eyes crinkled again. "Your choice."

She stayed where she was. Her leg thrummed in time with her heart, pain radiating into her hip and back and down her leg to her toes. "My only choice today. Sit up and bleed or lay in the dirt." She swallowed back tears then. She didn't like feeling vulnerable or helpless—but that's exactly what she was. "I have pain relievers in my purse. And a phone. And a Taser."

He didn't say anything.

She didn't care. "But you're right. I don't have my purse." She sighed. "And, yes, I should have used my Taser."

"Wouldn't have made a difference," he said.

She stared at the darkened stairwell. "Maybe. I just froze. I locked up. Seeing Chase like that, blood everywhere. And then, Chase ran off." Her voice broke again. He'd left her. He'd left her, and now she was here, alone and bleeding. Her brother, big and bad and capable of far too many illegal activities, had run away. "He left me," she whispered.

The man groaned, almost a growl, and stood.

Olivia lay perfectly still, very glad there were bars separating them. The man paced, a strange metallic clink echoing every step, his attention returning to her again and again. Now that she could see him, she missed the shadows. He looked wild, like a caged animal. And the scars that covered his body, muscled from head to toe, promised he was dangerous—very dangerous. The look in his eyes, the predatory way he moved, the sheer restless energy that rolled off him, all sent a shiver of anticipation down her spine.

"Are you—" She stared at him, blinking. "Are you chained?"

One brow rose, but he didn't say a word.

He was naked, unarmed, and vulnerable—and chained to a wall? Where *was* she? And what the hell was going on? She curled into herself, wincing at the pull in her leg. The ground beneath her thigh grew hot and wet.

"Will you stay fucking still?" His impatience was obvious, his agitation startling her.

"Fine," she snapped back, pressing her eyes tightly shut.

The lights came on then, and Olivia forgot about everything. She pushed off the floor and pressed herself into the back corner of the cage, as far away from the door as possible. She ignored his muffled string of expletives and tried not to cry as the massive man that drug her here descended the steps. He was holding a tray as if bringing food to caged people in basements was a normal thing.

He opened the cage, set the tray down, and crossed to her. "You're still bleeding?" he asked, tugging her up by one arm.

Olivia swung at him. It was pointless, she knew it, but no one touched her—ever. No matter what.

He slapped her hard, knocking her back against the bars. "Knock that shit off. I was going to stitch you up, but maybe I should let you bleed a little longer."

Olivia saw stars—bright, shiny, white stars whirring in front of her eyes. She gripped the bars to keep from falling over. He was going to stitch up her leg? If he thought she was going to let him—

She was lifted into the air and slammed against the ground, knocking the air from her lungs. She coughed, unable to breathe. The stars were back again. And her leg ached.

He took off the T-shirt and she felt dizzy.

"That's a gusher," he said, tearing her pants. "You humans need to learn you're too breakable to try to fight back."

Humans? She didn't have enough breath to say the word out loud. Not yet.

"I'll get a needle and some thread. Don't move," he growled, his pupils dilating darkly and his mouth pulling down.

Olivia couldn't have moved if she wanted to.

Not when the giant left or the door shut or when the guy in the next cage started talking to her.

"Don't move," he repeated, like she was going to jump up and run. "You're bleeding. A lot. Just stay calm and still."

"O-okay," she managed, still coughing.

"Dammit," he bit back.

The door opened and the giant's heavy footfalls announced his return. She lay there, her lungs still burning, when he bent over her, tying her wrists with a rope. "You move, it'll hurt worse," the giant grumbled. "Hold the light up," he snapped, offering the end of the rope to someone.

Olivia realized they weren't alone. A young woman was with them, her face sharp and hard. She stared down at Olivia with pure contempt. "Why are you sewing her up, Byron?" The girl tied the rope to the cage wall, forcing Olivia's arms taut over her head—stringing her up.

"Cyrus says so."

"Because?" the girl asked.

Byron looked at her. "That's all the reason I need. It's all the reason you should need, you hear me? Hold her ankles so she doesn't move."

The girl nodded then, her expression growing wary. Cold fingers gripped Olivia's ankles and tugged, forcing her leg straight and making her scream.

The girl smiled. "She's so fragile."

Byron grunted, focusing on his work.

Olivia felt the pierce of the needle and swallowed back another cry. She couldn't escape the pain; it was all there was. Poke, the tug of thread, another poke, more thread. Over and over.

By the time Byron stopped, she was a shaking, sweaty, bloody mess. When he tugged the zipper of her hoodie down, she barely reacted. But his inspection was quick and callous. He had no interest in her, unlike the girl peering over his shoulder.

"Not so fragile," the giant said. "She has scars." He pointed as he spoke, yanking her jacket zipper down and rolling her to her side. The rope chafed her wrists, pulling skin.

She bit back a groan, catching sight of the man in the cage next to her. He leaned against the wall, no care in the world. But his eyes were hard, staring at her with something hot and angry.

"No other injuries," Byron said.

"She won't die?" the girl asked.

Byron stood, dropping her hoodie back on top of her. "Guess we'll see. If he keeps her around."

He flipped her over, the ropes popping her back into place—bouncing her leg in the process. Olivia gagged, the food she'd eaten what seemed like a lifetime ago lodging in her throat. They untied her quickly, leaving her where she was and slamming her cell door behind them as they left.

She lay there gasping, the vague sounds of a struggle further disorienting her.

She turned onto her side, groaned, and threw up all over the stone floor. Rolling onto her back took the last energy she had. Her eyes drifted shut, offering a kind of relief. Maybe, just maybe, she'd wake up and this would all be the worst nightmare she'd ever had.

Chapter Two

Mal rolled his shoulder, the socket still tender. While he'd been watching everything in the goddamn woman's cage, Numb Nuts had come into his, shoving the broken blade back into his shoulder—and dislocating his arm for good measure. He was going to kill the motherfucker slowly and enjoy it. His arm was back in, but he didn't have the strength to dig the blade back out. And he was going to have to dig deep for the strength because of all the fucking silver.

He slid down the wall and sat staring at the woman—his wolf's rage and frustration at an all-time high.

She'd been strong, stronger than he'd expected her to be. That was a quality he could respect. His wolf, however, wanted to hunt down the Big One and rip him to shreds. The Big One had a name now. Byron. Byron the fucking butcher. Mal's almost visceral reaction when the ass-hat had tugged the woman's jacket free had shaken him, deeply. For a second he believed he could break his chain, silver or not, if Byron laid a hand on her. His wolf wasn't about to let that happen again.

He tried to relax, to prepare for what he needed to do. But as soon as he closed his eyes, the lights came on.

The girl came down, nervous, opening the woman's cage and grabbing the untouched tray. Mal had been slowly working on her, using every opportunity he got to charm her into sharing little bits of information with him. She liked him, his wolf knew that—enough to sneak him something special to eat now and then.

"Anything left?" He kept his voice soft.

She looked at him, her cheeks flushing. "I'm not supposed to."

He grinned. "It's okay." He stood, then moved to the cage, his hands resting on the bars, palms up. If he could get the tray close enough, he could get the metal fork. If he could get the fork, he could try to free the lock on the collar. And if he could open the damn collar…

He sighed, forcing himself to relax. "How's your day?"

She stepped closer, holding out the tray. "You've seen it." She nodded at the woman on the floor. "All this fuss over a human woman. And her brother."

"Why?" Not that it was any of his business, but he—his wolf—wanted to know.

"I don't know." She shook her head. "Cyrus left hours ago," she whispered. "You'll be left alone for a while." She frowned, glancing at the stairs.

Cyrus was gone? That would make things easier. "Or the other three will make sure I'm not around when Cyrus gets back."

She stared at him in sympathy, stepped forward, offering the tray to him. "Byron's passed out drunk. Cyrus made the others go on an errand. I think they're supposed to bring back her brother." She glanced at the woman. "You can rest."

He took the food, slipping the fork under the slice of bread, and smiled. "Sleep would be nice. And food." He held up the slice of turkey and bread he'd swiped. "Thanks."

"I don't like how they treat you, not that they care what I think." She smiled at him, biting her lower lip. "You should know, not all of us are threatened by your pack, you know? That killing your pack is the answer. Cyrus keeps saying he'll have answers soon, now that he has someone on the inside." She shrugged. "Some of us hope there's a chance for peace. There's room for us to coexist. Maybe even become allies."

Mal paused then. Someone on the inside? With Finn and the pack? He had to stay calm, had to think. Peace? Was she kidding? As long as Cyrus lived, that would be impossible. And killing off a pack's Alpha hardly fostered pack unity. It was more likely to lead to outright war. Since all he cared about was ripping them to shreds, a war sounded fine to him. Not that he was going to argue with her. She'd helped him, even if she didn't know it. He nodded, keeping his opinion to himself.

She smiled again and hurried up the stairs, flipping off the lights and closing the door.

Mal counted to five and got to work. The fork bent and twisted, but the keyhole on the collar was too small. He cussed, focusing on the chain then, sculpting the metal fork until it jimmied the locking mechanism. Slow. Silent—closing his eyes until he nudged the spring pen up and open. Once he'd pulled the bolt from his collar, he rolled his shoulders. He was wearing a silver collar and had a four-inch silver blade in his shoulder, but he wasn't going to let that slow him down. There was no time to get the blade out now. He had to move.

The cage door lock was old. It didn't take much effort to get it open.

He stood staring at the stairs, unable to move because of his wolf. *It* wasn't leaving without the woman. He growled, wishing there was a way to muzzle the damn thing. Now was not the time for the wolf to get territorial. She was just a woman, for fuck's sake, nothing more. He had enough slowing him down without taking her with him.

He wasn't going to do it. But his wolf wouldn't go. Flashes of his own pack leaving him were all the reminder he needed. He yanked open her door, his fury giving him the strength he needed.

He stooped, growling, "Wake up."

She shook her head.

"Now, dammit."

She frowned, her eyes heavy-lidded and swollen. When she saw him, she slammed her eyes shut.

"We're leaving," he said. "Can you walk?"

Her eyes went round, then. "What?"

"Walk?" he repeated, glancing at the door.

She pushed up, taking the hand he offered and letting him pull her to her feet. She swayed, tried to take a step, and crumpled. He caught her.

"Right," he snapped, swinging her over his bad shoulder. "Fuck, shit, dammit." He shifted her to his other side.

"I can walk," she argued, wriggling and twisting on his shoulder.

"No, you can't." He stared around the room, looking for something he could use as a weapon. Anything. "Keep still and be quiet." There was nothing. He scaled the steps, remembering that the fifteenth stair squeaked and avoiding it. The door wasn't locked, making him hesitate. Was the girl setting him up? This woman? It wouldn't be the first time they'd done this. He almost shrugged the woman off his shoulder and left her behind. But his wolf didn't budge, and time was ticking away. There wasn't much he could do about it now. He'd gotten this far, he wasn't about to turn back now.

The door opened on silent hinges. They were in a hallway, and the scent of pizza, beer, and dish soap flooded his nostrils. He glanced both ways, relieved the woman over his shoulder had gone limp. Maybe he was lucky and she'd passed out. At one end of the hall was what looked like a kitchen; the other was the front door. The front door was too obvious, so he headed toward the kitchen. Byron probably wasn't sleeping it off in the kitchen.

He walked as softly as he could, aware that the woman was moving. He squeezed her thigh and she went still.

A quick inspection revealed a dated and tiny kitchen—and a back door. Escape with no hint of trouble? It was too fucking good to be true. His senses sharpened, reaching out, looking for threats.

The girl was humming, washing dishes at the sink. She had the radio playing, softly. As nice as she'd been to him, she wouldn't let him leave—they all feared Cyrus too much. He didn't hesitate. He approached quickly, picking up a coffee cup and bringing it down on the back of the head. She crumpled, but he caught her, laying her on the ground without a sound. He straightened slowly, the silver slowing him down.

He did a quick search of the kitchen. Duct tape, kitchen towels, and a bottle of whiskey went into a mesh shopping bag. He grabbed cash from a purse hanging on a peg on the wall and a small tool box sitting on the floor by the back door. Damn, but his shoulder was on fire, his body racked with shaking. Time was up. With a quick glance down the hall, he slipped out the back door and into the cold, black night.

Trees.

Miles and miles of trees.

No hint of civilization—no scent of concrete or asphalt, no distant engines on a highway or signs of a nearby homestead. Nothing smelled familiar… Just clean, fresh, cold air and nature. He hurried into the tree line, farther into the woods. He didn't know how much longer they'd have before their escape was discovered, but he wanted as many miles between them as possible.

After a few hours of running, he scented pursuit. They were being trailed. Not by werewolves—but wolves, moving quickly. The local wolves might not be as welcoming as the ones on his pack's reserve. They'd find out soon enough. He needed to rest before that happened.

"You're bleeding," the woman's voice was slurred and unsteady.

"So are you," he answered.

"You're naked," she said.

"Enjoy the view." He needed to find cover.

"I grabbed this." She reached around his side.

"A coat?"

"It's cold." Her arm wavered, then dropped. "And…it was all I could reach."

"You're lucky you didn't knock anything off or make noise." His eyes swept the forest, his pace slowing.

"Does that mean, 'No, thanks then'? Or, 'Wow, how considerate. Thank you.'" Her irritation was amusing. "Or even, 'I appreciate the offer.'"

He chuckled.

"You're not cold? It's really cold. I can't feel my fingers or my toes."

He thought she'd been shivering because of her injury. "Adrenaline, I guess." That and the whole werewolf thing.

"Guess I don't have any." She poked his side. "Not trying to be ungrateful for breaking me out, but any chance of a break? My head is going to burst."

He didn't answer. She was hurting. He was hurting. He needed all his strength if the pack tracking them decided not to be friendly. He moved deeper into the woods, shifting her into his arms as he pushed into a patch of thorns and shrubs. She groaned, her head lolling back against his chest and her eyes pressed shut.

"Everything's spinning," she murmured.

He waited for her to open her eyes then set her on her feet, propping her against a tree and taking the coat she'd carried. The coat was massive, probably motherfucking Byron's. He spread it out on the ground then looked at her. "Better?"

She nodded, pressing her hand to her head. "Still dizzy."

His attention swept the trees. The wolves were closing in—he could smell them. "Sit down." He pulled the tool box from the bag. A pair of needle-nose pliers. Good. He looked her way—she leaned against the tree, eyes shut, breathing shallow. "Sit?" he repeated.

"No," she said, not moving. "Okay. In a minute."

He gripped the needle-nose pliers, took a deep breath, and slid the long metal pinchers into the cut on his shoulder. Numb Nuts had done a good job this time. He had to dig, damaging more tissue before he gripped the blade with the pliers.

"Oh. My. God." Her voice was soft. "What are you doing?"

He gritted his teeth and pulled, groaning as the blade slid free. The pliers and knife blade fell onto the coat with a wet splat, his blood scenting the air. He was already feeling better. The healing was slower, thanks to the collar, but he would recover. Which was good because the wolves were here.

• • •

Olivia clung to the tree. If she let go, she'd wind up face-first on the ground. She was dizzy, her leg was on fire, and now this—watching this complete stranger dig in his shoulder with a pair of pliers. Blood poured over his back in thick ribbons, but he didn't pause. She saw him tense, then the clean, quick pull of his arm, and the horrific sight of a jagged blade emerging from the gash. He dropped the tool and deadly looking weapon on the coat, sinking down—shaking.

She hugged the tree tighter, sucking in long slow breaths.

Now was not the time to fall apart. So she didn't know what was going on, or who these people were, or what, exactly, they wanted with her. But the more immediate question was, what was happening? And this guy? He'd rescued her but...why had he been *chained* to his cage? Was he that bad? Or were their captors just perverts?

Should she be freaking out? Because she was, even though she was too weak to run. And even if she could, where would she go? Home no longer seemed like a safe option.

"Come here." It wasn't a request.

She shook her head, then stopped, the world tilting and swaying.

He sighed, stood, and crossed to her. Her hold on the tree tightened—a fact he didn't miss. His brow arched. "We're not alone. I need you with me." He tugged her arms free and swung her up in his arms.

"I can walk." She tried to wriggle free, his recent makeshift surgical procedure vivid in her mind.

"No, you can't," he argued, carrying her to the center of the coat. He set her down, tilting her head back and looking in her eyes. "You're running a fever." He sighed, his gaze sweeping her face. "How do you feel?"

Was he serious? She shook her head.

"Bad?" he asked.

She glanced at his shoulder, blinking. "Worse than I thought." She stared harder. "I thought—I'm delusional." There was a cut on his shoulder, but there was no way the blade she'd seen had been inside it.

A snap in the trees made him spin to stand in front of her.

It wasn't the first time she'd been face-to-face with his butt. Hanging upside down over his shoulder, she'd had nothing else to look at on their trek to freedom. It was impressive. But then, so was the rest of him. His muscles were intimidating, the number of scars on his body assuring her they weren't purely for looks. Her gaze traveled up, taking in the mess that was his back. A scar ran along his side, between his shoulder blades, and below his waist. Maybe he'd had a skin graft? Whatever the reason, the man had been through serious trauma.

Tonight included.

Her head was pounding. Her accelerated pulse thrummed in her ears, so deafening she almost missed the nearby howl of a wolf. His words came back to her then. *We're not alone.* Was it too much to ask for a break? And a nap? And maybe some antibiotics or something? Like a blanket. "When you say we're not alone—you mean *wolves*?" she whispered, terrified once more.

"They're curious," he murmured back, as if it was no big deal.

She peered into the dark that surrounded them, her heart coming to an abrupt halt at the dozens of round eyes staring back at her. She shifted closer to him, petrified. But the slight effort stole her strength. Resting against his leg hadn't been the plan, but he was solid and warm and oddly comforting. Even if he was naked. And wearing a silver collar. This was the most peculiar night of her life.

She shivered. "I don't want to be eaten," she mumbled.

He chuckled. "I'll try to remember that."

Her arm twined around his leg, her vision wavering. "Why aren't you scared?" she asked. She was scared. Of… everything.

"They don't want to hurt us. They want to make sure we won't hurt them." His hand brushed the top of her head.

"No threat here," she murmured. "Promise." She blinked once, then again, so weak she couldn't stay upright. Her arms slipped free, and she fell back on the coat. She stared up at the stars, shivering, the world spinning. Pressing her eyes shut didn't help. Snatches of the last few days flickered. Her brother Chase being beaten to a pulp. Throwing herself between her brother and the giant. The blade cutting through her thigh and slicing up. Her brother leaving her. Where was Chase? Was he safe? "I need to find my brother," she said, opening her eyes.

The man grunted, standing over her—a gorgeous naked sentry. "The one that left you?"

Good point. "He's in danger," she added, unable to tear her gaze from him. She'd never seen a naked man before. Being a virgin these days was a rarity, but her love life was cursed, with a dead boyfriend and a dead fiancé to prove it. It didn't help that her brother was super-protective.

"And you're not?" he asked, glancing down to find her staring at him. His jaw clenched tightly.

"You just said they wouldn't hurt us," she whispered. "Besides, I'm not sure any of this—or the last however long it's been—is real." She reached out, poking his leg before stroking along his muscled calf. His skin quivered beneath her touch…or was she imagining that, too? She'd never been this imaginative before. "You *feel* real. Are you dangerous?" She thought about the chain and collar.

"You have no idea." He sounded dangerous.

She closed her eyes. "I can protect myself. I've been kickboxing for six years so I can kick your butt. Normally."

He snorted. "You're a *pain* in my ass."

"Then why not leave me in the cage? You didn't have to carry me out here." It was so cold.

He made an odd growling in the back of his throat, forcing her eyes open again. He was staring at her, unguarded and slightly terrifying.

"Brought me out here to feed me to the wolves?" she asked.

"Then I would have left you." His words were hard.

She was shivering, her teeth clacking together. She wrapped her arms around herself but couldn't curl up. Moving her leg wasn't an option—it hurt too much. If she had a choice, she'd avoid experiencing more pain tonight.

His gaze left hers, searching the utter darkness that surrounded them. He seemed to ease, somewhat, before looking back at her. "Fucking nightmare," he muttered, laying down at her side.

"I thought so," she agreed. "None of this is happening." It was a relief. None of it was real—but she could enjoy the good parts. She moaned with pure delight as his arms came around her. He pulled her back against the wall of his chest, enveloping her in blissful warmth. She moaned again, snuggling closer. How could his imaginary touch make her feel...better? She didn't know, she didn't care. She wanted more. Her hands covered his arm, pressing his hands against her stomach and holding on to him. She wriggled closer, pressing herself flush against him.

"Stop," he growled, his arms tightening around her.

"You're warm." She looked back at him, his expression mesmerizing. He was fierce and angry and so handsome.

"You're soft." His harsh whisper rolled over her. "And helpless."

"Good thing you're here to protect me," she said, her eyes growing heavy-lidded. In his arms, with the solid beat of his heart lulling her to sleep, she had no care in the world.

He chuckled. "Who's protecting you from me?"

She forced her eyes open, staring at the man more shadow than flesh. "What are you going to do to me?"

He groaned, his eyes shutting. He pressed the hard length of his arousal against the curve of her hips. "Don't tempt me."

"Really?" she asked, curious. She was oddly light-headed. Not dizzy or disoriented—more euphoric. "Even after the whole breaking free, running for hours, and cutting open your shoulder? You have energy for...that? This is the strangest dream."

He leaned over her. "I always have energy for that. You keep wriggling your ass, I'm not going to turn down your offer."

"I'm not offering anything." She frowned. "I'm freezing."

He brushed the hair from her forehead, pressing his palm against her skin. His touch felt cool on her face, so she turned into it. "Shit," the word was a growl. He shifted, the cold air slicing through her in his absence. "Drink this." He pressed a bottle to her lips. "It'll warm you up. Might take the edge off the pain."

She swallowed, the alcohol burning all the way down.

"Again," he said, pressing the bottle to her lips.

She drank deeply, and a hot, heavy warmth filled her. Her brain was so foggy and thick. But his strong arms were back, his touch warming her through and easing the aches and pains crippling her moments ago. The alcohol probably helped, too…

"Try not to move," he rasped.

"'Kay." Her tongue felt thick. She didn't want to move. She was deliciously warm. "Better." She touched his cheek, her fingers tracing his mouth. His hand grabbed her wrist, holding her hand away from him. "It's a dream. Maybe I should offer."

He shook his head. "You need sleep." But she heard the rasp in his voice. Could he want her? It *was* her dream so the odds were in her favor.

No. Not at all. It was the alcohol.

She blinked, wishing there was more moonlight so she could see him. She drew in a deep breath and whispered, "I don't think I'm going to survive this. And I'd really like to have sex, at least once, before I die."

Chapter Three

Mal stared down at the woman in his arms. Running with dead weight wasn't easy. Especially when he had to make sure he wasn't jostling her wound. He didn't need a medical degree to know she was getting worse. Sweat streaked her forehead and made her hoodie damp. And the scent of her blood… Infection raged. His wolf was on edge, worrying over her. Not that he was offering up any advice on how to make this situation suck less. Or that there was a damn thing they could do to help her. If Hollis had been here, he'd have her patched up and on her feet in no time. But Hollis and Finn and the rest of his pack were God knows how far away.

Thinking of Hollis reminded him of what the girl told him. Motherfucking Cyrus. The Alpha of the motherfucking Others had planted someone in Finn's pack? How was that possible? How did Finn not know, not sense, that there was danger? He didn't want to worry about them—they'd left his ass. They could fend for themselves. But there was a part of him—his wolf—that refused to desert them. If they were in danger, he needed to tell them.

"Ice cream," she mumbled, her voice high and petulant. The mumbling was nothing new, but she hadn't mentioned ice cream yet. "It's hot."

He sighed, holding her still, glancing at the snowflakes that had begun to fall. They took shelter under some trees, long enough to pry the collar off. She started thrashing around so he'd had no choice but to pin her down. She tried to pull away, so his grip tightened. All the tossing and turning had stressed her wound, making it ooze—announcing their presence to the whole fucking planet.

"Chase..." Her voice broke. "Where are you?"

"Hush," he said.

Her hands gripped his shoulders. "Please don't leave me."

He frowned. That's exactly what he should do. Leave her. But his wolf wouldn't let that happen. The more worked up she got, the more protective it became. He didn't like the effect she had on his inner beast. Rage. Aggression. Hunt. Kill. These were things he and his wolf could see eye-to-eye on. Worry. Apprehension. Fear—no way in hell. Not over some nameless chick who probably wasn't going to make it another twenty-four hours. His chest grew heavy at the thought.

"Please," she repeated, desperate and fragile.

"It's fine. I—I'm here." He ground out the words. The wolf wanted him to say something else, something calming and soothing. He pressed his lips together.

It didn't matter. She wouldn't remember. If she even heard him now, which was unlikely.

She crumpled against him. From rigid and clinging to limp and pliant. It was so quick he panicked a little. Was she dead? Dammit.

He rolled her onto her back and pressed his ear to her chest, trying to shut out the sweet scent of her skin and the hint of flowers from her silky hair. Her heart beat. Rapidly, uneven... Unconscious. He rested his head, slumping in relief and wishing Hollis were here. Not that he was especially fond of the uptight son of a bitch, but Hollis was a doctor. He wouldn't lay here, holding her and worrying, letting her bleed—it was all pointless.

Her fingers slid into his hair, startling him. "You're so warm."

Not unconscious. Her voice washed over him—and the wolf. He closed his eyes, allowing himself a moment's weakness. He couldn't remember the last time someone had touched him with a gentle hand.

"Thank you," she murmured. "For getting me out of that place. I don't know who they were or what they were going to do to me, but I know it was bad."

That sounded almost coherent. He looked up at her. "You're awake?"

"Doubtful. If I was awake there wouldn't be a naked guy on top of me." Her fingers kept stroking his hair. "And I wouldn't be lying in the woods." She paused. "Or in so much pain."

He grinned; he couldn't help it. "So, you're dreaming?"

She nodded, her fingers slid along his neck. "Well..." She seemed to think about this. "Why am I wearing clothes when you're not?"

"It's cold," he said. It'd be better if he could shift. He could keep them both warmer that way.

"You're being naked makes even less sense, then," she argued. "Besides, I'm not cold."

He pressed his palm to her forehead. She was still burning up. "Is that the only reason?" he asked, racking his brain for options. If he'd learned one thing in the last few months, it was finding motivation to fight. She needed big motivation. "Chase? What happened to him?"

She shivered. "I'd rather this was a good dream."

"Chase is bad?" he pushed.

She made an angry little sound at the back of her throat. "No. Sometimes. I love my brother, but I'm so mad at him."

Mal grunted. He knew how that was. Not that he loved Finn or the rest of his pack. Being part of a pack was more binding, more permanent, more complicated. And irritating as shit. But he did know all about being mad. Pissed as hell was more like it. "He did something?"

"I jumped in between him and that mountain of a man and got stabbed. He left me." Her voice grew soft and thready. "He left me… Alone."

Those words did something dangerous to his wolf. Before, the stupid animal had felt some sort of misguided defensive instinct. Now—Mal knew he was in trouble. The wolf wanted blood, specifically Chase's. The surge of fury that raged through his blood was welcome, but the cause was not. He didn't give a shit about Chase. He was a dick for leaving his sister, but Mal had enough to deal with without developing some sort of guardian complex for this girl. The wolf had other ideas, though. He wanted to make Chase suffer. He wanted to rip into him. Mal sighed.

"What sort of brother does that?" Her tears were sudden and hard, shaking her body. "I… I put up with a lot from him." She was sobbing.

"Goddammit," he hissed. "Stay still."

"It's your fault. You mentioned Chase…" She slid her arms around his neck and buried her face against his neck. "I wanted a good dream."

He held her close, one hand at the base of her spine, the other pressed firmly between her shoulder blades. Somewhere deep inside he ached for her. They had this betrayal in common, too. It was an ugly reality to accept. He needed her to calm down, to relax. She responded, slowly easing. Her sobs lessened enough for him to say, "Tell me about this good dream."

She sucked in a sharp breath. "It wouldn't be here."

"Where would it be?"

"In a bed, with soft sheets and lots of blankets." She broke off. "And maybe mirrors." She sighed.

He eased his hold so he could look at her, reeling. Was she serious? Her eyes were pressed shut, her features relaxed, and a slight smile on her face. "A sex dream?" Maybe she was still slightly delusional.

Her smile grew. "Yes, a sex dream. Virgin, remember?"

She'd said a lot of things, very few of which he'd listened to. He froze. The wolf froze. "You've never had sex?"

Her eyes popped open. "Virgin." She pointed at herself, shivered, and slid her hand between them. "Now I'm beneath some naked, hot, hero guy. The leap to a sex dream doesn't seem that surprising." She smiled.

And dammit, he smiled back at her. "Mirrors?" The wolf wanted to wrap itself around her, warm her up… Claim her. Mal swallowed, forcibly ignoring the wolf.

She pressed her eyes shut, a nervous giggle escaping. "Dream. So of course it will be amazing and we'll look gorgeous."

It was his turn to chuckle. "Right." He looked at her—really looked at her. She was pretty. Her body, pressed against him, was tempting—even when feverish and delusional. Men would have wanted her. Plenty of men. The wolf growled.

"I feel weird." She pressed a hand to the side of his face. "Really weird." Her hand trembled. "Am I going to wake up?"

She was asking him? How the hell was he supposed to know? What was he supposed to do or say? He cleared his throat, wrapping his fingers around her wrist. Her pulse was erratic. If he could leave her, he might be able to determine where they were—how close help was. As much as he hated to admit it, she needed help he couldn't give. "You need to be strong." It was all he could do now.

"I am strong. I don't feel very strong," she murmured.

Her body was weakening, but her mind was sharp. She'd need it to fight.

Her smile was slight. "Is it really as magical and life-altering as people say it is?"

"Sex?" Mal bit out.

She nodded weakly.

"It's been a while," he grumbled, smiling at her laugh.

"Are you avoiding the question?" she asked.

He sighed. "Yes."

"Yes, you're avoiding the question? Or yes, sex is magical and life-altering?"

He was losing control of this conversation. "What's your name?"

She opened her eyes. "Oh. My name is Olivia Chase."

"You talk a lot, Olivia Chase."

Her eyes were huge and fathomless. She grinned. "You have a name?"

"Mal," he murmured, appreciating the slight dimple in her left cheek. He was wrong. She was more than pretty. She was *vital* somehow. Real and human. And dying.

"Mal. Can you do me a favor?" she asked.

"Depends. What?"

"Talk to me?" Her blink was sluggish, like her lids were weighted. "Feels like I'm underwater, like my head's breaking the surface only part of the time. Maybe hearing your voice will help me stay afloat."

What the hell was he supposed to talk about? "I'm not a conversationalist."

"I sensed that." She sighed. "Never mind."

His wolf growled, thoroughly disappointed. He'd been trying to give her the motivation to hold on, then when she told him what she needed he couldn't find something to say? "I'll try."

She smiled. "Thank you."

It was a hell of a smile. Soft and sweet and inviting. The whole virgin thing was very hard to believe. Harder not to think about. "You ever been kissed, Olivia Chase?" he asked, his voice gruff.

Her eyes widened. "Not properly."

"How about improperly?"

"I'm not sure I know what that means?"

•••

Olivia held her breath, her fingers clasping the back of Mal's neck. Why was he looking at her like that? Was he going to kiss her? And why was she so excited about the prospect of being kissed by some dangerous naked man in the middle of the woods?

"I *am* dreaming," she murmured.

"You are," he agreed.

The pad of his thumb traced her lower lip, mesmerizing her with its warmth and texture. Her lips parted, drawing a sharp hiss from Mal. Had she done something? Everything was liquid and hot—in a good way. Breathing was becoming a challenge. But the way he was looking at her… The flare in his dark eyes made her forget about the shooting pain in her leg.

"Mirrors are overrated," he said.

Her heart thumped. "Are they?"

He nodded. "But, since you're dreaming, I'm going to kiss you."

"Properly or improperly?" Her voice shook.

The corner of his mouth curled up. "I only do improperly."

"Oh good." Her fingers slid back into his hair and tugged him down.

She thought she saw a flash of surprise on his face, but then his lips were on hers and she didn't care. Feather light—

her turn to be surprised. But there was nothing soft about his kiss. From light to demanding, his mouth descended, his tongue sweeping her lower lip and invading her mouth. He devoured her, and she never wanted him to stop. Breathing wasn't necessary, but holding on to Mal was. Not to push him away, but to draw him closer.

She liked the feel of his arms cradling her, the slide of his hands under her shirt and along her back. She wanted to arch into him, to be closer… It wasn't enough.

His teeth nipped her lower lip before he sucked it into his mouth. He pressed kisses up the side of her neck, along her throat, then latched on to her earlobe. She moaned at the feel of him, of her skin, engulfed in his warm, wet mouth.

"Dammit," he bit out.

Seconds later, the world was cold and painful again.

"What happened?" she asked, her hand searching for him.

"Stop," he growled. "You need to stay still. You're bleeding again."

"I am?" she asked, still dizzy from the effects of his mouth and hands and…everything.

"You are." He sounded angry—and breathless. "We need to move again."

"You're mad?" She was all tingly and euphoric, and he was angry and ready to hit the road? That was disappointing.

"I am."

"Oh," she murmured.

He sat with his back to her, illuminated by the moon. The moon was enormous. It was missing a slight sliver, just the edge. But out here, it was like a second sun. Of course, the light of a thousand stars helped. She blinked. And…it was snowing? Why wasn't she cold? Right, she was dreaming. "I'm ready to wake up now," she whispered.

He looked back at her and stood, swinging her up into

his arms.

"I didn't mean to make you mad."

He started walking. "You didn't. Pissed myself off just fine." He paused. "You asked earlier where we are. I have no idea. Someplace up north, far north. Maybe Alaska."

"I go to school in Alaska," she said. "I just started."

"School?" He looked surprised.

"Getting my doctorate," she answered. "Anthropology."

"You're from Alaska?" he asked.

"No." She was so tired. She'd been tired for the last year or so. And stressed. There were things you couldn't unlearn, couldn't erase from your mind, no matter how hard you might want to.

He wrapped the coat around her. "You're shivering."

"Am I?" she asked, immediately turning into him and placing her hand against the warmth of his skin.

His broken groan startled her. "Stop moving," he hissed, shifting her against him so her head rested on his chest. "Relax."

She did, instantly. With him close, there was no choice. She felt comfortable, safe—protected. And she was so, so tired.

"Why Alaska?" His voice was fading.

"My brother," she answered, his steady pace rocking her. "One of his clients lived there—he said it was nice. He was always moving me around. Now I think maybe it was because someone was looking for him. Or me?"

His hand rhythmically stroked her back. "What does your brother do?"

The frustration she'd been fighting with the better part of a year boiled up. "A year ago, I'd say he sold foreign and luxury items. He took over my father's company when Dad died. Suddenly, he was going by Chase, not Eddie—his real name. It's like he's a rock star or gangster or something? He's making new *friends* and keeping odd hours and more protective than ever. Chase decided to change things up. I don't know exactly what he's doing. I'm not sure I want to know. Last time I was home, something was wrong. Late night calls, people coming and going at all hours, Chase always stressed. And now shady guys with big knives are involved." She paused. "I'm not sure that answered your question."

Mal's grunt was the only answer.

"I think my brother's the bad guy, Mal." She chewed on her lower lip, the sting of tears burning her eyes. "I don't know what to do, you know? These people that did this to me—do I go to the police? Do I report them and, in all likelihood, hand my brother over as well?"

No answer.

"Are you listening?" she whispered.

"Yes," he growled. "I'm listening to every damn word you're saying. Give me a minute." His arm tightened, just a little.

She smiled.

"This client in Alaska—do you know them?"

"No… Chase and I have money, Mal." She lifted her head. "Do you think that's what this was about? Money? Were they going to ransom me?"

"You're moving," he bit out.

She rested her head again, relaxing in his hold.

"It's possible. Why was Chase there when you were attacked?" he asked.

"I don't know. I had no idea he was coming. I had the flu and was walking across campus from the med clinic, and there he was, waving at me. Next thing, this guy pulled up in a van. He and Chase started talking, they fought, and the guys started shoving Chase. I ran up then, put myself between them, and you know what happened."

"You didn't hear anything they were saying?" he asked.

"Something about a bad shipment, not what he'd promised." Olivia burrowed closer. "Aren't you cold?" she asked, her hand stroking his chest.

"No." His hand covered hers, stilling it.

His heart beat under her ear, the steady thump a soothing lullaby. She'd almost drifted off when his voice woke her.

"Olivia? Did you hear me?" he asked.

"No," she murmured.

"It might have been a kidnapping. Or payback against your brother for this faulty shipment."

"I was almost asleep." She yawned.

"I thought you said this was a dream," he pointed out.

"Payback?" she asked, her brain still foggy from sleep.

"Chase's visit wasn't planned?" Mal asked. "But this happened at your university?"

"Right."

"Then they were there for you." The razor-sharp edge in his voice jolted her awake. His hand slid beneath her shirt, pressing his palm against her back, as if he understood she needed comfort—that his touch would give her what she needed.

There for you. What did that mean? What would they have done to her?

Clearly these people were capable of horrible things. She felt her wrists, remembering the sting of the rope—the feel of the needle in her flesh.

When she'd first seen Mal, he'd been chained to the wall, beaten and bruised and so menacing she'd wanted to hide from him—if she'd been able to move. They'd done that to him. And yet, he'd rescued her.

"Why did you save me?" she asked, holding her breath.

"I almost didn't," he said.

She smiled. "But you did. With a knife in your shoulder. And no clothes. Not knowing a thing about me."

He stayed silent.

"Mal?" she pushed.

"I had to," he whispered.

Chapter Four

He bolted awake. Something was off. How long had he been asleep? Not long, surely.

It was cold. Damn cold, even for him.

A sound? Animal.

A predator. Big.

Screaming.

Mal sat up, his senses sharpening instantly.

He glanced at Olivia—Olivia. The place beside him was empty. She was gone. His heart stopped, the world grinding to a complete stop.

Fuck no.

Where was she? He jumped, scanning the site, ears reaching, nose seeking. A trough in the overnight snow. She'd been pulled away? Some blood—her blood—leading away, into the trees.

It was her screaming. He could hear her. Olivia. *Goddammit.*

The sound gave the wolf permission to take control. Mal welcomed the wolf, embracing the burn of stretching muscles and snap of rearranging bone. The wolf would find her, bring her back, and make sure whatever had her would regret taking her from him. He was running before the shift was complete, his claws still splitting through the new fur of his paws as he covered the ground.

The scent was animal. Not human.

Whatever had Olivia, it wasn't the Others.

Sharp, musky, pungent. Bear.

The wolf ran faster.

He and the rest of Finn's pack were bigger than the average timber wolf—bigger teeth, bigger ears, bigger everything. And strong. Dangerously lethal. It made him a merciless killing machine—one most animals feared. Maybe that's why the bear had been dragging Olivia away. It had sensed that Mal was a threat.

He charged through the trees, following the tracks—*too much blood*—until he saw her. Olivia, crying, her arms flailing over her head, her hands tearing at small saplings seeking some sort of hold. It wouldn't make a difference. A grizzly bear lugged her behind. Without him, Olivia didn't stand a chance.

He didn't hesitate. His howl split the air, adrenaline and power coursing through him.

The bear turned, dropping Olivia's leg, and reared up. It was big, posturing, baring its teeth and roaring.

Challenge accepted.

Mal glanced at Olivia, her blood turning the white snow a brilliant, horrible red. She was crying, trying to crawl into the trees. He wanted to yell at her to stay still—she was bleeding too much. And then the grizzly's frying-pan-size paw sent him a good fifteen feet into the air and back—it's claws leaving gouges deep in his muscles.

Mal jumped up, circling until he could spring onto the bear's back. He sank his teeth into its shoulder, unable to reach its neck, and was rewarded by the hot tang of blood in his mouth. The bear tried to shake him loose, but Mal leaped free, taking a hunk of the bear with him.

All the rage he'd been suppressing took over. The urge to kill, the spurt of blood and the weakening of his foe, was all that mattered. Rational thought vanished in a haze of blinding red fury.

It wasn't a quick fight. The bear was big. But Mal was determined. He wore it down, nipping and clawing, aiming for arteries or a debilitating blow. When the bear grabbed Olivia by the ankle, Mal's fury knew no bounds. Having his back leg snapped didn't stop him from sinking his teeth into the bear's throat. He held on until he felt the give of artery and tendon. It was done. The bear released Olivia and hobbled into the tree line, Mal let him go.

Mal ran to Olivia's side. He circled, sniffing her. The bear had torn into her wounded leg, its teeth leaving an angry open wound. It was a miracle she wasn't already dead. The wolf howled again and again, unable to bear the thought of losing her.

And dammit, neither could Mal.

He whimpered, desperate to save her.

"I give you permission to eat me," she muttered, blood covering her chest and leg. "If you'll let me die first, please?" She was serious, he could tell. If he'd been in human form, he'd laugh—then tell her to be strong. But with her wounds, she couldn't tough this out, and no tourniquet would make this better. Something hard and jagged settled into his chest.

Save her. It was a plea.

No, he couldn't do that to her. Death was peaceful…

She held her hand out, startled when he pressed his head into her hand. Why did her touch have to ease him?

"I don't want to die," she said, crying then, covering her face with her hands and sobbing uncontrollably.

Don't let her die. The wolf pleaded.

He couldn't leave her alone to deal with this. He shifted quickly, knowing he'd feel it in his muscles and joints later. "Olivia?" he gasped.

"Mal?" Her voice was panicked, her hands dropped from her face. "Run, Mal! You have to run. There's a wolf. And a bear."

"Hush," he argued, inspecting her injuries while fighting for control.

Save her. His wolf demanded it.

"Don't…hush me. I'm dying, I think." She stared at him, her hazel eyes clear and huge in her pale face. She'd lost so much blood. "You're a gorgeous man, Mal. I'm glad I got to kiss you before I die." Her hand rose, trembling, so he took it in his.

"You're a beautiful woman, Olivia Chase." He cleared his throat, knowing he should swallow back the words that tried to force their way out. Death was a natural part of life. People died all the time. Sometimes naturally, sometimes not. Olivia Chase was a sweet girl, someone who'd had something horrible happen to her. But that didn't mean he was supposed to step in and change her fate. He'd promised his pack. He knew how fucked up this life was. But the words came out anyway. He couldn't stop them—maybe he didn't want to. "Let me save you," he whispered.

There was nothing his wolf wanted more.

A furrow formed between her brows. "Save me?"

"The life you know won't exist anymore." His voice was raw. "It will be harsher, more violent." She stared at him, fading. "You have to decide now, Olivia."

She blinked, coughed, a trickle of blood spilling over her full lower lip.

"Fuck it," he growled. She was out of time. He stood back, shifting again, rushing through the transformation out of sheer desperation. When he looked down at her next, he was a wolf, and she was staring at him in shock and awe.

"Mal?" she croaked. "No way. You're…what?" A slight frown formed as her eyes drifted shut.

Mal growled, ignoring the pain in his chest. His gaze swept her body. Her leg was already damaged—one more bite wouldn't change that. He bit into her right thigh, whimpering at her cry, at the way she tried to pull away from him, at the taste of her blood in his mouth.

In that instant, his eyes saw through hers. He saw himself—his wolf—biting her leg. Felt the nightmare pain, biting cold, and bone-deep weariness. Flashes of Olivia bombarded him. Memories, sensations, experiences, hopes, and dreams. Saw her brother Chase and knew him. Heard his own voice assuring her, "I'm here." Felt her response to his kiss. God, she'd ached for him. It crowded in on him, drowning him, until there was a single pinpoint on a blanket of white—Olivia on the snow below him.

He shook his head, nudging her with his nose.

She was breathing steadily, a slight hint of color on her cheeks. He'd infected her, so he knew what was coming. A fever, shakes, nightmare-like delusions—things she'd already been dealing with. Her first change would happen in two days, with the full moon. After that, she'd be able to change at will, if she learned to control her wolf.

His wolf snorted. They had an understanding. Mal might not always agree with his wolf, but he didn't hold him back, either. The animal had instincts that had never led him astray.

Turning Olivia didn't make much sense but…it had been necessary. In that moment, there had been no choice. Now he was a pack of two. He had a responsibility to Olivia. And, oddly, that didn't bother him. But finding safety before the Others found them did.

...

Olivia was walking in the snow. Her toes were blue, no longer capable of feeling the cold. What little clothing she wore was shredded and covered in blood. She was looking for something, desperately. She tried to call out again but couldn't make a sound.

The bear lay dead, eyes rolled back in its head, mouth hanging open. Odd. It was twitching? The massive torso—shoulders—jerking where it lay.

The head of a white wolf popped up. Red covered its nose, strands of blood and drool connecting the wolf to the carcass it feasted on. Pale eyes speared hers, sharp and mesmerizing and soulless, flooding her with terror and holding her hostage.

Instinct told her to run—to get away from the wolf. But it, the wolf, wouldn't let her. It leaped atop the bear, peering at her, its tail swishing in agitation. The wolf sniffed the air then tilted his head back and howled.

The air seemed to shiver around her, freeing her from whatever spell held her. She dropped, crumpling into the snow and wrapping her arms around her knees.

The white wolf was circling her, its menacing growl making the hair on the back of her neck stand straight up. He would hurt her; she saw it in his eyes. And he, the wolf, was excited—baring his fangs at her when she dared look him in the eye.

It pissed her off.

Rage, an unfamiliar emotion, consumed her, fueled by every hurt or insult she'd ever buried deep inside. Her parents. Her sweet fiancée John. Her sweet boyfriend Mike. Chase, for dragging her all over the place and leaving her at the mercy of that man. The bear, for attacking her. Splinter images of every injustice from elementary school to adulthood filled her with a living, breathing fury.

She could fight this wolf.

"Don't." Mal's voice was at her ear. "Stay calm."

The white wolf howled again, tempting her to go against Mal's advice, until her body was wracked by blinding agony. Pain. That was all there was.

"Olivia," Mal whispered, "I'm sorry."

She couldn't focus on Mal or his words or the wolf or… anything. If she was dying, she'd like it to be over—now. Why did it hurt so much?

"Stop fighting, Olivia. It will be over soon," he pleaded.

That was good news, but it didn't stop her from crying, mostly from the pain. But there was a small part of her that understood her life was almost over. She curled in on herself, hoping to find a position that hurt less—if there was one.

"I'm here." Mal's voice.

She wasn't alone. "Mal?" She thought she was screaming. It was a whisper.

"Listen to me." Rough and deep, rich and soothing. "It's the infection. What you're seeing—it's not real. We're in a cabin…there's a hole in the roof. Snow's coming in."

She turned toward his voice, calming at the feel of his skin against her cheek and nose. His arms were around her. She could smell him, feel him, but she couldn't see him. Her eyes were open, she was blinking, but it was pitch black.

"Bear's dead," he murmured.

Which was good news.

"Should be safe for now," he added. "Time to get your strength back." His fingers stroked along her neck and shoulder.

It was amazing. She arched into his touch.

"You're healing," he whispered, his fingers running down her arm, pausing to rub here and there. "Scratches are almost gone."

Scratches? Wasn't she bleeding to death? Somehow,

scratches didn't matter. Neither did bleeding to death. She wasn't hurting because of his touch. Why had he stopped?

"Fucking Others. Fucking bear. Fucking moon," he growled, his fingers tracing the length of her thigh. "Fuck," he whispered.

She didn't know what he was talking about. He was massaging her thigh with strong, deep strokes. It was heaven. Of course, there was a very real possibility she was in heaven. Did that mean Mal was dead, too? He'd died saving her from the bear?

He couldn't be. She whimpered.

"Rest, Olivia," he added, his tone sharp, his breath brushing her forehead.

She relaxed against him. Her fingers and hands tingled—she flexed, breathing easier. Arms, too. Heavier than normal, but mobile. Resting held no appeal. Now that she wasn't feeling so disembodied, she realized Mal was holding her in his lap. She pressed her nose to his collarbone, placed one hand on his chest, and blew out a shaky breath.

He tugged her closer. "This is going to be a problem."

Her dying? Yes, it was. Because, even though she hated pain and fear and being chased and attacked, she really didn't want to leave Mal.

"I won't be a problem," she whispered, her throat raw and hoarse.

He chuckled. "You already are." But he didn't sound upset about it.

Chapter Five

Mal's wolf was driving him bat-shit crazy. He got that Olivia was theirs. He understood that keeping her safe was important. They were a pack, that's the way it went. So why wouldn't it shut up about her?

And why had she taken precedence over revenge?

The only thing that kept him from losing his mind in that godforsaken cell was imagining vengeance. In detail. Regularly.

Every time a silver needle was imbedded beneath a fingernail or claw. Every bone they'd broken, high-decibel sound they'd blasted him with, and knife they'd used on his fur—he could hardly wait to return the favor. By the time Mal became immune to one torture, they'd find something new. They knew how far they could push him without killing him. They'd told him to beg and they'd stop.

Spilling his guts about Finn and his pack wasn't an option. No matter how pissed he was at them for leaving him behind, he'd never give them up to Cyrus and the Others. Never betray them the way they'd betrayed him. He was stubborn—

his wolf was more so. No fucking way he'd beg. Ever. They'd never know they'd broken him, even if they managed it.

After they'd pummeled him senseless and left him bleeding, chained to that wall, he'd plan how he'd take them down one by one.

Killing Cyrus wasn't enough. The motherfucker would know what it was like to be skinned. How it felt to heal, only to endure injury again and again. It would be his turn to wake up drenched in sweat and vomit, remembering the slide of that thin blade against his shoulder blades and along his spine. It would be Mal's turn to look into Cyrus's eyes and smile.

But now the fight had gone out of the wolf. All it wanted to do was be close to Olivia. If she was out of sight, the wolf grew angry and restless. The only time the damn animal seemed happy was when he was touching her.

Like sitting around all day was an option.

He didn't know how long they had before the Others caught up to them, but there was no doubt they would. They'd taken him hoping to get information about Finn's pack. When it became clear that wasn't going to happen, their motivation changed. Getting information was secondary to hurting him. That's when things had turned personal.

When Olivia had passed out after he'd bitten her, he'd convinced his wolf to leave her, probably because the beast knew it was for her safety. He'd saturated the site where they'd spent the night with bear blood, hoping to buy them some time. Between the smell of her infection and the bear, it *might* work. If they were really lucky, the Others would believe Olivia had been eaten. Then they'd only be after him. It might be possible for Olivia to avoid having the Others trailing her day-in and day-out for the rest of her life.

But what the hell would her life look like now?

She was in graduate school. She could go back to that.

What else?

Her brother? No loss there. As far as Mal was concerned, the son of a bitch could believe she was dead. He'd brought this down on her—maybe not the werewolf thing, but the attack and kidnapping. But why? What the hell were the Others doing with someone like Chase? He'd only seen flashes of him in Olivia's mind, but he hadn't struck Mal as a criminal mastermind. He'd seemed desperate. What sort of business could Chase have with the Others?

It might be worth digging into, for his pack's survival. Whether *his* pack meant him and Olivia or the rest of Finn's pack, he wasn't ready to address. Not yet. For now, he was still tied to Finn. They needed to know Cyrus had a spy, that they were in danger.

Finn wanted the Others off their backs as much as Mal did. They both had something to lose. Finn had his wife and pups and he had...Olivia.

He stared at the sleeping woman, that strange yearning ache tightening his chest.

His wolf growled at him, irritated that he insisted on sitting across the cabin from her. He sat six, maybe seven, feet away, and the wolf was pissed as hell. It wanted him to curl up around her, to ease her—and him.

Mal didn't like it.

He'd be damned if his wolf told him what to do. They might be one, but *he* was in charge. And getting attached to her any more than he was already was a bad idea. There was still a chance she'd leave. Yes, he'd first have to teach her how to shift, how to work with her wolf, how to control her instincts. But then? There was no reason for her not to have a somewhat normal life.

His wolf growled again, so agitated Mal felt on edge.

"Chill the fuck out," he hissed.

But the wolf was ignoring him.

He'd planned on carrying her out of here this morning.

The more distance between them and the Others, the better. But she'd been so feverish he couldn't do it. She had periods of wakefulness, or so he'd thought. He'd learned quickly she was delusional, and the best thing to do was keep his distance.

His wolf had approved of the way she'd clung to him, pleading with him to hold her close. And he'd tried. But she'd been too soft, too sweet. When her fingers slid into his hair, her silky lips latching onto his neck, Mal had wavered. Her touch reminded him of a time before he'd been turned, when things like peace and happiness were still possible.

Too bad he hadn't met her then.

She was tossing on the makeshift mattress before the fire, soft cries and whimpers ratcheting up his wolf's anxiety.

Mal sighed, stood, and crossed to her. He crouched at her side, hesitating briefly before placing a hand on her shoulder. She shuddered and stilled. His wolf was satisfied, the smug bastard.

"I didn't say I didn't want to be close to her," he whispered, arguing with his wolf. "I'm saying it would be better for her if we weren't."

But as soon as the words were out of his mouth he was lying at her side, tugging her against him, and easing into a deep sleep.

...

Olivia was warm. She burrowed under the blanket, her fingers stretching in the thick fur that covered her. Each silky hair was distinguishable from the next, had its own texture and weight. She sighed, moaning softly.

"How do you feel?" asked a voice she didn't immediately recognize. It must be Frank, one of her roommates' boyfriends. He was always on their couch, eating their food. He was nice—just a freeloader.

"Shh, Frank, I'm sleeping," she said. "Whatever flu meds they gave me—wow, talk about a trip."

Frank chuckled. "Really?"

"But I'm feeling better," she said. "Just let me sleep."

"We need to move," Frank said, closer now. "If you're up for it?"

Her dream-guy's voice. The dream-guy's scent. Mal. Oh, his scent. She stiffened. "Am I up for it?" she asked, opening one eye.

Mal was sitting beside her, smiling. No one had a right to smell better than fresh-baked chocolate chip cookies. But he did. And, she noted with disappointment, he was wearing clothes. Overalls, flannel shirt, and boots. He was the sexiest lumberjack in the world.

Other scents reached her. Cedar, smoke, leather, dust. She wasn't used to being so scent sensitive, but she *was* recovering from the flu. They were in a small cabin—rustic was a generous description. But there was a fire going, and she was comfy on the cot, beneath a pile of what looked like animal pelts.

Animals... She felt dizzy, disoriented, and closed her eyes. "How much of what I dreamed was real?" She peered at him, her nerves stretching thin and tight.

"We can talk about that later." His eyes were surprisingly light brown, almost caramel. It had been hard to tell what color they were in the dark. In the light of day—God, he was absolutely gorgeous. "Let's go."

"No." She jumped up. Did she want to go? Not really, but apparently, he did. She froze then, looking down at her leg. "Holy crap." Her jeans were shredded and crusted with dried blood. Her hoodie was stained, too. She bent over, pulling the denim aside, remembering. An oblong cut—the knife. Some crisscross scratches and a few deep gouges—the bear. And two perfect punctures... She reached around the back of her thigh: two more. A bite.

This was real?

All faint scars, healed and white.

She swallowed, staring at Mal. The wounds were real? The air seemed to thin. He'd bitten her. He, as a large black wolf. A large black wolf that had saved her life. "None of that was real? It can't be." Her voice was soft, unsteady.

"We'll talk later," he said softly, watching her. "Put on the overalls and coat." He nodded at the too-big jean overalls and the coat. The coat she'd taken the night they'd escaped. "It's not safe."

She nodded, using the length of rope he offered as a belt to keep the pants around her waist and then slipping into the coat. Her mind was in overdrive. For one thing, there were far too many questions in her mind. Who was Finn? And the Others? There was more—she was loved in a way she'd never thought possible. Was that real? It felt real. Maybe she was still a tad delusional after all. And what was this voice in her head? She couldn't quite make it out, but…something was talking to her, like a subconscious thought. Her conscience?

The most obvious question, though: Should she be afraid?

She knew the answer. No. She didn't fear Mal. If anything, she wanted to be near him, to trust him. Whether or not that was the wisest choice seemed irrelevant. Which was concerning. She was normally a cautious, methodical type. She didn't rush into things or act rashly. Trusting some guy who was comfortable running around naked in the middle of the woods was…out of character. But if her choices were going with Mal or returning to the creepy cave to suffer who-knows-what, she'd go with Mal. For now.

She'd been sick. Delusional. None of that had happened. It was impossible. Especially now, in the light of day. But her fingers fell to her thigh, tracing the scars beneath the rough denim fabric.

Mal stuffed a few items into a weathered backpack then shrugged it onto one of his incredibly broad shoulders. He was bigger in the daylight; whether that was a concern or a comfort remained to be seen.

"Where are we?" she asked, needing to focus on something.

He shrugged. "A hunting cabin. Gave us some shelter, clothes, and some useful supplies." That was all she got. Apparently, breaking and entering wasn't a big deal to him. Maybe his days always included being stranded in the middle of nowhere saving girls from bears as a giant wolf, all while hiding from someone who wanted to do very bad things to him.

Oh my God. What it wrong with me? Was I drugged?

None of this made sense. None of it.

"I've officially gone crazy," she mumbled.

"No, you haven't."

"Are you sure?" She hugged herself. "I have plenty of evidence to the contrary. And I feel…different."

He glanced at her. "Better?"

She frowned. "Better than what?"

"Than you were ten hours ago? You look a hell of a lot better."

She couldn't ignore the pleasure his slight compliment stirred. Yes, she *could* ignore it. She should ignore it. Something was *seriously* wrong with her. "When I had blood poisoning in my knife wound or a grizzly was using me as chew-toy?" she asked, sitting down on the cot. She remembered burning and searing, the rub of teeth on bone. Her bone. "That happened? It all really happened?"

He didn't move. "Yes."

She stared at him. "How can I *not* be crazy? *We* not be crazy?"

The hint of a grin tugged at his mouth. "Trust me."

She arched a brow but slowly nodded. She *trusted* him? Because that was the most logical thing to do. Not that she had a choice. Right now, he was keeping her safe.

"Let's go," he said again, heading out the door.

She stared at the open doorway before following, tugging the oversize coat tight around her waist. The sun was blinding, bouncing off the white snow and hurting her eyes. She held her arm up, shielding her eyes and taking in their surroundings. Mal, however, was already a spot—rapidly disappearing into the distant trees.

She jogged to keep up, able to do so without growing winded. A new development. So was the fact that she could see the buds on the tree branches and hear the flutter of the birds in the boughs high overhead. And smells… There were all sorts of smells in the woods, some far less pleasant than others.

After twenty minutes of silent walking, she asked, "Where are we going?"

Mal glanced at her.

"I know you're not used to talking, I get that. But it would make things a little easier on me to know I'm not in this alone. I'm scared. Freaking out. Right now, even though you've tried to tell me otherwise, I'm pretty sure I've been drugged, or I'm having an out-of-body experience, or I'm in a coma in a hospital somewhere and this is all in my subconscious. Whatever the reason, you're here—proof that it wasn't all in my head. I guess the scars are, too." She drew in a deep breath and tried again. "I know once we're safe you're going to dump me off at the nearest bus station, and I'll have to figure things out from there, but until then—"

He stopped, his irritation obvious. "I'm not dumping you anywhere." He looked—hurt?

He wasn't going to ditch her? Why not? It was obvious he didn't like her. Not that she wasn't thankful for all he'd done.

"I didn't mean—"

"We have a lot of ground to cover today." He started walking again.

She followed, trying to calm the torrent of images, conversations, emotions, and flashes swirling in her brain. Snippets of conversation she'd never had. Smiling faces of men, people she'd never seen. Sex. She stopped walking. She'd never had sex, but she felt the rough scrape of nails on her sides. She blew out a deep breath, looking around her. All she saw was Mal's retreating back. She walked on, her mind jumping ahead to taking a shot. The burn of whiskey down her throat.

Throat. Panic skittered across her skin, every nerve drawn tight. Having her throat cut. No, torn out by a wolf. Quick bring-her-to-her-knees pain blinded her. A big white wolf. She grabbed her throat, the image so real and intense, and leaned against a tree for support.

"Olivia?" Mal was there, his hands gripping her shoulders.

That voice was back in her head. It said Mal's name. She pressed her hands over her ears.

"What is it?" he asked. "What hurts?"

"Nothing hurts. I… There's a voice, talking in my head…" She glanced at him.

His eyes narrowed. "Saying?"

She frowned. "I…I can't tell. It's muffled or far away—" She broke off then blew out a deep breath.

He let go of her, stepping back.

"Wait. I tell you I hear a voice and you ask me what it's saying. No worry over the fact that I'm hearing a voice." She stepped forward, her patience snapping. "Please tell me what's going on."

"It's your wolf," he said. He wouldn't look at her.

She wished she were still leaning against the tree. "My *wolf*?" she whispered.

He nodded.

"What does that mean?" she asked. "My wolf? I don't have a wolf. You— " She shook her head. "And the rest of it?"

"The rest of it?"

"The man with the red hair? And the white wolf? Why am I seeing things that didn't happen to me?"

"It's me," he said. "From the bite. That's how I know what Chase looks like. You had a cat named Fudge, hate brussels sprouts, and loved your mother more than anyone else. And when I kissed you, you didn't want me to stop." A low growl edged into his last words, making her toes curl and her heart thump. "Keep moving."

His words set her in motion, without thought. He was in her head? Because he bit her. She frowned. It was all too much. If they'd stop walking long enough for him to clue her in on everything, then she wouldn't keep slowing them down.

Mal had his throat torn out? There was more, waiting at the edges of her subconscious. Might be best not to let it all in at once, not yet. It might be better to come to terms with the fact that she'd been bitten by a...a *werewolf* before she started digging into Mal's psyche.

Worrying about what was happening to her was no good. Did she have every reason in the world to freak out? Yes. Yes, she did. But it wouldn't change anything. It wouldn't make this easier. Panic hovered, ready to take over, if she let it. She sucked in a deep breath, clearing her mind of all the images and sensations she couldn't wrap her mind around—not yet. All she needed to know right now was Mal had saved her. And now, he was taking care of her. She heard the voice in her head then—her *wolf*—and paused. He would always take care of her because, according to her wolf, he was important.

Chapter Six

Mal glanced back over his shoulder again. Olivia was still following him. Quiet. Too quiet. She was frowning, a deep crease between her brows, and it worried him. He vaguely remembered how it had felt, being newly turned. It was confusing—disorienting.

He'd wanted to save her, not change her. He wasn't Alpha material—that was all on Finn. No one should lean on him, follow his orders, or look to him for leadership. But now she did, even if she didn't know it yet. And there was no way to undo it. He hoped she'd shift her loyalty to Finn when they reconnected. But his wolf wasn't too fond of that idea.

The wolf was perfectly clear what it was after: Olivia. For the first time, Mal couldn't give his wolf what he wanted, and he knew it was going to make life difficult. Nothing like having someone in your head, pushing, second-guessing, doubting, and making him do things he wouldn't do on his own.

Like turning Olivia.

No, dammit, he wouldn't have stood by and let her die. Blaming his wolf was pointless.

All that mattered now was getting somewhere safe soon. Otherwise, they were both as good as dead. He'd like to think they'd left the Others behind, but he knew better. He had to head south, or they'd end up in the ocean. And while there was a hell of a lot of land to cover, there were plenty of Others. If the Others wanted to find him, it wouldn't be hard to do.

Would they be looking for Olivia, too? That was a separate question. He'd like to think she was a victim of circumstance versus a specific target, but he couldn't be sure. He wouldn't search Olivia's memories, even if it might explain her abduction. Violating her privacy and trust didn't sit well with him or his wolf.

Neither did her unusual silence.

"Your brother," he said, waiting for her to catch up to him. "Why would he deal with werewolves?"

She frowned at him. "He didn't."

"The men keeping us in those cages? The man that stabbed you? Werewolf. Like us."

"Right." Her eyes widened, the sheen of tears startling him. "Werewolves. Like us."

"Jesus." He'd made her cry. "Don't cry."

She wiped frantically, sniffing and turning to hide her face. "I'm trying to stop."

Way to make things worse. He was an asshole, but sometimes he forgot just how good at it he was. Considering her life had been ripped to shreds in a forty-eight-hour period, crying was a normal reaction. He could *try* to be less of a dick. "You can cry," he murmured.

"Oh good," she said, sniffing, her breathing shallow and broken.

He tried to turn her, to hold her, but she shrugged him off. "Olivia?"

She shook her head, knocking his hand away a second time.

"Dammit," he growled, tugging her into his arms and holding her close. "Cry." He closed his eyes, her silent sobs chipping away at his forced indifference. Guilt crushed in on him, forcing him to explain. "If I hadn't bitten you—turned you—you would have died. My wolf wouldn't let you die."

She clung to him, her soft curves and sweet scent a temptation he wasn't sure he was strong enough to ignore. But he held her until the tears ended and her breath was coming in hiccups.

"She likes your wolf," Olivia said.

"She who?" he asked.

"M-my wolf." Her voice wobbled then.

"Shit," he growled out. "Tell her he's an asshole."

Olivia laughed. "We both know that's not true." She wasn't crying anymore, but she wasn't letting go of him.

Then again, his hold didn't seem to be loosening, either.

"Mal?" she whispered.

"Olivia?" He buried his nose in her hair to draw her scent deep.

"Can I ask you some questions?"

"Some?" he asked, willing himself to let go. His hold didn't ease.

"Some," she repeated, her arms sliding around his waist.

He liked her sigh, the way her breath fanned across his chest. "Two."

"Two?" she repeated.

"You can ask me two questions," he clarified. They needed to keep moving. If he could find a phone—then what? Was he going to call Finn? Like the bastard would come. Chances are he was knee-deep in puppies and too busy making more to give a shit about him.

"Do you have a mate?" she asked.

Mal's brain came to a screeching halt. "No." They were not talking about mates. His wolf, selfish fucker, was ready and willing to talk about it. Mal, however, would never do it—never. "Next?"

There was a slight hesitation before she asked, "Will I ever see my brother again?"

Mal drew in a deep breath, fighting his wolf until his hold eased on her. He didn't like how empty his arms felt, how cold the air was. But he stepped back, ignoring the fact that he took her hand in his. "No."

"But?"

"He's connected with the Others. Until we know why and how, you'd be putting yourself in danger."

She was staring at him. "The Others?"

"Two."

"Mal, please." She tugged his hand.

He looked down, studying the way her fingers threaded through his, locking them together. Like his bite. She had no idea she was his pack now, or what that meant. She could have a family, children, and a life—but if he called, wanted her to do something, she'd have to obey. They were forever tangled up in each other. She should know about the Others.

"The Others are our enemies. The cage. Your kidnapping. The guy that stabbed you. They will hunt us down and hurt us." He spoke clearly. "They know how to hurt, trust me."

"I do." She nodded.

Those two words gave him pause. She squeezed his hand, smiling.

"Can you tell me where we're going?"

"Too many questions." He smiled back.

"Dear God, it's just not fair," she spoke so softly he had to lean forward to hear her.

"What?"

"Nothing."

He frowned. "Tell me."

Her eyes went round. "You're gorgeous. When you smile,

I-I think about that kiss. I want you to touch me." She tugged her hand free, her hands fisted at her side.

He stared at her, then her mouth. Her words had an immediate impact, making him hard and throbbing. "We need to keep going," he ground out.

His wolf didn't want to move. His wolf wanted to do exactly what she'd said. To touch her. Fine, he'd appease them both. He stepped closer, taking her hand in his—touching her. The contact of her skin against his felt too good. Too natural. He cleared his throat and held their hands up between them.

Her slow smile weakened his resolve to stop there. She nodded, squeezing his hand.

"You ready now?" he asked.

They walked for a good ten minutes before she asked, "Mal?"

He grinned. "Olivia?"

"Do you think my brother knows they're werewolves?" she asked. "I'm not sure he did. Sort of hard to believe this is real."

"Maybe," he agreed. "The Others use intimidation as incentive. I guess it depends on how in he is with them, what sort of goods he's supplying them. I'd think showing him what they are and what they're capable of would keep him in line." He glanced at her. "Any way to find out what he was getting them?"

"I'd need a name to start with," she said, looking at him.

The Others tarnished everything. Just telling her his name felt wrong. "Cyrus." Mal spat out the word.

Olivia paused. "Cyrus White?" she asked. "Creepy guy with pale eyes and light blond hair and a problem respecting personal space? Chase called him the Norwegian giant."

The hair on Mal's arms went up. "You've seen him?"

Olivia shot him a perplexed look. "We ran into him when I was touring Northwestern. Had dinner with him." She grew quiet, thoughtful.

"What are you thinking?" he asked.

"Chase was scared of him." She moved closer to Mal. "Too scared to turn down his dinner invitation. He wanted me to pretend I was sick to get out of it. Then he changed his mind and wouldn't let me go to the bathroom by myself, or even leave his side. It was a long night."

Mal hated Chase a little less. The guy was still in serious trouble when they met, but he'd tried to keep her safe from Cyrus. Initially. "Was it a long time ago?"

"Six months," she said. "We'd stopped by a bar to have some drinks and listen to some local music before dinner. Anyway, he was there."

"At the bar?"

She nodded. "Chase totally freaked out, spilled his beer. They made small talk, and Cyrus offered to take us to dinner." She stopped. "Chase monopolized the conversation, I remember that. Stepping on my toes when I was going to talk. Cyrus gave me his card and told me if I ever needed work or help with school to call him."

Mal's gut churned. She'd been in the same room with the man that had skinned him, beaten him, and ripped his throat out. She'd been having dinner with a monster, defenseless. "What did you do?"

"Chase told me Northwestern wasn't the place for me, and we left that night instead of the next day. I sort of wrote the thing off and assumed Mr. White was just some weird eccentric guy." She shrugged.

"They never brought up business?"

She stared off at the horizon. "The only thing I remember was something about Russian dolls." She stopped, smiling. "That's it! I remember now, that's why I thought he was super creepy. He's a doll dealer or something, buys and sells dolls from all over the world. The better condition, the more money.

He spent thirty minutes talking about a sealed, early-edition fashion doll and how in demand they were. It was just weird."

"Dolls?" Mal repeated, thoroughly confused. "Cyrus had you kidnapped because your brother screwed up a doll order?" The collecting part, Mal believed. But whatever Cyrus was buying and selling from her brother, it wasn't dolls.

•••

They'd been huddled across the highway for an hour, her stomach growling so loudly she worried they'd attract bears. But then she remembered what Mal had done to the last bear and decided they were okay.

"How do you know if there's danger?" she whispered.

"You tune in," he said, clearly searching for the right words. "You'll feel it. It's like a ripple in the air. A wave. When a wolf is near, you'll know."

"Even from here?" she asked.

He nodded.

"The scent says whether it's your pack or not?" she asked.

He nodded.

"But we're waiting?" She'd learned that if she just kept asking questions, she'd find out what she needed to know. "Even though you don't smell anything and there's no ripple in the air."

He nodded.

"Because…?" She waited.

"You," he said. "They don't know you made it. That you're a wolf."

She sat back against the rock. At this point, she didn't want to acknowledge that last part. He could be the wolf. The bad guys could be wolves. But she wasn't. She *was* starving, and she could have eaten an hour ago. There was more to it. Something else was preventing him from going to that diner.

But what? Whatever it was, maybe he needed to do it alone. "I'll wait here. That's easy." She smiled.

He frowned.

"What?"

He shook his head.

"If I'm here then you don't have to—"

"Then you're unprotected," he argued.

She stared at him, flushing from head to toe. With all the sensory changes taking place in her body, it was a relief to know attraction and affection hadn't changed. Well, it had, but in a good way. It was amplified. And right now, the fact that he worried about her filled her with pure joy. "I'll be fine."

He growled, staring back at the truck stop.

"Tell me this is weird for you, too, please," she said.

"What?" he asked, not turning to look at her.

She wasn't sure how to put it into words. There was a connection between the two of them now. Her wolf told her part of it was the bite. So it was nothing really, but it was totally something. "Me and you," she managed.

"Yes," he agreed.

She giggled.

He looked at her then, smiling—and taking her breath away. She could almost feel his lips against hers, almost remember the way he tasted. Her breath hitched as she stared at his mouth, the ache in her stomach startling her. She shook her head.

He groaned. "You're thinking about what you said earlier?"

She kept shaking her head. Yes, that was exactly what she was thinking. But she didn't want to admit it. "No. I'm thinking about something else."

"You are?" he asked.

She stopped shaking her head. "No." It was a whisper.

"You can't lie to me a little?"

"I can't. Lying is the worst possible thing a person can do." She managed a nervous laugh. "You want me to lie to you?"

He shook his head. "No."

His dark eyes drew her to him. She liked being close to him, even if the air was thinner somehow. She tore her gaze from his, fighting for breath. "I won't lie to you," she whispered, glancing his way.

He was staring at her.

"Any change? Ripple? Wave-thingy?"

He shook his head. "All clear."

"Then let's get food. If we don't eat soon, I might just attack you."

Mal grabbed her wrist and led her to the highway. By the time they were inside the diner, his posture was ramrod stiff, his don't-mess-with-me expression giving the waitress pause to even seat them. When she finally did, he asked for a booth in the back corner.

"Stop glaring at people," she whispered, hugging the long coat tight. "No wolves, no worries." She hoped that was the case. They'd been walking all day, her need for a cheeseburger, french fries, and a milk shake was out of control. "Besides, the way you're acting will only draw more attention."

He glanced at her then, cocking an eyebrow.

She smiled. Tension rolled off him. Should she be worried, too? Her wolf was quiet—oddly so. "Thanks for feeding me."

He shook his head, but he rolled his head and blew out a long, slow breath.

They placed their orders and sat in silence. The longer the silence stretched, the faster his tension returned.

"What do you do?" she asked him. "When you're not saving me?"

He shook his head. "This and that."

"If you give actual answers, I won't have to ask you millions of questions."

"You've definitely exceeded two." He accepted the water the waitress placed on the table with a nod.

Olivia stared at the massive burger with pure delight. She took a bite and groaned at the delicious flavors tickling her taste buds.

He sat back, watching her with an odd look on his face.

"What's wrong?" She dabbed her mouth with a napkin and swallowed. "If you're not going to eat, you could talk?"

He ate a french fry.

If he wasn't in the mood to talk, she'd eat. "I'm starving. I don't think I've ever been this hungry in my entire life." She shrugged and took another large bite of her burger.

He grinned. "You're getting ready for tomorrow night."

She swallowed, taking a long pull off her chocolate milk shake. "Yum. What's tomorrow night? Oh, the moon." She ate a french fry, her enthusiasm dampened. As much as she was enjoying what was happening between the two of them, there was that whole other thing. Being a werewolf. Being a monster. That was her life now. "It's going to hurt, isn't it?"

He gave a vague, nod-shake of his head. "Nothing you can't handle."

"Are you saying I'm tough?" She ate two fries and picked up her burger. Even his compliments didn't ease the knot of apprehension in her gut.

"Yes."

She smiled slightly, her mind spinning again. Upset or not, it wasn't affecting her appetite. Her plate was empty and she accepted the offer of apple pie and ice cream without batting an eye.

Mal opted for coffee, black, his gaze bouncing around the room. He was agitated. From the images she'd glimpsed in his memories, there was an obvious cause. His pack. Their betrayal. That he might need them now would be hard to accept. She was having a hard time with it, and she didn't even know them—not personally.

"There's a pay phone. Are we calling them?" she asked.

He focused on his coffee cup.

"They're your pack," she whispered. "I feel it."

"They think I'm dead."

She studied the hard set of his jaw, the tightness bracketing his mouth and eyes. They'd hurt him deeply, but he was too proud to say as much. "So does Chase," she murmured. Her brother. His pack. "Thinks I'm dead, I mean. Maybe we should run away together? Someplace sunny and tropical? Do werewolves do okay in tropical climates? Or would the Others follow us?"

He cocked an eyebrow. "What is it about silence that scares you?"

She opened her mouth then closed it, refusing to take the bait. She could be quiet. But her wolf chose that moment to argue. Her wolf said Mal liked hearing her voice, that it chased away the hurt in his heart.

"I think you should call them," she said. "Let them know you're alive."

Mal stared at her for so long she worried she'd crossed some line. It was hard to accept they'd only known each other for two days—still harder to accept that in another twenty-four hours her world would never be the same.

Chapter Seven

Mal stared at the pay phone, torn between tearing it off the wall and just ripping the receiver free. For all he knew, it didn't work anyway. He picked up the handset. Dial tone. He glanced at Olivia in their booth. She was staring around the diner, battered and bruised and beautiful.

Calling Finn would get them out of here.

Calling Finn would make her safe.

Finn needed to know there was an Other in his home, listening to everything they did and said.

And, as unlikely as it was, maybe her odd interaction with Cyrus could provide insight into the Others.

He dropped a coin into the phone and dialed. It rang and rang and rang.

"Hello?" It was Hollis.

He'd been holding his breath, but Hollis answering made it easier. "Hollis?"

The line crackled. "Who is this?"

"It's me," he murmured, clearing his throat.

"Jesus Christ! Mal? Is that you?" He sounded muffled.

"It's Mal. On the phone."

"I need pickup," he said. "I'm in Alaska. A truck stop. Honey's Diner."

"Alaska?" Hollis repeated. "We're on the way. It's damn good to hear from you. Damn good."

"Plus one," he said. "We have a new pack member."

There was silence.

"Tomorrow will be her first change," he added.

"Got it," Hollis said. "We'll get there as soon as we can. What's the number?"

Mal read the numbers off the payphone. "Thanks."

"We didn't know, Mal. Jessa thought you were dead. We all thought you were dead." The anguish in Hollis's voice clutched at Mal's heart.

They did miss him. There was that.

"Not your fault," he said. Finn was the Alpha. He should have known, should have sensed it. If something happened to Olivia Mal would know. Because, for now, he was her Alpha—it was his job to know. As much as he wanted to forgive Finn, he didn't know if it was possible. The betrayal was so deep he wasn't sure he could truly be a part of them anymore. Guess he'd find out soon enough.

"Any threat in the area?" Hollis asked, clearly relaying from several voices in the background.

"Thirty-four hours ago. Left them unconscious in a house in the middle of nowhere, miles from here."

"Good," Hollis said.

He hesitated briefly before adding, "Cyrus said he has someone there, with you on the inside, Hollis. Any ideas?"

There was a long silence. "No. Maybe he was just trying to get in your head?"

The motherfucker had definitely gotten in his head. Maybe Hollis was right. He sure as hell hoped so. "Maybe."

"We'll call when we're fifteen minutes out. See you soon."

"Soon," he said, hanging up the phone. He felt it then: the pack. That internal leash tying him to them. Irritated or angry, betrayed or furious, it didn't matter—they were still a part of him. Even if he wished that weren't the case.

"How'd it go?" Olivia asked, leaning against the wall behind him. "Are we meeting them somewhere?"

"Finn will fly in," he said, glancing at her. It had been the two of them until now. Since she was his responsibility, he owed her some information. "We should talk."

Her brows rose. "We? You mean, *you're* going to *talk*?" She smiled. Then she frowned. "Wait, is this a good talk or a bad talk?"

Watching her was fascinating. Her features were fluid, revealing her thoughts before she said a thing. And she said plenty. But it was his turn. When she opened her mouth to say more, he pressed his fingers to her lips to stop her.

Touching her mouth was a bad idea. Her lips were silky soft. The shudder that rippled from her head to her toes told him she was eager. She'd said she thought about his kiss and wanted more. This touch, light as it was, was all it took to warn him he might want the same thing. He traced the shape of her mouth, the line of her jaw, cursing his stupidity but unable to stop touching her.

Her hand fastened around his wrist, holding on to him. She wanted him; he wanted her. But his wolf—her wolf—complicated things.

And things were getting dangerous.

"We're not doing this," he hissed, pressing her back against the wall. "You hear me?"

She nodded. But her gaze was fixed on his mouth.

He gripped her shoulders. "Olivia?" The desperate hunger in her gaze had his wolf howling and him reeling. She shouldn't look at him like that. She didn't understand that she was playing with fire.

The air crackled between them, wrapping them together in a way that made him forget anything else existed. His wolf wanted him to give in. Dammit, he wanted to give in.

"Mal," she whispered. "This isn't the ripple-wavy thing, is it? This is just more of the me and you thing?"

His nod was stiff.

If he were smart, he'd drag her back to their table and wait for Finn's phone call. He'd put space between them, stop touching her. But he'd relied on his instincts for so long.

He tilted his head, running his nose along her temple and across the bridge of her nose. Her lips were soft beneath his, but her hands gripped his shirtfront fiercely. She was shaking, but dammit, so was he. His lips lingered, absorbing the flavor of her—the feel of her. When his fingers slid into her hair, he didn't know. The silken threads caressed his fingers. In a hard world, Olivia was the embodiment of soft. One he wanted to protect. One he wanted to claim.

He stiffened slightly, his wolf's demand echoing in his ears.

Olivia would never be his mate.

His grip tightened on her hair. But it was Olivia that wrapped her arms around his neck and pulled him to her. It was her lips that clung to his, urging them apart so her tongue could trace the length of his and almost bring him to his knees. She was the aggressor, her fingers tugging his hair, her moans greedy and frantic.

Her lips fastened on his neck, her tongue and teeth nipping and sucking until his earlobe was bathed in the heat of her mouth.

"Fuck," he bit out, grinding his granite erection against her. "Goddammit."

She hooked one leg around his waist, her mouth seeking his.

He lifted her, her legs wrapping snug around his waist as

he gripped her hips. She had a firm ass, one he'd love to feel without her denim overalls between them. Hell, he wanted to touch all of her, naked and warm on a bed—with mirrors if she wanted them.

His wolf was ready, damn near whimpering.

Mal froze, burying his face against her throat. "No more." The words were hard and cold.

She was gasping for breath in his arms, her legs still tangled around him, her nails biting into his scalp. He disentangled her, holding her by the shoulders until her gaze cleared and her cheeks were bright with embarrassment. It wasn't her fault. He wanted her so bad it hurt to let her go. His wolf craved her more than anything. That was going to make this whole pack of two thing more difficult than he'd anticipated.

The sooner Finn got here, the better.

•••

Olivia washed her face for the third time. Never in her life had she been as mortified as she was right now. Or as confused.

What was she thinking? She'd practically climbed up his body and attacked him. It was sad—considering how easily he shut her down. Of course he would shut her down. She was acting crazy.

Because this was crazy. All of it. Whatever Mal said was wrong. She was losing it.

She stared her reflection in the eye. How long had it been since she'd done something normal like wash her face and look at her reflection? It felt like years.

But the last few days had been relentless, and it showed. Her matted hair stuck out, in need of a brush. Or some scissors. Dark smudges shadowed her eyes. Her lips were dry and chapped. Wearing the large trench coat she'd taken for Mal didn't help. She looked like a homeless person—a deranged homeless person. *This is how crazy looks.*

It made more sense to believe she was in a coma somewhere, dreaming. Maybe she'd had a reaction to her flu meds. Maybe she'd saved her brother from being mugged and knocked her head. Or maybe she was dead, and this was some sort of purgatory she'd have to earn her way out of.

But believing in werewolves—being a werewolf—made no sense.

As a student of anthropology, she'd learned the importance of tiny details and hypotheses. Sometimes it was necessary to suspend doubt, to suspect the unlikely, to find the truth. But this was asking too much.

"Pull it together, Olivia," she said loudly, to her reflection. "Wake up."

There are no such things as werewolves.

How could she dismiss what she'd seen? Rather, what she *thought* she'd seen. If, and it was a big if, she'd been attacked as badly as she'd imagined, she'd be dead. Right? Right.

And Mal had been in a cell. Naked. He'd carried her out, into the snow, naked.

She covered her mouth, trying to stop the slightly hysterical laugh from slipping out.

What, if any of that, was real?

Mal was real. She pressed her fingers to her lips. All too real. The way he watched her. His growl of a voice. The way he shielded her, protected her, over and over.

She stared down, shrugging out of the coat and draping it over the sink. Her hand shook as it ran along her thigh. She could feel a scar, raised but smooth, through the denim. She untied the rope belt and held the fabric back to inspect where she'd been wounded, and sucked in an unsteady breath. Scars like that took a long time to heal.

How long had she been in the cabin?

"Olivia?" Mal banged on the door.

"One second," she called out, overwhelmed with indecision and fear. What was going to happen to her? She ran for the stall, falling to her knees by the toilet as her stomach violently rejected its contents.

The bathroom door slammed into the wall, and Mal stood, staring down at her.

"Five minutes?" She held her hand up. "I can't have five minutes alone?"

His features relaxed. "You're sick."

She leaned back against the stall, closing her eyes. "I'm fine."

He snorted, crossing his thick arms over his broad chest.

She glared at him. Sure, he could look like *that* when she looked like some extra from a zombie apocalypse movie. "I've had a rough couple of days."

He paced the small room, his hands on his hips. "You've done well." He didn't look at her, but his words were soft.

She rested her chin on her knees, peering up at him. "Can I ask you something?"

He kept pacing, his nod quick.

It took all her energy to ask, "Can I go home?" She swallowed, trying again. "Can I pretend none of this happened? I want to go home and to un-know the things threatening my idea of the world. Please?"

He crouched by her, tilting her face toward his. "No."

"You can't keep me against my will—"

"I can bend your will to mine, Olivia." He sighed, stroking her cheek. "Whether you like it or not—whether I like it or not—your home is with me."

She frowned. She didn't like it. And yet, part of her really did. "For how long?" *Why was everything so confusing?*

He took her hand in his, pulling her up. "You need a shower."

She tugged her hand free. "Did anyone ever tell you to

work on your bedside manner?"

"No one has ever complained about my bedside manner." He grinned.

He was going to tease her? Now, when she was having an emotional crisis? He had no idea how close she was to running. She could always make a scene—surely some truckers would come to her defense if she said he'd taken her against her will. Then she could leave…

Stop it.

Why did the voice in her head have to be so damn bossy?

"Shower?" he asked.

"Now you have magical werewolf shower powers?" she asked.

He stared at her, in shock, before laughing.

It was her turn to stare. If his smile was mesmerizing, his laugh was dangerous.

His dark eyes swept her face. "Here." He shoved a bag at her, still chuckling.

She peered inside. "Clothes?"

He nodded. "After your shower," he murmured.

Apparently, there were showers in the truck stop, sort of like a drive through car wash, but for people. It resembled a closet with soap and shampoo dispensers mounted to the wall.

"Take your time." Mal's voice. "I'll stand watch. Knock when you're dressed."

She stared at the door, lost. She was listening to him, trusting him, looking to him to take care of her. And even though the voice in her head was telling her that was the right thing to do, she knew it couldn't be.

She kicked off her boots and stripped, all too happy to be rid of her dirty clothing. The water was hot, and the soap, all musky and bracing, left her skin refreshed and tingling. She scrubbed her hair until it was thickly lathered then let the water rinse it all down the drain. She stood under the dryer, wiping away as much of the residual water as she could. Her new wardrobe hung in a plastic bag on the back of the door. No bra or panties—but he had done his shopping in a truck stop. She slid into navy sweatpants, a white T-shirt that read *Truckers Do It on The Road*, and thick socks before tugging on her beaten boots. She shoved the bright pink hoodie back into the bag for later.

She knocked and opened the door.

Mal came in then, shutting and locking the door behind him. "I need five minutes," he said, tugging off his clothes before she had time to think. Words like, "Stop," or "Wait," or "Let me give you some privacy," never made it out of her mouth. Instead, she stared at his naked back, stunned.

"I can leave." Her voice shook.

Soapsuds ran down his back, skimming over the twisted scars to caress the firm curve of his buttocks on the way to his thighs.

"No." He ran his fingers through his hair. "Stay. Safer," he said, washing his face.

She blew out a deep breath and leaned against the wall. Safer? Only because he didn't know what she was thinking. What she was wanting. What would he do if she shoved all her new clothes back into the plastic bag they'd come in? What would he do if she pressed herself against his back and explored every inch of him?

Yes, her world had been turned upside down but…

He turned to face her, eyes shut, head tilted back under the shower.

Oh my God. Look away, look away, look away.

She couldn't do it. His body was perfect. Hard. Cut. It was like he was sculpted, the movement of his arms only showcasing every muscle. Shoulders, chest, stomach…her gaze wandered, following the dark trail that began at his navel and descended lower. Mal was big. All she could do was stand, and stare, and concentrate on breathing.

Her hands pressed flat against the wall. Cold as the tile was, she was on fire.

He shook the water from his hair and wiped his eyes, blinking away the water drops that clung to his thick eyelashes. And when he looked at her, she feared sliding down the wall to the floor. From relaxed to tense, his hands fisted at his sides, and his breath powered from his chest. He shook his head, jaw clenched.

She forced her gaze up, at the ceiling of the small stall.

But it didn't help.

He wasn't standing under the water anymore. He was inches away.

Chapter Eight

Her T-shirt was wet. With no bra, he could see the hard peaks of her nipples jutting against the thin cotton. And every gasping breath she took made them sway in invitation. It was an invitation every fucking cell ached to accept. The small sampling he'd had of Olivia left him craving more. It would be easy to finish what they started, to tug her pants off and wrap those silky thighs around him. Skin on skin, his hands gripping that firm ass as he showed her just what she'd been missing. Her out-of-control want for him was the only foreplay he needed.

Not that he'd act on it. Fuck no.

The words—*Truckers Do It on The Road*—added insult to injury. He shook his head again, unable to stop staring at her shirt, her breasts… He blinked, forcing his gaze up. Parted lips, dazed eyes, and flushed cheeks weren't much better.

"We're not doing this." His words lacked conviction. Because he—his wolf—really fucking wanted to do this. Her. Now. Hard. Until they were too tired to move or breathe or think. He swallowed, hands fisting against the urge to reach for her.

She nodded, still pressed against the tile, her breath still powering out of her, making her breasts shimmy and bounce in the most distracting ways.

"Goddammit," he muttered, ignoring the wolf and turning back into the shower. He blasted the cold water, spewing obscenities out long and loud until he'd cleared his head and his rock-hard erection eased.

He didn't look at her as he turned off the water, dried off, or dressed. His body was all too willing to respond to her. "Finn should be calling soon." Just saying his name helped Mal shift gears from horny to pissed. Pissed was better.

She didn't say anything.

He glanced at her, pulled her new pink hoodie from the bag and tossed it to her.

She caught it.

"Put that on." He nodded. "We're trying to avoid attention."

She glanced down at her shirt, frowning. "It's your fault."

He groaned. She was in the state she was in because she wanted him. And he was fucking walking away. His wolf was having a fit.

"I didn't pick out the shirt," she added, irritation replacing hunger.

He chuckled. Right, the shirt. "Just…cover up."

She tugged on the oversize hoodie, pulling up the excess material. "It's big."

Meaning she was drowning in material and her nipples weren't on display. Good. He was breathing a little easier when he pushed open the door. A quick look both ways told him it was clear, so he waved her forward. She hurried by him, leaning away when she squeezed through the doorway.

There was an old guy with a bag under his arm waiting for the shower. He looked Olivia up and down and shot Mal a wink. Mal ignored the urge to punch him and led Olivia back through the truck stop and into the diner.

The waitress nodded at them as they sat at the table they'd vacated. But once they were seated, Olivia sort of slumped into the booth—bleary-eyed and agitated. "Try to sleep," he said.

"Not tired," she said, stretching her arms out in front of her on the table and yawning.

He shook his head.

"I thought you said we needed to talk?" she reminded him, stretching her arms over her head then rolling her neck. "You never said if it was a good talk or a bad talk." Her small smile was teasing. "Are you breaking up with me?"

Mal couldn't stop his smile.

But then she was staring at his mouth and he knew, immediately, what she was thinking—and wanting.

"Want something?" the waitress asked, making them both jump.

"Coffee," he said.

"Same." Olivia nodded and tugged the bowl full of creamer and sugars toward her. She started stacking the creamer cups.

Mal watched her fingers, the slight tremor of her hands, how her hazel eyes focused on her work. He liked watching her, her laugh and smile. "Finn's the Alpha," he said. "He started it all."

She stared at him, turning a creamer cup over and over. "How? He"—she glanced behind her—"bit you?"

He nodded.

"You guys weren't born this way?" she asked.

He shook his head. "Finn's son is the only one of us that was born."

Her eyes went wide. "You can have children? With other werewolves? Or women?"

"You're the only female werewolf in our pack," he said, waiting for the waitress to serve their coffee before continuing. "There were five of us. Finn was infected first— "

"Who infected him?" She dropped the creamer packet on the table.

"His brother was an archeologist. There was an accident, Finn got stuck by a bone." He shrugged. "It infected him. And he infected us."

She frowned. "Why would he do that to you?"

"You sort of lose your head with the first change," he explained.

"I'll be on, like, a killing spree?" The question was whispered.

He leaned forward. "You'll be fine, Olivia. I'll make sure of that." He hadn't meant to take her hand again, but her fingers threaded with his. "We'll be safe at the reserve."

"Where is the reserve?" she echoed, still nervous.

"He has a few. Big one in Minnesota. Smaller one in Montana. Another in Wyoming. Finn's loaded. He bought half of Minnesota and started a wolf refuge, a place where Hollis could search for a cure without drawing attention."

"Makes sense." She looked at their hands, twined together. "The reserve isn't a reserve? It's a cover?"

He shook his head. "There are wolves there."

"Tell me about the pack. There were five?"

"Finn, the Alpha. Me. Hollis—he's sort of the resident doctor and wolf expert. Dante and Anders."

"And Finn's son?" she asked, releasing his hand to sweeten her coffee.

"Oscar." Mal nodded. "He was a baby. Finn's mate was expecting." He'd known Finn's mate a few days before she'd been kidnapped by the Others. In that time, he'd felt the bond between Jessa and Finn. It had been amazing—and terrifying.

"So, they've been together for a while?" she asked.

"That's nice."

He shook his head. "Oscar had a different mom. The Others killed her. Jessa was helping Finn take care of the baby when…when they became mates."

Olivia arched a brow. "I'm assuming that's different than your average human relationship?"

"Wolves mate for life." He muttered the words, sat back, and drank his coffee.

"She's a wolf?" she asked.

He shook his head. "Just his mate."

"I'm confused."

"Join the club," he answered. "He didn't turn her. At least, he hadn't when I saw her last. They are the good guys. The Others are bad. Cyrus, their Alpha, is a twisted son of a bitch I can't wait to rip to pieces." He looked at her, eyes narrowed. Except now, ripping Cyrus to pieces was no longer his top priority. "Since being turned, life's revolved around staying alive and protecting my pack. Which is you."

She smiled. "And Finn and the rest of them."

"We'll see," he said, not ready to let them back in yet.

"How long have you been gone?" she asked softly.

He shrugged. It could have been weeks or months. "Too fucking long."

She took his hand again. "They must have been missing you."

He stared at their hands, watching her fingers stroke his, the way they smoothed across his knuckles and the length of his thumb. He grabbed her hand, holding it securely in his. "If someone had you, I'd go after you," he said. "My wolf wouldn't let me give you up. Not without a fight." His words were thick. "They never came."

Olivia slid around the booth bench, pressing herself against his side. "They thought you were dead."

"That's bullshit. An easy answer," he grumbled. "You'll

understand once you shift. Your wolf, my wolf—there's a sort of sharing of thoughts and emotions—" He broke off. He wasn't sure how it would be between them, or if he was ready to be vulnerable with her.

She was smiling at him. "You must hate that."

He stared at her, reaching up to tuck one soft curl behind her ear. "I do."

Hazel eyes, warm and searching, bored into him. The longer she stared, the more curious he became. "What are you thinking?" he asked softly.

"Are you sure you want to know?" Her answer was equally soft.

He arched a brow. "You're not thinking about sex again?"

"I wasn't." Her cheeks flushed. "But thanks for taking me there again."

"What were you thinking?" he asked, refusing to lose himself to thoughts of Olivia and sex.

She cleared her throat. "Part of me wants to run screaming from the diner—far away from all of this." She swallowed. "I want my life back, without wolves, rules, bad guys chaining people in cells, being mauled by bears, and you. No matter how calm and sane you appear, there's nothing sane about *any* of what you're telling me." She sucked in a deep breath. "I miss home. Television and takeout Chinese food, fuzzy slippers and naps and lousy roommates and unreliable brothers. I want boredom, security, and safety. The *known*. None of this."

His wolf whimpered. "And the other part?"

"Wants to take away the hurt and anger in your heart." She shrugged. "I want this bizarre connection between us to be real. Which is ridiculous. I've known you for, what, a few days? I'm still confusing simple human emotions—like lust for love. Even I know it's not possible to fall in love over the span of a few days, so this you and me thing is all wolf. But it's so intense." She stopped. "Honestly, I still keep expecting to wake up."

He wished she were dreaming. Then none of this would be real. He didn't want to be here any more than she did. He didn't want to be responsible for her, for any of this. And he sure as hell didn't want to hear her say things like *love*, not to him. "You're awake," he mumbled. "So, pick one."

"I didn't think there was a choice," she said, cradling her cup with both hands.

He looked at her. "If there was, what would you pick?"

She spun the cup slowly in her hands before meeting his gaze. The air grew heavy again, weighted by the magnetism of their connection. He was rooted there, waiting for her answer—terrified and hopeful.

The phone rang.

• • •

Olivia glanced at Mal. Whatever was being said on the telephone, he didn't look happy. But, to be honest, he rarely looked happy. He was a master of the blank expression, with the occasional don't-talk-to-me-or-I'll-hurt-you glare thrown in. There was also the look of confusion she brought out in him…and the other look. The one that made the pit of her stomach warm and liquid and her toes curl and her lungs empty.

She shook her head, mulling over his question—which hadn't been a real question. If this was real, all of it, of course she couldn't leave. And, improbable as it was, she was beginning to believe that might be the case. She took a bracing sip of hot coffee—

An odd shiver shot up her spine, from her tailbone to the base of her skull, a flash of heat—a warning. The air around her seemed to ripple. A ripple. Something she'd never felt before, something that made her feel nauseated and uneasy.

She stood, knocking the table and spilling her coffee onto the speckled laminate. Her gaze swept the room as she tugged her hood up. No one else was there. Not yet. Her gaze fixed on Mal as she made her way to him in the phone booth.

His expression made the hair on the back of her neck stand straight up. Tension rolled off of him, his posture ramrod stiff. "They're here," he said into the phone, pausing briefly. "Now."

"Mal?" A whisper was all she could manage.

He pulled her against his side, easing her at once. "We'll be there. Get her out of here. No matter what." He hung up the phone, his gaze sweeping the room. "In the truck stop." Grabbing her hand, he headed down the hall to the bathroom. He locked the door behind them, eyes narrowing as they inspected the window placed high in the wall. "Can you fit?" he asked.

She nodded, accepting his help as he gave her a boost. "Mal—"

"I'm right behind you," he said, shoving her up. "Go."

She didn't want to, but somehow she was pushing the window wider and crawling out into the snow outside. The air was cold and clean, the ripple less pronounced. Breathing was easier, but there was nowhere to hide—and her gut told her to hide. The fluorescent exterior lighting seemed too bright, almost as if its sole purpose was to announce her presence. The urge to run grew, so that the sudden touch of Mal's hand on her back made her jump.

"Stay calm, Olivia." Mal grabbed her hand and tugged her behind him.

She was struck by how silently he moved. While she was shuffling along, tripping over her own feet, every footfall echoing, he crept between the semis on soundless feet, alert and ready for—she wasn't sure she wanted to know.

He stopped occasionally, forcing her to brace herself or

teeter on tiptoe to avoid plowing into his back. And every time, Mal reached back to steady her.

By the time they reached the edge of the parking lot, her nerves were shot. She didn't like feeling clumsy. She wasn't clumsy. She did yoga and took her kickboxing classes regularly. But doing yoga in studio or kickboxing in the gym hadn't prepared her for running for her life. And the voice in her head, the one she was beginning to recognize as her wolf, was certain that was the case.

She did her best to follow Mal's example. She moved when he did, breathed when he did, and tried not to act like she was on the verge of a panic attack. When they reached the cover of the woods, he stopped.

"Your heart's racing," he whispered.

"I'm sorry?" she squeaked.

He turned to face her then, his hands clasping her shoulders. "Controlling your fear takes time. You're doing great."

"I am?" she asked, stunned.

He nodded, rubbing her shoulders. His gaze wandered beyond her to the truck stop and its blindingly bright parking lot. Snow was falling, carpeting everything in white.

"Are we safe?"

His grin was tight and his voice was low. "That's always the question."

She stepped into him. "Mal? Are we?"

He glanced at her. "Close your eyes."

"What?"

"Close them," he repeated.

She did, instantly.

"Concentrate—tell me if what you felt is gone." His voice was low and deep, lulling her into submission. "Are we safe? Or are they still here?"

Olivia stood still, but her mind was racing.

"Focus. Take slow deep breaths and concentrate." His breath stirred the hair by her ear, his heat was at her back, one hand resting on her stomach. "Don't overthink this. Just listen."

Focus. On Mal. His warmth, his touch, the even brush of his breath at her temple. But getting lost in him wasn't what he was after. And even though she appreciated the comfort he offered, she'd never had much luck relying on people. Focus.

She heard the snow falling.

The gears of a truck shifting.

A bell? The truck stop door opening.

People talking. Inside. Not just people.

Something else. Something different.

The newcomer's heartbeat was a little faster, a little stronger than the others. A wolf.

"Inside," she whispered. "Just one?"

His hand pressed her back against him, blanketing her in warmth. "Little things like scent, pulse, and breathing are important. Sweat is more potent—sour—with stress. Pulse is strong and rapid when hunting. When breathing is shallow and rapid, chances are they're hunting a scent."

Olivia listened again. "Shallow breathing."

"He's still looking," he said. "Let's keep moving."

She opened her eyes, her senses processing. It felt like having an all-over rug-burn, prickly and sensitive. All the newness prodding. All overwhelming.

"Olivia?" he whispered, turning her in his arms. He was so close, so solid.

"Out of sorts." She ran a hand over her head, pressing her fingers to her forehead to silence the sounds. "And noise." It was a dull roar, voices, noises, rolling over her in waves. Her equilibrium was off. Her nerves stung. "Just so much feeling." It didn't explain things, but it was true.

His arms were heavy around her, steadying her. She

leaned into him, pressing her eyes closed and shutting out everything but the solid *thunk-thunk* of his heart. Her hand rested on his chest, absorbing the rhythm—and the comfort of him. *Because nothing said comfort like cuddling with a werewolf-man.*

"Look up," he whispered.

His softly spoken words had her looking up. Her breath caught, stunned by the brilliance of the stars in the sky. Never in her life had she seen a night so clear. Midnight blue, patches of pitch, scattered with a million brilliants. The clarity was startling, the black deep and vast and breathtaking. It was oddly exhilarating.

The moon was massive, almost full.

"Tomorrow?" she whispered. "Should I be scared? Excited?" Her fingers gripped the thick flannel jacket he wore. "Because I feel really lost."

He didn't say anything. What was there to say? But his hand stroked the length of her back and that was enough.

"I'm going to be okay?" she asked. "It's okay if you lie to me, Mal. It's just…I really need to think this is all going to be okay."

"I don't lie," he argued, his tone sharp.

"Mal," she pleaded, tugging on his shirt and staring at him in the dark.

"I never lie," he repeated.

Those words washed over her, buoying her spirits and making it easier to breathe. For a man that used words so sparingly, those three words were exactly what she needed to hear.

"You're going to be okay." His hand gripped hers, tugging her forward. "Let's go."

To the refuge.

Where she'd be surrounded by werewolves—or crazy people that believed they were werewolves. Considering tomorrow was the full moon, she'd know soon enough if she should be scared of the crazy or the wolves. But then, she'd be a wolf, too, so there would be no reason to be scared.

How was any of this okay? Nothing felt *okay*. She didn't remember what okay was at the moment. Just fear and confusion and total sensory overload.

Mal's fingers threaded with hers. *You're going to be okay*. His words weren't the easiest to believe, but she believed him anyway.

Chapter Nine

Mal wanted to shift. He'd kept his fury caged since they'd taken him. No matter how many times they'd beaten and left him bleeding and full of silver, he'd refused to give up. Vengeance gave him something to fight for. A purpose beyond giving the Others entertainment. Now he was free. He could shift whenever he fucking felt like it. But one thing was stopping him.

Olivia.

Not that it was her fault. No, dammit, she was blameless in all of this. Innocent. A quality he'd almost forgotten existed.

If Olivia weren't there, he'd wait for the motherfucker to come out. His wolf would stay out of sight, toy with him, then bleed the son of a bitch out and rip him into pieces so small it'd be impossible to identify who or what he once was.

But Olivia was with him.

There was no choice. He'd tuck tail and run back to Finn. Even if it was like rubbing salt in a big-ass wound. She was his responsibility. Warning Finn about the Others was his responsibility, too, dammit. He hoped Hollis was right—that the pack's safety hadn't been compromised. But he needed to find out for himself.

He glanced over his shoulder at Olivia. She stared, wide-eyed, around her, moving quietly and staying in his tracks. Her hand clung to his as they trudged through the snow, following his lead without thought. And he liked it a little too damn much. Maybe it was his wolf pressing his agenda on the man. Maybe it was the unnerving attraction they shared. Maybe it was because she was a decent human being that deserved to live. Whatever it was, he was beginning to—grudgingly—like having her around.

And that made things so much worse.

His wolf already knew. The traitor jumped ship before they ever got out of that damn cell. As far as he was concerned, Olivia was his pack. Worse, the animal wanted Olivia as his mate. No matter how badly Mal objected to the latter, the wolf wasn't giving up.

They walked until the chattering of Olivia's teeth was too hard to ignore.

"Cold?" he asked, teasing.

"Y-y-yes," she tried to snap back.

Knowing she was miserable wasn't amusing. Cold as it was, he'd no doubt that adrenaline and fear was ramping up her reaction. He tended to block memories of Finn's attack, being turned and the horror that followed. It had been bad—a waking nightmare. Sensory overload, mood swings and exhaustion, excitement and terror. He'd had time before his first shift to come to terms with what had happened and understand what to expect.

Olivia had no idea. All she had was his word…and her wolf. He could sense her waiting on the periphery of Olivia's mind, eager to be fully realized. Pure energy and enthusiasm, naïveté and endless strength—tomorrow night was going to be one hell of a ride.

She froze, going perfectly still and drawing him up short. The sound was faint at first. His wolf knew what it was before he did.

"Is that a helicopter?" she whispered, pressing herself against his side.

He was impressed. She'd heard it before he had. "Finn."

She relaxed against him.

They might be about to get rescued, but they weren't out of danger—not yet. And relaxation was the last thing on his mind. The louder the helicopter grew, the more agitated he became. The pack was coming for them, so why wasn't he happy? Why couldn't he forget the hurt and anger their desertion caused? It was a splinter festering deep, one he couldn't ignore—not yet.

Maybe it was a good thing. His anger had given him the fight to survive the shit-storm of captivity. The future was still uncertain. Just because they were excited about his homecoming didn't mean they'd welcome Olivia with open arms.

Maybe calling Finn had been a bad idea. He'd been taking care of them just fine on his own, and Olivia was smart, her instincts were kicking in. They'd be a good team—he could tell. Except that wasn't fair to her. Keeping her to himself, living on the road, on the run—she deserved better. Once she'd settled in with the pack—with Finn—Mal could do whatever the fuck he wanted. On his own.

His wolf whined then growled. Leaving Olivia didn't sit well with his inner beast.

The chatter of her teeth pulled him from his internal argument. He glanced down at her, frowning. She was watching him, her face too shadowed to reveal what she was thinking. Which could be a good thing. "What's wrong?"

She shook her head.

"Tell me," he urged.

The helicopter was in view now, a spotlight sweeping the newly fallen snow.

"You're w-worried," she managed. "About me? Where I-I fit, what to do with me?"

He sighed.

"Because you're not sure you still belong with this pack? Or because of the you and me thing?"

He shook his head. "Because I don't know what's best for you."

"So, making me a werewolf suddenly renders me incapable of making my own decisions?" she asked, the hint of anger creeping into her tone.

He growled. "Can we do this later?"

She let go off him, wrapping her arms around her waist.

He waited, but she stayed silent. In the grand scheme of things, her bad mood didn't matter. Hell, being pissed was more effective than being scared. Not that he was going to let anything happen to her. He shook his head, tugging her into the clearing behind him and shielding his eyes from the beam of light…

A ripple. A warning.

His wolf recognized the scent. The one tracking them, an Other. The wind had shifted just enough to give him cover. Enough to let him get too damn close. He shoved Olivia behind him and turned, scanning the darkness.

Was he alone? It was unlikely.

Glowing white eyes waited in the shadow of the trees. One pair so far. That was good.

"He sees us," she said, her fingers gripped the back of his jacket.

Mal hesitated. He couldn't let the wolf go. The Others were uncertain how many were in Finn's pack, and that's the way they wanted to keep it. That might have changed since he'd left, but he wasn't going to risk it. Add Olivia's presence, healthy and alive, and they'd know he'd turned her.

"Mal?" she whispered.

"Stay here," he said, knowing the helicopter was overhead. "Dante is here. Sad eyes, floppy hair. Go with him."

"No, Mal—"

"Go with him," he snapped. She didn't understand, not really—not yet. But she would. The bastard couldn't get away.

She released him.

He shrugged off his coat, the shift already running over his flesh and stretching his muscles. It wasn't easy, he was agitated—worrying about Olivia, worrying about not getting the wolf before it ran. He fell forward, grunting against the snap of bone, the shift of vertebrae and joints. Claws tore through knuckles. Flesh gave way to fur. His heart picked up, his breath pulling the rival wolf's scent deep into his lungs. His ears cocked forward, tuning in to his adversary.

The hunter had become the hunted. And Mal's prey was braced for a fight.

•••

Olivia wanted to throw up. Watching Mal tear apart was mesmerizing and terrifying. Hearing each snap and pop, the wet rip of skin and scent of blood—this was Mal. Her Mal. His beautiful body split wide to leave something different. She wanted to block out the sounds and un-see what had just happened. But she couldn't. Even the spinning blades of the helicopter and the whir of the engine didn't drown out the sounds of his shift.

Mal was gone. And breathing, thinking, moving, was impossible.

When hands gripped her shoulders, she jumped, screamed, and shrugged away from the touch.

Mal—the wolf—stared back at her, the thick black fur of

his neck bristling. She stepped back, unable to stop herself. *This was Mal.* This was *Mal.* Mal was a big, scary black wolf growling at her. No, not at her. The man behind her. She looked—a man in a harness, holding a rope. From the helicopter.

"I've got her," the man said, nodding at Mal.

Mal snorted and tore across the snow, leaving her behind.

"Dante," he said, extending his hand.

She stared at his hand, his face, and stepped back. "Sad eyes," she muttered, glancing at him. "Dante?"

The man nodded, studying her. "You are?"

She stared after Mal, her heart throbbing. He couldn't leave her. She was supposed to be with him, at his side—no matter what he was facing. The urge to follow him was powerful, pulling her forward.

But Mal's command echoed in her ears. "Go with him."

Where the tears came from, she didn't know. Incredible sorrow and pain engulfed her. He'd left her. Left a hole right through the middle of her. He wasn't supposed to leave her—not ever.

The hand returned to her shoulder. She didn't like it, didn't want anyone to touch her.

"He'll be back," Dante said. "Trust me."

She nodded, fighting the urge to go and the hold Mal's words had placed on her.

"Your name?" he asked again.

"Olivia Chase." She sounded…angry. Because she felt angry. At Mal.

"Let's get you into the helicopter," Dante said.

She glared at him. "No."

"Mal said to go with me, Miss Chase," Dante reminded her.

Her eyes burned violently. He had told her to go. She sniffed. "Fine."

He held his hands up. "I'm going to snap you in," he said, offering her the harness.

She nodded, staring into the darkness.

More eyes.

"Dante?" she whispered. "Do you see them?"

"Aw, shit," Dante groaned.

A howl split the night, sending her to her knees. It was impossible to breathe or see or think. Mal. Growling, snarling, whimpers. A howl cut short. Mal. She didn't realize she'd screamed his name out loud until Dante told her he'd be fine.

She didn't know how Dante managed to get her into the harness, or how she wound up in the helicopter, leaning out the door, waiting.

"Two more?" she asked. "Three?"

Dante stared out into the dark, his posture growing more agitated.

She held on to the handle by the door, leaning as far as she could without falling. She might be a werewolf, but something told her she wasn't ready to follow Mal out into the fight. Even if part of her, a very big part of her, wanted to do just that.

If she concentrated she could hear him—his heart beating, the ragged gasp of his breath. Adrenaline sliced through her, kicking her own heart rate up.

It lasted too long.

And the noise—primal, feral, terrible—echoed in her brain and flooded her blood with an energy she didn't understand. A quiver ran along her spine, making her twitch and tingle. She itched under her skin. Her joints felt tight and her brain pulsed.

Amid the howls, whimpers, and growls, she searched for some sign of Mal.

Dante's eyes narrowed, his gaze focused on something she didn't see. "Stay here. I will help him, but you have to stay here."

"Don't leave him." Her words were hard, a hoarse

demand.

He nodded then jumped from the helicopter.

"What the hell?" a voice crackled over the intercom.

A shot rang out, so loud she covered her ears. Another followed.

Dante lay, naked and human, on the ground below the helicopter.

She stared at Dante's lifeless body, a large red patch forming on his newly bared chest. He'd been ready to shift when the bullet made impact. Now he was vulnerable and alone.

She heard a howl and saw them, wolves, circling the tree line.

Where was Mal? There was no way he could rescue Dante and protect himself from the circling pack. Mal's howl split the night, and desperation washed over her. She had to do something.

"You need to land," she called to the pilot.

The voice crackled, "No can do—"

"Now," she argued. "They need help."

"Shit, damn, ass, stupid." The voice continued insulting the state of the world, but the helicopter was landing. It was fast, the ground rising to meet them with a jarring impact. Then the cockpit door opened and and a man came out. Outfitted in riot gear, an automatic weapon in each hand and a belt full of knives, he seemed almost excited.

He nodded, winked, and climbed through the helicopter door before she moved a muscle.

She jumped out, helping lift Dante's unconscious form into the helicopter.

"Hurry," the man urged. "They're almost on us."

Olivia didn't let his words get to her. She couldn't. She was too busy looking for Mal.

"Where is he?" she asked.

"He'll be okay."

"We are not leaving him. Do you hear me?" she shrieked. "I don't care if I get eaten waiting."

The man grinned. "No need to get all riled up now."

But Mal's wolf was running toward them and everything snapped back into place. The hole was gone. The fear, too. He planted his feet, the fur on his neck and shoulders bristling as he faced their attackers.

"That's his way of telling us it's time to go," the man said, pulling her into the helicopter.

She almost argued, but Mal climbed in after them.

Second later, the helicopter was rising in to the sky, the rapid whir of the blades drowning the frustrated howls of the wolves they left below. She didn't know whether to hug him or punch him, so she curled into herself. But Mal's nose slid between her face and knees, his whimper pulling at her heart. She hugged him close, losing her fear in the feel of his soft fur against her face. He pressed against her, a low rumble in his chest, sniffing her hairline and throat.

"Is he okay?" she asked Mal. "Dante?"

The wolf groaned, moving to Dante's side, sniffing his wounds. He sat, staring at her, then Dante.

"I'm not a nurse," she argued, crawling forward to peer at the wound in Dante's chest. "I heard two shots."

The wolf grunted, a sharp woof.

She looked at him. "It's sort of rude, isn't it? To shoot at each other instead of fighting it out as wolves. Sort of underhanded."

Mal's wolf grinned. He did—that's the only word for it.

"What?" she asked, turning back to Dante. She pressed her ear to his chest. "His heart sounds good." She hesitated, remembering what Mal had told her. "He's calm. Even his breathing is normal."

"Takes a lot to kill a wolf," the voice crackled. "I'm Gentry, by the way."

"Are you a wolf?" she asked.

"No." He laughed. "But I sure love running with the crazy-ass-motherfuckers."

She sat back on her heels, sighing.

"It's fucking good to see you, Mal," Gentry added.

"Damn good," Dante whispered from the floor. "Damn good."

Mal was up, ears cocked forward, nuzzling Dante's face. Dante laughed, patting the wolf's neck with an unsteady hand.

"What'd I tell you? Tough sons of bitches," Gentry said.

Tears were streaking down her face. Tears? Why now—when he was safe? When they were safe? Now was not the time to lose it.

"They know about her now," Dante whispered.

She stiffened.

Mal's brown eyes met hers. As a wolf, Mal was more expressive—more in tune. There was regret in his eyes, and worry. She shook her head, sliding across the floor to rest against the metal wall of the helicopter. It vibrated violently beneath her head, the tinny echo sending painful sparks into her skull, behind her eyes.

What was wrong with her?

Her temples were pounding. A sudden dull ache bloomed at the base of her neck and crushed in on her head. Never in her life had she felt so alone. Or helpless. Her wolf had wanted to help him. She'd wanted to help him.

"Finn has a plane waiting to take us to the refuge," Gentry's voice crackled again.

The rest of the ride was silent. She concentrated on the pulse in her head, on *not* thinking about how Mal's body had contorted and twisted. Or the fear that she would never truly be safe again. That Chase was in danger—or the bad guy. Or that she was falling in love with a werewolf.

When they touched down on the tarmac, Mal nudged her

from the helicopter. She and Gentry helped Dante make the short trek to the waiting jet.

Mal followed, a gorgeous shirtless, fatigue-pants-wearing man. But in his brooding gaze, Olivia caught sight of his wolf. She didn't resist as his arms came around her, as he pulled her close with a sigh. He shivered, the muscles of his shoulders tensing as she nuzzled his neck. It was instinctual. Natural. Nothing more. Offering him comfort was the right thing to do. And the soft grumble at the back of his throat told her he approved.

"Let's get the hell out of here," Gentry said, disappearing into the front of the plane.

Apparently, he could fly both helicopters and airplanes. And use all sorts of weapons. And he liked it. Just one more crazy thing at this point.

"You'll heal faster if you can shift," Mal said.

"Silver," Dante pointed at the wound in his chest. "Went through, but there's traces left—I can feel it."

She winced, so did Mal, and Dante grinned. "You want to tell me what happened?" Dante asked softly.

"How long?" Mal asked, pulling her onto the couch beside him.

Silence fell.

"How long have I been gone?" he repeated.

"Three months." Dante's voice was thick.

Fury coursed through her. Her gaze bounced from Mal to Dante. "You left him in that place for three months?"

"Olivia— " Mal's voice was low.

"Don't you dare tell me to be quiet." She cut him off. "That's not right, leaving you there for so long." She glared at Dante, her emotions all over the place once more. But seeing Dante's sadness, and the pain on his face, made her instantly regret her hostility.

"I agree," Dante said.

"But you're not the Alpha, are you?" she whispered, directing her anger at Finn—the one who *had* left Mal.

Dante exchanged a look with Mal, a look she didn't understand.

"No, Olivia, he's not." Mal's voice was coaxing, almost pleased. "So be nice to him."

She frowned, tearing her gaze from Dante to look at Mal—really look at him. Scratches covered his bare chest. A bite covered the ball of his shoulder and the side of his neck. She ran her fingers over a deep bruise on his cheek, wincing at the blood that trickled from his right ear. "Are you okay?" she managed, truly concerned.

He smiled as he smoothed the curls from her shoulder, his warm gaze exploring her face. His gaze locked with hers, hot and bold and yearning. There was no mistaking the hunger in his eyes as he stared at her mouth, or the subtle shift of his hands on her body.

"Your mate has spirit," Dante said. "It will make tomorrow night easier."

Mal's eyes narrowed. "She's not my mate," he bit out, jaw clenching.

Dante shook his head. "Holy shit, here we go again. Guess denial is the first step in finding a mate," he mumbled, loud enough to be heard.

Mal's dismissal cut through her, stealing the warmth he'd given her only seconds before. Dante was a wolf, yet she didn't have the same odd reaction Mal's presence elicited. She had yet to meet Finn or the rest of the pack, but she suspected it would be the same. What was between her and Mal was different—even if he didn't want to accept it.

Accept it or not, Olivia was adrift in loneliness. Nothing made sense. Nothing. But letting her fear take over wasn't productive. Fear wasn't going to rule her—she was stronger than that.

Chapter Ten

Mal's grip tightened on her, without thought. She was trying to put distance between them, probably pissed again. Distance was good. She wasn't his mate, she was his pack. And he needed to remember that—for both their sakes. But the wolf wouldn't let him.

Tonight had scared the shit out of him. When Dante fell, he'd been too far away to get to him. But seeing the helicopter land, watching the Others close in, knowing Olivia was inside… He'd left the fight to get to her. He'd had no choice. She was exposed, at risk, in danger. No fucking way.

Now the Others knew she was alive. It was safe to assume her scent revealed the rest: Olivia was a wolf. What that meant for her, for them, he wasn't sure. But it sure as hell wasn't good. There were too many unknowns. Mal, his wolf, didn't like unknowns.

"Damn, Mal," Dante's voice was thick.

Mal stared at his friend, his family. His chest grew heavy, and the familiar dread that had tightened his stomach since they'd left him eased. "Glad you're okay." He'd spent a lot of nights wondering how things had turned out—if anyone else had been lost in the fight.

Dante swallowed, answering Mal's unasked question, "You were the only casualty."

Mal shot him a look.

"Jessa said you saved her," Dante went on. "She blames herself."

Mal shook his head, Olivia stiffening in his arms. He ran his hand down her back, offering comfort—taking it in return. Jessa wasn't the one that left him swinging from that tree. Logically, Mal understood. Finn would pick Jessa, his mate, over him. But it wasn't always easy to think logically when you're chained to a wall getting your ass kicked by two sadistic werewolves.

"Ellen said you were dead," Dante said.

"Ellen?" Mal growled, his hand stilling on Olivia's back.

"She is—was—one of the Others. I don't fucking know where exactly she fits." Dante paused. "But she's helping Jessa through her pregnancy."

Mal stared at Dante. He'd never considered they'd *welcome* an Other into the pack. "And we're trusting her?" Cyrus's plant was in plain sight?

"Not all of us." Dante frowned. "It's an uneasy truce."

"Un-fucking-believable," he mumbled. Finn gets a mate and loses all judgement? Another reason to steer clear of the whole mate mess.

His wolf growled. Olivia slid from his lap. Maybe she sensed his agitation. Or maybe he was squeezing her a little too hard.

"Seeing you—your throat torn out—" Dante broke off, shaking his head. "No one should have survived that."

"I did." He rested his head against the seat, breathing through the pain and anger Dante's words stirred. Maybe he was right. Maybe he shouldn't have survived. There'd been times he wished he'd died. The last time, strung up, back newly skinned, something inside him cracked wide open. He'd wanted to give up—until Cyrus had given him a knife to end his own suffering. But the smile on the fucker's face had been too smug. Mal had thrown it at him, slicing through the bastard's ear, and lost his one chance to make the pain go away.

Olivia's hand took his. She didn't face him or move closer, but her fingers wrapped around his. He was hurting. Touching her made it better. It was simple and honest. He pulled her hand into his lap, breathing easier when she leaned against his side.

His wolf was pleased—Mal ignored him. "How is Jessa?" She'd been nice enough. He hoped she'd survive life as the mate of their messed-up pack's Alpha.

"Due anytime now," Dante said.

"She going to make it?" he asked. The mother of Finn's first child, the result of a hookup and failed birth control, had died when baby Oscar was born. Her cause of death had been a mystery—the Others or due to the abnormal pregnancy. If it was the latter, there was reason to worry about Jessa's life.

Dante shrugged. "Sure as hell hope so. Finn's losing his shit as it is."

Olivia yawned, drawing his attention. She was worn out—she had every right to be. She was facing the biggest change of her life. Throw in new scents, new sensations, new threats—her nerves had to be shot. Him acting like a moody asshole wasn't helping.

If he were the sort of guy that apologized for being a dick, this would be the time.

"You look tired." Dante led them to the waiting plane. "It takes a couple of hours to get to the Montana refuge. You can sleep."

The plane's interior was chrome and leather, soft lighting,

every modern convenience. The exact opposite of where he'd spent the last three months. Now the hiss of the air, the thrum of the plane beneath his feet, the shift in the air, plucked at his senses. He'd rather shift—trek through the woods and let his neglected senses take over for a while. He gritted his teeth, the space closing in on him.

Olivia's presence grounded him. She looked as dazed and lost as he felt, but the slight smile she shot him, soft and trembling, made him wonder why he was fighting this. Not just her, but his wolf.

When they landed, he'd run until his wolf collapsed.

•••

Olivia sat on the edge of a long sofa. Her fingers plucked the edge of the cushion, tracing the seam of the buttery leather fabric. It smelled clean. Not clean like the fresh night air or the towering pines. But sterilized. As the door of the cabin closed the air seemed to thicken, weighing her down—making her clammy.

"There's a bedroom," Dante offered. "Or a bathroom, if you want a shower?"

A shower. On a plane. Because Finn was rich. And, apparently, rich people had showers on their airplanes. She glanced at Mal, her mind flooded with images of him naked, covered in soap suds, and glorious.

Clear her head, that's what she needed to do. Focus on drowning out the white noise so she could sift through the emotional minefield in her head.

After being alone with Mal for so long, the confined space and extra bodies pressed in on her until she almost missed the snow, the dilapidated cabin, and the endless trees she'd found comfort in. She should focus on that—the quiet black night of the forest. Not the mad beat of her pulse reverberating through her spine and neck, making her head throb. She blinked, pressing a hand to her temple. She was vaguely aware of Dante and Mal talking, of Gentry's southern drawl over the intercom, but to her it was white noise. A deafening, whirring buzz that challenged her focus.

"Here." Mal's offer of a glass of water startled her but she took the glass and nodded her thanks. He sat by her, his hand wrapping around hers and soothing the fight rising within her. "Olivia." His voice was low. "Look at me."

She blinked and frowned and stared at the ceiling, but eventually she had to look at him. He was too beautiful. Light brown eyes burned into hers. His jaw locked, lips pressed flat—as if he was holding something back. Everything about him was restrained.

"We'll talk when we get there," he said to Dante, pulling her to her feet. "Right now, might be best if we got some sleep."

It didn't take long for them to find the bedroom. But once inside the lavish room, she stared in astonishment. No more chains or dark basements, bloody snow or truck-stop showers. It seemed ridiculous they were here. How had she ended up with strangers who were werewolves, headed toward some wolf refuge owned by the billionaire with a fancy plane. Who happened to be the Alpha of the pack. Their *werewolf* pack.

Her lungs emptied, each fingertip going tingly, while cold sweat ran down her spine. All of this was wrong and completely illogical. But the voice in her head—her wolf—didn't want her to worry. *Her wolf?* The door shut behind her, but she didn't turn to face Mal. How could she? She was on the verge of an emotional implosion.

His hands landed on her shoulders, causing a full body shiver. "Sleep?" The word brushed her ear.

Sleep? She shook her head, too worked up to think about sleep. Her brain was too busy short-circuiting to sleep. She'd rather fight, argue, anything to let out some of her unexplained aggression. "Stop trying to control me, Mal."

"Olivia." He turned her, tilted her head back. His gaze searched her face, a furrow forming between his thick brows. "You—"

"I frustrate you, I know. I'm a nuisance. I'm spiraling out of control, and you don't know what to do with me," she whispered, watching the play of emotions on his face. "Honestly, I don't know what to do with me, either."

"You *amaze* me," he finished. His hand cupped her cheek. There was warmth in his gaze, a heavy, delicious warmth that erased the jagged edges from her hurt and temper.

Her heart thumped. He cared about her, she knew it. Her wolf, vague and unfocused as the voice was, knew it, too. Things seemed to click into place. "But you're going to leave me with him—with Finn—aren't you?" she asked. That was why she was afraid. That was what was wrong. She couldn't do this without him.

He frowned. "I'm going to do what's best for you." His hands slid down her shoulders and released her.

She shivered. "That's not an answer," she whispered, her gaze falling to his lips. It was the only answer she was going to get.

He steered her to the bed. "We'll talk later. Now, sleep." He yawned and kicked off his boots. She watched him stretch, immediately distracted by the angles and edges of his torso. Was it normal to have so many abs, or was that a werewolf thing?

He dropped his pants and sat, naked, to pat the bed beside him.

She stared. He was naked. He was totally naked. And this was the first time they'd been alone without the fear of being ambushed or mauled. She could stare at him, set aside her frustration, for the few hours they had together before landing. This was their time, a time to get acquainted without the rest of the world pressing in on them. Looking at him was easy, but the looking turned to wanting and difficulty breathing and hot, aching hunger—

"Olivia." There was a hint of warning in his voice. A hint. "Sleep."

"Like actual sleep?" She sounded like a disappointed child. "But you're naked," she mumbled.

He grinned. "It's how I sleep."

Fine. "Then that's how I sleep, too."

His eyes narrowed, the muscle in his jaw clenching tight. He wasn't stopping her.

Hands trembling, she tugged her hoodie over her head and dropped it on the floor. She kicked off her boots, avoiding his gaze when one of them stuck, almost tripping her. The sweatpants were loose—tugging the knot free made shimmying out of them easy. The white *Truckers Do It on The Road* T-shirt was long enough to cover her, but they both knew she wasn't wearing anything underneath.

His hands fisted in the comforter.

She'd reached for the hem when his hands tugged her close between his legs. The heat of his muscular thighs against her bare skin was glorious. She closed her eyes, hands braced on his shoulders.

"You're going to make me do something I'll regret." The anguish in his voice drew her attention. He was sad, so sad.

"Mal?" She cupped his face, resting her forehead against his. "No regrets." It was hard to say the words out loud, but she had no choice. "Distract me. Make me feel good, alive. Please. My body is hungry for you—"

He moved swiftly, his big hand tangling in her hair and pulling her down to him. His lips were brutal and desperate as they sealed with hers. And she loved it. Her mouth parted, and she was stunned by the shock of lust that wrapped around her. His tongue against hers. His other hand sliding up, stroking behind her knees, lightly caressing up her thighs.

He growled, rolling them and tugging her beneath him.

Breathe. Her lungs ached. Never in her life had she been so consumed with sensation. And it was oh-so-good. His back under her hands, muscles and heat. His lips devoured hers, moving on to her neck, soft, hungry, relentless. Mal's scent was the ultimate aphrodisiac. Breathing him in made her body throb and ache in the best way possible. His chest pressed against hers. Her shirt was in the way—she wanted his skin again her, wanted no space between them.

He must have been thinking the same thing. Her shirt was across the floor in seconds. Mal sat back, staring down at her, wild-eyed and breathless. He groaned, his hands running down her sides, along her hips, and back up her stomach. One hand cupped her breast, stroking over the skin, plucking the tip gently as his gaze locked with hers.

She arched into his touch, unable to sever the hold he had on her. In his eyes was truth. He wanted her as much as she wanted him.

She thought he said, "Mirrors," before rolling away from her.

He didn't go far.

The exquisite stroke of his tongue against her knee had her moaning in earnest. His hands parted her legs as he kissed and licked the bend in her knees and up the soft skin of her inner thighs.

Her hands fisted in the blanket, waiting—hoping—uncertain. But then his fingers brushed through the fine thatch of hair between her legs, parting her sensitive flesh to stroke the most intimate part of her body. She was throbbing, aching. And his touch was divine.

He growled, his finger stroking against the tight nub again and again.

Her body bowed, responding without thought to his caress. When his finger slid inside her, she moaned again. This was Mal, joined with her physically—even in such a small way. On the inside, in her heart and mind, she'd accepted he was a part of her. An essential part. One she would fight to hold on to—no matter how hard he resisted.

Chapter Eleven

Watching Olivia writhe beneath him was hot as hell. Her nipples jutted up, begging for his mouth. He gave her what she wanted, what he wanted. He ran his nose along the swell of her full breast, his tongue teasing the puckered tips until she was gasping. She was so beautiful, so abandoned. Her lips parted, her ragged breath filling the room as he sucked her nipple into his mouth. She tasted so damn good. He took his time, learning what made her whimper—what pleased her most.

All the while, his finger was buried inside of her. Where he belonged.

His wolf was pacing, crazed with the need to claim her. She wanted this, the wolf insisted. She wanted to be his mate.

Mal kissed his way down her side, sucking hard enough to leave a mark on her creamy skin. His wolf would have to be satisfied with marking her skin. He went lower, tracing the arch of her hipbone, nuzzling the juncture of hip and thigh and easing her legs wide. Seeing Olivia so hungry for him, so exposed, almost shook his resistance. He wouldn't bury himself inside her, wouldn't please the wolf, no matter how much he ached for it. Instead, he slid another finger inside of her. She clenched around him, the breath powering out her chest and leaving him trembling. His dick so hard he knew he'd be hurting if he didn't find some release.

His mouth latched on to her upper thigh, his teeth grazing the skin. When she reached down, her hands tangling in his hair, he smiled. She might not know what she was asking for, but he did.

His tongue skimmed over the tight bundle of nerves, driving her crazy. So good, like honey, pure honey. He wanted more. Every time he sank his fingers into her, his dick throbbed. She was tight and wet and ready for him. He couldn't stop, couldn't leave her—touching her was all that mattered.

She is ours.

He tried to shut the wolf out, to lose himself in the taste and feel of Olivia. But the knowledge that no one else had touched her this way was powerful. A surge of possessiveness gripped him, shaking him to the core. No one but him. Ever.

Not yet. He'd promised himself she would never be their mate. He couldn't allow it. She deserved better.

Her fingers tightened in his hair, pulling his head closer.

He worshipped her, frantic to claim her in some small way. His tongue worked her over, pulling moans from the back of her throat. His fingers, tightly enveloped within her, stroked deep—drawing little gasps of pleasure. It was his mouth that made her fall apart beneath him. Nipping and sucking her clit, his tongue drinking in the taste of her as her body clenched and shook with the strength of her release. She grew soft and limp, her hands sliding from his hair.

Laying between her legs, his cheek resting on her thigh, it was hard to ignore his rock-hard dick and raging hunger. He ran his fingers over her, watched as her body clenched. The urge to bury himself deep, to finish what he started, wasn't easing. Better to remove himself from the situation than lose his control.

She wrapped her legs around his waist. He growled, his hands on either side of her face, holding himself above her. So close—so fucking close he could feel her heat.

Olivia smiled at him. "Wow." She was all smiles. "Really. Wow."

All he could do was grunt as he tried like hell not to think about arching into her.

Her smile faded. "Are you mad?" she whispered.

He wasn't sure how to answer that. Staring down at her, all flushed and rosy and shuddering with aftershocks, wasn't helping. God, he wanted her. No, he wasn't mad. But admitting he was horny as hell, on the verge of losing it all over her stomach, probably wasn't a good idea. She was too caught up in her orgasm to realize what she did to him. For him, right now, she was all silk curves and smiling invitation. An invitation he couldn't accept. His, "No," was a snarl.

"No?" she echoed, her fingertips running down his sides.

Goddammit. Her touch sent a shudder down his spine, causing him to jerk away from her—pressing his painful hard-on against her thigh. She froze, her eyes going round as her gaze traveled across his chest and down his stomach to examine his erection. When her gaze met his, her breathing was unsteady.

The unexpected feel of her fingers stroking him was heavenly torture. He pressed his eyes shut and groaned, arms stiffening, braced over her, too stunned to move. Not that he wanted to move. Hell no. This could work—this was what he needed. Her fingers closed around his shaft, sliding up, tracing the sensitive tip, and gliding down again. Arching into her hand was the natural thing. She understood, her grip tightening ever so slightly as she slid from root to tip, over and over. Her lips fastened onto his chest, her tongue stroked his nipple, and all the while her hand was leading him to surrender. His breathing grew frenzied, his thrust matching the rhythm of her stroke. His eyes popped open, boring into hers while her hand kept working.

"Mal," she whispered. Her cheeks flushed pink, her red tongue darting out to lick her lower lip.

He came hard and fast—lost and found in a way he knew he'd pay for later. His blood roared, pure pleasure shooting through his veins and holding him rigid in her grip. It went on and on, draining him of his tension and anger. The calm that followed was unexpected.

She was smiling, looking far too pleased with herself. Her hand hovered over her abdomen, one finger tracking through the evidence of his release across her belly. All he could do was stare, his erection returning with a vengeance. She was incredible. Sexy, eager, generous—his.

"I do this to you?" she asked.

He nodded, once.

"You don't like it?" she asked, her brows arching high.

He nodded again, smoothing a curl from her forehead. Like wasn't the right word. Terrified worked.

She frowned. "Is this a normal human thing? Or is the craving a wolf thing?"

"I don't know." He was still a little breathless. But her question made him panic.

Her nose wrinkled. "Oh."

Relief washed over him, and his wolf. Because he was a stupid ass. "I'll be back," he grumbled, pushing off the bed and crossing to the bathroom.

He found a washcloth and ran it under warm water, then returned. She lay in the middle of the bed, eyes closed, arms stretched over her head, legs parted. Pure sensual abandonment, and one helluva temptation. He glanced down at his cock rising to attention, and sighed.

"Mal," she said, far too eager. "I-I don't need mirrors."

He sat on the side of the bed, wiping off the smooth plane of her stomach and all evidence of his weakness. "You need sleep," he murmured. He carried the washcloth back into the bathroom and rinsed it in the sink, avoiding his own reflection in the mirror. How could he stay mad at Finn for breaking his word to them when he couldn't even follow through on a promise he'd made to himself? He rubbed a hand across his face, instantly distracted by the lingering scent of Olivia on his fingers.

Her scent.

He turned, staring into the bedroom. Olivia was already asleep, curled onto her side. And even though he knew there were things to discuss, this was where he wanted to be. He slid between the sheets and fitted her tight against him. She stretched slightly, her back arching against his chest, the delectable curve of her ass tilting toward his more than willing erection. He buried his nose in her hair, pressed his hand against her belly, and let himself imagine what it would be like to have Olivia as mate.

...

Olivia didn't want to wake up. She was warm and relaxed, Mal's breath stirring the air above her ear. He was sound asleep, his body twitching occasionally. How long had it been since he'd slept? Her nightmare situation had lasted no time at all compared to the three months he'd spent in that place.

She closed her eyes, relishing the calm.

It was time to wrap her head around what was about to happen. Meeting Finn and the rest of the pack would change everything. Again. As much as she wanted to believe Mal wouldn't leave her—especially now that they'd shared whatever *this* was—her stomach churned all the same. And instead of pushing the issue and getting a direct answer, she'd let *this* happen. And, oh my goodness, had she happened. She sighed, a full-body shudder reminding her of the pure bliss Mal had introduced her to.

Blissful for her, maybe not so much for him? He'd had sexual experiences before. What she'd considered a life-changing event might not rank in his top ten. Her euphoria took a sharp dip. Not that she wanted him to stay for purely physical reasons. She just wanted him to stay—with her.

He wouldn't leave her right away. If he did go, it would be after she'd been accepted by Finn's pack. A pack she didn't know. There was *so* much she didn't know. With Mal's tight-lipped disposition, getting answers from him would be a challenge. And time was running out.

"What's wrong?" His voice was gruff.

She jumped. "Nothing. You were sleeping."

"I was," he agreed. "Your heart is pounding."

"And that woke you?" she asked, smiling. Was it wrong that she loved how in tune he was to her?

"Apparently." He stretched, his hard angles grinding against her back in a most distracting way. "What's wrong?"

No point lying. He'd figure it out. "Thinking. About things. This Ellen person. I saw your reaction."

He groaned.

"I understand. Why trust her? If she's an Other—"

Mal's voice was harsh, biting. "The girl in the house said Cyrus had someone on the inside."

The warmth drained away as she pulled out of his arms and rolled onto her stomach, staring down at him. "Wait. She's working for Cyrus like a-a spy?"

He shrugged.

"But that's what you're thinking?" she pushed.

His half-hearted nod made the hair on the back of her

neck stand straight.

"Why would Finn be okay with this?"

He shrugged again. "Dante said she was helping Jessa. Her well-being is all that matters to Finn." A slight furrow marred his brow as his gaze dipped, skimming her neck and shoulder. He ran a hand over his face and sat up. "We'll know soon enough. We landed."

Olivia froze. True, the steady roar of the engine and low vibration had stopped. She sat up, tugging the sheet around her, and watched as Mal pull on the pants he'd discarded earlier. Words rushed up, clogging her throat. In a few minutes, he'd walk out, and she might never have the chance to say all the things she wanted to.

He tied his boots and stood, his dark gaze meeting hers. "What?"

She shook her head.

His eyes narrowed. "Nervous?"

She nodded.

"Don't be." His tone was soothing.

"Everything I've ever known is gone. I'm going to a strange place, full of strangers, possibly a bad guy—er, girl—to be left." She tossed off the sheet, stooping to collect her clothing. "Oh, and don't forget about the full-moon skin-tearing wolf-monster thing I get to experience." She tugged on her white trucker T-shirt. "You're right, no reason to be nervous. None, whatsoever."

Mal sighed. "I didn't mean—"

"You're going to sigh at me?" She jerked the sweatpants tight.

Mal's hands covered hers, working the knot free and tying it more comfortably at her waist. His fingers grazed her stomach, leaving her tingling. "I'm not leaving you."

"Not right away," she interrupted, suddenly breathless.

His hands settled at her waist. "Let's take this one step at a time."

She looked up at him, the heat in his gaze stealing some of her anger. "Step one?"

"Meeting Finn and his pack." One of his hands slid under her shirt to stroke the skin of her stomach.

She shivered, her body tightening with instant yearning. One touch and she was lost, swaying into him. As distractions went, it worked well. When his hand slid up to cradle her breast, she was gasping. The light flick of his thumb against the erect tip had her holding onto him. A broken groan slipped from his mouth, inflaming her even more.

"This isn't normal male-female wolf interaction, is it?" she asked.

Hs stiffened. "Did Dante—does he make you want him?"

She blinked, surprised by the razor-sharp edge of his voice. "In the twenty minutes he was shot and bleeding and mostly unconscious? No. So far, you're the only that makes me like this."

He blew out a deep breath and stepped back, his gaze searching her face.

Was he disappointed? "Is that what you want?" she whispered. "For me to feel this way with someone else?"

"No." He bit the word out, so harsh Olivia jumped. "Let's go." He clasped her wrist and led her from the room, not bothering to turn back—or release her.

Olivia couldn't stop her smile then. He might not be happy about the effect she had on him. But he wasn't denying it. And that was a good place to start.

Chapter Twelve

Gentry drove, so Mal sat in the front passenger seat, his attention seeking out Olivia in the visor mirror again and again. She was squished against her seat, making as much room for Dante as possible. He wasn't doing so hot, the silver in his body making him weak and green. If he thought it sucked now, he was going to have a hell of a time when they dug the metal out. It had to be done so Dante could shift and heal.

The sooner they got there, the sooner he'd have to face facts. Him and Olivia. There was a small part of him that hoped she'd bond with another wolf—a very small part of him. Which would likely result in his wolf trying to kill whoever it was. She'd been worried about Dante, but not overly so. As big an asshole as that made him, Mal was relieved.

Is that what you want? For me to feel this way with someone else?

She hadn't been prepared for his response. Hell, *he* hadn't been prepared for his response. But as soon as the words were out, he knew the answer. Not just no, but fuck no. Having this much space between them with another wolf present was driving him crazy, a weakness he was doing his best not to reveal to Gentry or Dante.

He alternated watching the road and checking on Olivia. She seemed to shrink into herself in the morning sun, staring out the window with wide eyes, her brain in overdrive. Her wolf could sense what was coming and wasn't making it easy on her. Once the shift was over, both Olivia and her wolf should be more at ease with their new status. For her sake, he hoped that was the case.

There'd been some improvements since he was last at the refuge. The fencing was higher, threaded through with razor wire and some high-tech cameras and sensors, but the ivy-covered cinder-block walls were just as tall and thick as they'd been three months before. Only now they didn't offer the same sense of protection.

"New security?" Mal asked as they approached the refuge entrance.

"Brown went on an upgrade rampage after we got his daughter back." Gentry glanced at him, steering Finn's state-of-the-art, bulletproof SUV through the massive reinforced metal gates of the refuge. "She's pretty messed up."

"Who is Brown?" Olivia's question was hesitant.

Mal's tone was soft. "Brown is Finn's head of security. Good man with an axe to grind. Eight years ago, the Others killed his wife and took his daughter."

"She barely talks, acts like a cornered animal most of the time." Gentry paused. "They turned her."

Mal stared out the windshield, processing this new development. Brown's daughter had been bitten by the Others, making her an Other. Where did her loyalties lie? She'd been a captive for so long, it was a legitimate question. Could being liberated from her abductors allow her alliance to move from one pack to the next? The unknowns were piling up again.

"She's a wolf?" Olivia asked.

Gentry nodded. "Just like you, missy," he said, all southern charm.

Mal glared at him.

"But the only wolves in Finn's pack are you"—Olivia pointed at Mal—"Dante, Anders, Hollis, and Finn?"

"And Oscar," Dante added, his voice hoarse.

Gentry chuckled. "Cute little thing, too."

"Oscar is Finn's son," Mal reminded her. "The only natural-born wolf among us."

Olivia nodded, her hand absentmindedly rubbing her leg. "And Jessa is expecting a baby…wolf?"

Mal nodded. One more thing that needed defending. What the hell was Finn thinking? It was bad enough when he'd knocked up some hookup in the first place. She'd died because of it—leaving a son to be raised by their pack. Adding a mate and kids to the mix was asking a hell of a lot, from all of them. His actions dragged all their wolves into his emotional free-fall—taking one more choice from them. He flexed his hand, the familiar prickle of anger skimming across his skin.

"How are you involved, Gentry?" Olivia asked. "You're not a wolf."

"Never been invited to join the pack." He winked. "But, hell, as long as I get to blow things up and shoot my big guns now and then, I'm happy."

"You'd want to be turned?" Olivia's curiosity made Mal smile. He liked that about her, the way her mind worked, even if all the questions got irritating. If he was ready to face facts, and he wasn't sure he was, there wasn't much he didn't like about Olivia.

"Are you kidding me?" Gentry asked. "Who wouldn't want to let out their inner beast now and then, raise a little hell, kick a little ass."

"You make it almost sound good," Dante murmured. "Almost."

Mal glanced at Olivia in the mirror. She was smiling, her brows arched high in astonishment.

The SUV stopped, parking in a freestanding garage. Gentry climbed out, opening Dante's door. "Lend a guy a hand?" Gentry asked.

Now that they were here, Mal was torn—the need to fight and run versus the pull of the pack. It had been so long, he'd almost forgotten the feeling. But now, with Dante hurting and vulnerable, he couldn't shut it out. Mal gritted his teeth and came around the vehicle, hooking Dante's other arm over his shoulder. He stared at Olivia. "Stay close." He knew he sounded like an overbearing dick and didn't care.

"She's safe," Dante rasped. "Try to relax."

Mal kept his thoughts to himself, relieved that Olivia took his other hand and stayed close by his side. She was safe because he was with her. But he knew someone inside was a traitor. He knew to be careful. He was the pack hothead, the reactionary one. He could walk in and start hurling accusations, stir up a shit-storm of suspicion. It's what he wanted to do. But he wasn't willing to place Jessa, the baby, Oscar, and Olivia in immediate danger. For now, he was the outsider, something he could use to get the lay of the land. Until he knew who Cyrus's go-to was, what they were after, he'd stay alert—and close to Olivia.

They'd made it to halfway across the yard when Hollis opened the front door. He sprinted out to meet them. "What happened?" he asked, focusing first on the patient—he was hard-wired that way.

"Motherfuckers opened fire." Gentry shook his head. "Never done that before. Some shifted, some didn't. Ones that didn't, opened fire."

"Some sort of silver-coated bullets," Mal offered. "Sticks

in the wound."

Hollis's sharp green eyes met his, his smile unexpectedly sincere. "Good to see you, Mal." His awkward one-armed hug was abrupt. He took Dante's other arm from Mal. "Let's dig it out."

"Do I have a choice?" Dante groaned.

Hollis chuckled. "Not if you want to heal."

"Or shift," Mal added.

Hollis nodded. "Finn's coming out to greet you. Both of you." His gaze lifted long enough to find Olivia.

Mal ran a hand over his face. "Great."

"It'll be fine, Mal." Dante's voice was unsteady.

"Gentry, stay with me," Hollis said, leading Dante inside. "I might need an extra set of hands."

"That doesn't sound good," Dante groaned.

"It's not going to feel good, either." Hollis sighed.

"Way to sugar-coat it, Doc." Gentry chuckled as they disappeared inside the house.

Finn was coming? What the fuck was taking him so long? He was supposed to stand outside for him to make his appearance? He'd waited long enough. Might as well rip off the fucking Band-Aid so they could all stop feeling guilty. It wouldn't do much for his wrath. Mal grabbed Olivia around the wrist and pulled her toward the house.

"Mal." Her voice was soft.

He stopped.

She lifted her arm, his vice-like grip too tight.

"Fuck." He let go of her, rolled his head, and stared at the sky overhead.

"I know it's not much, but I'm here Mal." Her voice was confident, her fingers twining with his. "No matter what, I've got your back."

Her words pulled his gaze to hers, anchoring all his attention on her. She had no idea what her words meant.

The life she'd lived had been flipped to hell, her future was uncertain, and in a few hours, she'd be facing her first shift. Instead of freaking out or running for the hills, she was pledging her loyalty to him. For the first time in too long, loneliness didn't weigh him down.

•••

Mal's smile made it easier to breathe. "I'll hold you to it."

She nodded, offering him what she hoped was a reassuring smile.

However calm she appeared, she was a wreck. Her nerves were in overdrive, absorbing, filtering, processing more information than she knew what to do with. Questioning what was and wasn't real at this point was stupid. There was no denying this was happening. She could sense them, Finn's pack, inside the house. Mal was bracing for a fight. But whether the fight was with Finn or inside himself, she wasn't sure.

What she *was* sure of—she wanted to throw up. Throw up and pass out. Or run. Running would be good. She was hot, but cold. Starving, but nauseated. Everything was mixed-up—twisted and out-of-sorts. Her heart was on the verge of pounding its way from her chest. Her lungs ached for air. And her mind was spinning with distant voices, images, thoughts, and sounds that weren't hers. She was being invaded by something she couldn't see.

She fought the urge to slide an arm around Mal's waist, pressing a hand against his lower back instead. She knew his touch calmed her; maybe she had the same effect on him.

Beneath her hand, Mal's muscles clenched. She barely had time to register what was happening. One second he was there, the next he was gone. Then Mal, out of control and dangerous, was slamming his fist into another man's face.

Finn. She knew it was him, recognized him and what he was to her. Her Alpha. The link was instantaneous—new but unwavering.

The growl that ripped from Mal clutched at her heart. It wasn't just anger. It was heartbreak.

Finn stood, stunned, but made no effort to protect himself.

Mal didn't hesitate. His fist sank into Finn's side, a resounding snap and Finn's muttered *oof* echoing in the open air. A punch in the abdomen knocked Finn back several feet. Mal crushed Finn's nose, blood spurting all over the man's face and shirt.

She'd been furious with Finn on Mal's behalf. But this, this wasn't right. Mal would hate himself if he didn't stop.

But there was no one to stop him. Except her.

Mal kept pummeling him over and over until Olivia worried he might beat him to death. When Finn fell flat, Olivia moved. She ran across the yard, putting herself between them. "Mal." She placed a hand on his chest, searching his crazed brown eyes for some sign of her man. She hurt for him, ached for the wounds deep inside that hadn't healed. "Mal, please." She stepped forward, wrapping her arms around his waist and pressing her face against his chest.

He was panting hard. Thundering heart. Barely controlled. She closed her eyes, her hands stroking over his back again and again. If she concentrated on slowing her heart, on calming the agitation and fear in her mind, Mal might do the same.

Slowly, his arms drooped at his sides and his posture eased. Olivia let go of him, stepping back as he crumpled to his knees in the dirt.

Was Finn okay? She turned, staring at the bloodied face of the man Mal had been hell-bent on beating. Their Alpha. Her Alpha.

"You were going to let me keep going?" Mal's words

were hard and desperate.

Finn sat up slowly, spitting dirt and blood from his mouth. He nodded. "I deserved that. And more." The anguish in Finn's words stole some of the anger she knew Mal clung to. "Nothing I say—" Finn cut off. He shook his head.

The struggle in Finn's words cut deep. His regret and self-loathing was tangible, the guilt for what his choice had cost Mal. In Finn's pale eyes, Olivia glimpsed bone-crushing grief for what Mal experienced. Mal did, too. The broken look on Mal's face was too much. She reached out, resting her hand on his shoulder while resisting the urge to wrap herself around him.

"I'm glad you're home, Mal." Finn's voice was hoarse.

Mal grunted.

"You must be the new pack member?" Finn's pale gaze met hers as he wiped blood from his nose and upper lip.

She nodded, stepping back as Mal pushed himself to his feet.

"Olivia Chase," Mal answered for her, tucking her behind him. He offered Finn a hand and tugged him to his feet.

Finn glanced between them. "Welcome."

She nodded. "Thank you."

Finn smiled, gesturing to the house. "You can relax here. Whatever you need."

"I could use a shower." Mal sighed, swiping the dirt from his knees. "You should eat, rest up for tonight," he told her.

"Tonight is your first shift?" Finn asked, leading them to the front door.

She nodded again. "Should I be excited or terrified?"

Finn's crooked grin was charming. "Maybe a little of both?" He pushed open the front door.

"She'll do fine." Mal's fingers twined with hers as they entered the house.

The ripple in the air made her tense. Mal, too. A room full

of unfamiliar faces—and an unknown threat. The same ripple as the truck stop. She'd known there was an Other here, but she hadn't expected them to be *here* here. Who was it, and why weren't they caged? Guarded? Being watched? Did Finn and his pack not realize what they were capable of? Olivia's wolf was struggling for control. The need to hunt, to fight, was instinctual when it came to their rival pack.

"She'd have to be tough." A woman spoke, her odd accent hanging in the air. "You have their scent on you. You were with the Others?"

"They turned you?" Finn paused, glancing back at her in confusion.

"No." She shook her head, ridiculously relieved that Mal had been the one to make her a wolf. "Mal did. He saved my life."

A man spoke, his eyes wide. "Mal changed you? Mal, Mal? That hairy fella hanging on to you?"

"Anders." Mal nodded at the man, a small smile on his face. "You look good."

"Better than you, Mal. You going native? What's with all the hair?" Ander's hugged Mal hard. "I knew you weren't dead. Nothing can kill you."

"Why did you change her?" Finn asked. There was no hint of accusation, but the tightening of Mal's grip told her he didn't appreciate the question.

"She was dying." Mal's words were a growl.

"You saved her," a very pregnant woman said, smiling. Pregnant. Jessa. Finn's mate. Her alpha's mate. She was pretty, radiating warmth and welcome.

"Humans die. It is natural." The woman with the accent spoke again. "They're fragile."

"Who the fuck are you?" Mal snapped.

"Ellen." She smiled at Mal, a slow, lazy taunting smile that made Olivia see red.

Mal's answering smile promised pain and violence. "This is going to be fun."

Finn sighed. "Mal."

"Hi, Mal." Jessa crossed the room, hugging Mal. "Olivia, I'm Jessa. It's so nice to meet you."

"You as well," Olivia said, appreciating the woman's attempt to diffuse the tension.

"Ellen is helping out with my pregnancy," Jessa said. "So, please, play nice."

"When are you due?" Mal never took his eyes off Ellen.

"A few weeks," Jessa said.

Mal nodded. "I can wait. Anticipation's a good thing."

Olivia knew it wasn't an empty threat and almost felt sorry for Ellen. Almost.

Mal's smile turned genuine when he regarded Jessa. "You look good."

Jessa glanced at Finn. "Stop telling people to say that."

Finn held both hands up. "I didn't say a word."

Watching them was educational. Olivia watched people; it was what she did. And while it was clear they were deeply in love, there was more—something she couldn't readily identify.

"Are you hungry?" Jessa asked her. "I've got a mountain of food. Those full-moon munchies are wild."

"First shift can make a wolf blood-crazed," Ellen sounded off. "She'll need to be watched."

Mal's chuckle was hard. "*She'll* need to be watched? After you get put in your cage for the night?"

Ellen stood. "You know I'm right—"

"I know you're dead in a few weeks," Mal cut her off. "If you say one more fucking word to me or Olivia, you're dead tonight. Try me."

Ellen glared at him, her lips pressed tight and her nostrils flaring.

"Food." Jessa tugged Olivia's arm. "Please," she added, a

little desperately.

Olivia went, hoping Mal would follow. She understood his rage. She felt it, too. But none of Finn's pack had been through what they had—they couldn't understand. She hoped they never would.

"See, mountains." Jessa nodded at the stack of pancakes, massive tray of lasagna, and trays of muffins and breads. "Anders made a little bit of everyone's favorite. There's steak, chicken, and a turkey in the oven. You know, protein."

"Wow." Olivia took the plate Jessa offered. "But what about the rest of the pack?"

"They've been eating off and on all day. And tomorrow they'll be exhausted and worn out." Jessa smiled, piling pancakes onto Olivia's plate. "And ravenous all over again."

Mal, Finn, and Anders joined them. Thankfully, there was no sign of Ellen.

As she ate, Olivia focused on the dynamic, sorting through what had been said and left unsaid.

Jessa was calm, surprisingly so, considering her circumstances. Finn's first child had lost its mother in childbirth—that had to be unnerving. Yes, she was the Alpha's mate, someone to protect above all else. But she was also expecting a baby that was part werewolf. And since her pregnancy had more bumps that the average human nine months did, Jessa might need protecting. Questioning that never wasn't an option—and clearly a wolf thing—but Olivia was okay with it.

Anders was curious. His frequent glances and quick smile assured her he was a friend. He just didn't know where she fit.

Join the club. She smiled at him. He smiled back, winking.

Impatience rolled off Finn. Once they were sitting at the large wood plank table, he rested his elbow on it and stared at her. He wasn't trying to be rude; he was trying to understand.

"How did you meet?" Finn asked, his gaze turning to Mal.

Mal's attention remained on his plate. "She was in the cell next to mine." Mal's words were hard.

Finn winced. "They were keeping you prisoner?"

She nodded. "I'd been stabbed, and it was infected so I was sort of out of it. Mal carried me to safety." She hadn't realized how hungry she was until her first bite. The delightful mix of maple, butter, and pancake fluffiness was amazing. "It would have been easier if he'd let the bear eat me."

"Bear?" Jessa repeated, startled.

"A bear tracked us, probably from my injury. It dragged me from camp, but Mal came after me." She glanced at Mal. "By then, I was bleeding to death."

Mal's jaw clenched, his dark brown eyes crashing into her. He'd saved her again and again.

"We're talking about Mal?" Anders's confusion said it all.

Mal glared at Anders then shot a look at Olivia. She smiled in return, appreciating the way the corners of his mouth turned up in response.

She stared at her almost-empty plate. How had she eaten so much, so fast?

"Why were they holding you captive?" Finn asked, watching her.

"Bait?" It was the only theory that made sense. Finn would want to know about her brother, about her dealings with Cyrus—however small. But one look at Mal made her hesitate. He was concerned about Finn, about the safety of the pack. If Finn had been compromised in some way, she didn't want to be the one to share the wrong thing. "I-I don't know."

"Who knows what motivates the Others?" Anders said, taking a long swig of beer.

Finn nodded.

"Where is Brown?" Mal asked.

"He's with his daughter. She doesn't do well when the

moon is full." Finn sat back, shaking his head.

Olivia covered her mouth, yawning wide.

Jessa covered Finn's hand with hers. "She needs sleep, Finn. They both do."

"I have questions, too." Mal's voice was edged with tension.

Finn nodded again, his pale eyes locking with Mal's. "Whatever you want to know, Mal. I'm not keeping anything from you—I hope you'll do the same." He stood. "I'm glad you're back."

She waited for Mal to say something. If there was ever a time to share there was a traitor in their midst, now was it. But he didn't say a word. He stood, accepting Finn's awkward hug, then pulled her chair back.

"Your room is ready," Jessa said. "Get some rest."

"Thank you so much," Olivia said. "For everything."

"You're part of the pack, Olivia," Finn said. "I take care of my pack. Everything's going to be okay."

Olivia nodded, and the connection tethering her to this man strengthened. She didn't like it or understand it or want it, but she had no choice. Finn was her Alpha, and this was her pack. She didn't know how to come to terms with that. Or what, exactly, any of this meant. A part of her wanted to scream or run or argue her way out of this place and back into her reality. But she knew that wasn't going to happen. Now she had to figure out how to be okay in this life, with or without Mal at her side.

Chapter Thirteen

Mal paced the bedroom he was sharing with Olivia. Finn had to know they weren't mates. Was he trying to test Mal's control? Or had his sense of humor become seriously twisted since Mal left? Whatever the reason, he was pissed.

And so fucking relieved.

If she'd been in another room, it would be impossible to keep an eye on her or protect her. It had nothing to do with what he wanted or needed.

Bullshit.

His wolf was having a fucking field day with this. He was winning, wearing down Mal's resistance. Why not make her his? No one would touch her then, or challenge his claim to her.

Anders and Dante—hell, even Hollis—were his friends. They wouldn't pursue her. If she was his.

"All yours," Olivia said, emerging from the bathroom on a cloud of steam, wearing a long flannel gown. "So, Finn, he's mega-rich rich? Not that the bedroom on the airplane didn't sort of tip me off."

Mal laughed. "Head of Dean Automotive, lots of investments, lots of money. So, yeah, obscenely rich."

She grinned. "I got that. The bathroom seemed a little over the top for a wolf refuge in the middle of nowhere. Not that I'm complaining about the heated floors or the waterfall shower. Not in the least." She paused, rubbing her towel over her hair. "Where are we?"

"Montana."

"Makes sense. Wolves. Not overly populated."

"Finn bought this place after he was infected. The dig site where it happened isn't far from here." Mal sat on the bench at the foot of the bed. "Figured keeping it protected might prevent anyone else from getting hurt."

She sat beside him, the towel in her hands. "He's a good guy? Finn, I mean?"

Mal nodded.

"What Ellen said about tonight…" She stared at her hands. "Am I going to be dangerous?"

"Yes. We all are. We're wolves. Every time you shift, you'll have the urge to rain a shit-storm of pain on whoever stands in your way. You'll learn to control it."

"No training manual?" she asked, her attempt to tease strained.

He cradled her hand in his. "Tonight will be the worst. You'll be disoriented, confused."

"That's what happened with Finn?" she asked.

Finn had been out of his mind. He'd looked through them all, blazing with raw aggression and fueled by fear. One by one, he'd chased them down—no sign of the man he'd been. Mal's first shift had been nothing like that. "I think Finn went through something else."

"But that's how you were turned? And Anders and Hollis and Dante?"

"Yes." He wasn't going to lie to her. "Finn lost it."

She stood. "How do you know I won't lose it?"

"You can't hurt your pack. I mean, you can, but you won't. Your wolf will know there's no threat." He stood, too. "There are no humans nearby."

"Jessa?"

"Locked up and guarded." Mal shook his head. "After tonight it won't be like that. You and your wolf will connect and be one. You'll learn to shift when you need to, regardless of the moon."

"What about things I do consider a threat?" She glanced at him, anger burning in her hazel eyes. "Like Ellen."

"I won't stand in your way." He'd love to see Olivia kick the bitch's ass. "When you're ready."

"I won't be tonight?" She was too goddamn gorgeous, too soft and sweet, to be a monster. If he could go back—no, he wouldn't change a thing. She was alive and here.

He shook his head.

"Will you—will I be alone?" she asked.

His heart thudded. *Never*. He shook his head again. "I'll be there."

"With me?"

He nodded.

She smiled, covering her mouth as she yawned.

"Sleep," he said, nodding at the large bed in the middle of their room.

"Shower." She nodded at the bathroom, grinning broadly as she climbed onto the bed. She collapsed against the pillows with a sigh. "Heaven."

Mal agreed. But standing here staring at her was pathetic. He forced himself from the bedroom, stripped off the undershirt and pants he'd found on the helicopter, and stepped into the steaming shower. The hot water stung, but the rhythmic rain of water eased the knots of tension from his shoulders and neck. Things were far from settled, but there was comfort in being back with Finn and the pack.

Tonight, Olivia would shift.

Tomorrow, he and Finn would talk. Beating the shit out of his Alpha had taken some of the fight out of him, but not all of it. It was time he told the pack that Ellen was gathering information about Cyrus. They'd react. They'd want answers. Hell, *he* wanted answers.

While Mal had a hard time believing the bitch had anything of value to offer when it came to protecting Jessa, Hollis did. If they had to bide their time until the pregnancy was done, they could. But they'd be watching her, alert, and ready for any move that might come their way.

And before Ellen died, they'd make sure to extract every piece of information they could.

The only concern that needed immediate action was how she was contacting the Others. Finn wasn't stupid, their wireless and internet were locked-down hard-core. If she was getting information to Cyrus now, how was she doing it? Or was she planning on escaping, taking something with her besides information about them? What the hell would the Others want from them?

In the years since Finn's pack had been infected, the Others had found the refuge once. But the entire raiding party had been killed. The refuge was just that—a refuge from their enemy and a place to be what they were away from the prying eyes of a world that would never understand. If Ellen had already compromised their location to the Others, why hadn't they attacked? If she hadn't given them away yet, then Mal would do whatever was necessary to keep it that way.

He turned off the shower jets, dried off, and headed back into the bedroom.

Olivia slept restlessly, her features fluid in sleep, her lips parted and cheeks flushed, the sudden hitch of breath followed by a soft gasp. His wolf wanted to touch her, so he ran his fingertips along her brow, smoothing the furrow. She turned into his touch, sighing as he pressed his palm to her cheek.

He crouched by the edge of the bed, studying her face. He cared about her, and it scared the shit out of him. She was his mate—it's what he wanted and what his wolf craved. But being his mate meant more pain for her—something he wasn't willing to subject her to.

But he'd cared before. Loving her, Jude, had meant her death. Finding what was left of the woman he'd planned to marry haunted him. Hate had been the only thing that mattered. Hating the Others. Hating himself. Hating Finn. Hating life.

But he couldn't hate Olivia. Or leave her. What he felt for her was too big, too real. All the cold hardness he'd wrapped around his heart had thawed during his time with her. She'd woken him up, made him live, made him fear.

•••

The white wolf was following her.

She was running, but the snow at her feet was heavy and clinging—pulling her into the ground. It wasn't white snow, it was red. The tang of blood, sharp and burning, flooded her nostrils.

She could feel the breath of the wolf on the nape of her neck, smell the blood on his fur, and ran faster.

Air powered from her lungs, her claws tore up the ground. Claws. Fur. She was a wolf now. And her wolf didn't want to run anymore. She stopped, spinning in the blood-red snow to face the white wolf.

But she was alone. Completely alone.

Olivia sat up, the terror of her dream waking her.

"Olivia?" Mal's voice. Mal's hands running over her arms.

Mal's warmth as he tugged her back down beside him. "Bad dream." His voice was thick. "Just a dream."

She burrowed closer, wrapping her arms around his waist and pressing her face to his chest. His smell, his strength, made the trembling stop.

"What was it?" he asked, sounding more awake.

She shook her head.

"Tell me." His words were muffled against her temple.

She looked up at him. "I was being chased by a white wolf."

His hand slid through her hair while his arm tightened around her waist.

"I realized I was a wolf, s-so I turned to face him. H-he was gone." She sucked in a deep breath. "I was alone."

"It was a dream," he whispered.

"That felt real. The ground was red." She shook her head. "It felt *real*."

"Never happen." Was he smiling?

She blinked. "Okay. But—"

"I'd never let it happen," he said, interrupting her. Yes, he was definitely smiling.

She smiled, too, confused. "You weren't there."

He traced the side of her face with his fingertips, his eyes narrowing as they swept over her. His smile tightened then faded, leaving him looking vulnerable. "Which will never happen." His voice shook. "Never."

Any hint of lingering fear or confusion was gone. Mal's brown eyes bored into her, into her soul. She couldn't move, didn't want to. Right now, the only thing she wanted was to stay wrapped up in his arms and lost in his dark eyes.

Until he kissed her.

Soft. Gentle. The brush of his lips feather-light against hers, leaving her gasping. Mal, tender, made her ache, body and heart.

Her hands slid up his sides, his chest and neck. She cradled his face, her thumbs stroking the rough stubble of his cheeks and hard angle of his jaw. He pressed his forehead to hers, the slight shake of his head making her hesitate.

Then he was over her, the bed shifting beneath his weight. The tip of his tongue traced the seam of her lips, and she opened for him. His kiss was long and slow, his tongue and lips worshipping hers, drawing her earlobe into his mouth, nipping the length of her neck.

But then he stopped. "We have to go." He looked at her.

"What?" she managed. They were going somewhere? "I'm good."

He grinned. "It's getting late."

Late. "Oh." She pressed her eyes shut. Late as in she'd be turning into a wolf soon, not losing her virginity.

"I'll be with you," he said, still lying on top of her.

She didn't open her eyes. "Okay." She wanted him close, but she suspected his presence wouldn't make it hurt less.

"Olivia?" He was worried; she could hear it in his voice.

She opened her eyes, staring up at him. "Were you sleeping on top of the blankets?" The thick comforter she was covered with was squished between them, effectively pinning her beneath him—and separating them.

"Thought it would be a good idea." His hand smoothed the hair from her forehead.

"Because I might attack you in my sleep?" She frowned. Ellen's warning worried her more than the pain of the shift. She knew she'd survive that; she'd seen Mal do it. But she'd never be able to live with herself if she hurt someone else.

"No." Mal slid off her, sitting at the edge of the bed. "Because I might attack you."

She rolled her eyes, sitting up. "You're hilarious."

He stood, running a hand over his face. "I wasn't trying to be." He looked at her, the hunger in his eyes making her breathless. "I want you so damn bad. I think about the way you felt, hot and tight around my fingers. How you taste. Watching you come." His voice was hard, almost angry. He stared at her, his gaze devouring her mouth, his jaw muscle working. "I can't lose control with you."

Olivia's insides melted. She throbbed, his words pricking sweetly at the end of every single nerve. Memories crashed in of his scent, his mouth, and tongue. She blew out a deep breath, gripping the comforter in both hands. "Why?"

"I'm trying to be the good guy," he bit out.

"Don't be," she begged. "Please."

His nostrils flared. "Stop."

She kicked the blankets aside, her frustration mounting. "Stop?" She tugged Jessa's borrowed gown into place. "Stop what? Responding? Aching? It's you. *You* did this"—she pointed to herself—"to me. You made me crave things I never wanted before. You look at me and kiss me and say things that—Oh God—make me *burn*. You touch me and it's all I want. I don't know how to stop this. Don't tell me to stop. I don't want to."

"Fuck." He ran a hand over his face. "Tonight, you need to focus on shifting, that's all. You're right—this is my fault. I know better, and I shouldn't have kissed you."

"If you apologize, I will bite you," she snapped.

His jaw clenched, his hands flexing at his sides.

"Tonight. When I'm a wolf..." she clarified, stunned by his reaction. He wanted her to bite him? Not the response she'd expected.

"Relax. Being angry or upset can make it harder to shift."

"Harder? As in more painful?" she asked.

He nodded.

She'd try not to be upset if he'd stop looking at her mouth and acting like it was taking 100 percent of his concentration not to toss her onto the bed and do everything she wanted him to do. Of course, she could be reading him wrong, and he was just mad. But she'd seen Mal mad plenty of times, and this was different. Having him look at her that way was amazing, empowering, and frustrating. "Then *you* stop," she muttered.

He frowned. "What?"

"Looking at me like that." She hugged herself. "If you're not going to throw me on the bed and do what we both really, *really* want"—her voice broke—"you need to stop looking at me like that's what you want to do."

A sharp knock on the door made them both jump. "Get ready," Finn said.

Olivia stared at the door then at Mal. He'd recovered. He didn't look like he wanted to jump her now, he looked worried. She preferred the other. "What do I do? What should I bring?" Her head was spinning now, the reality of what was about to happen slowly sinking in.

"Nothing," he said, finally closing the distance between them. "We go to the woods, you shift."

"With Finn?" she asked, nervous.

"Yes." His tone was hard.

"And Anders and Dante and Hollis?"

"Just Finn and I," he said. "We'll help you find your footing."

"What do I wear?" she asked, tugging her nightgown.

"Nothing." His mouth tightened. "You'll be a wolf."

"Right." She grabbed the hand he offered, hating the fear that settled in the pit of her stomach. She was strong. Mal called her tough. And tonight, for him, she'd prove it.

Chapter Fourteen

Mal kept touching her. She was controlling her breathing, concentrating on remaining calm—and he was falling fucking apart.

"Where's Ellen?" He glared at Finn.

"With Anders and Dante."

"She's free?" he asked, tempted to tell Finn what he knew about Cyrus and Ellen.

"Yes. They keep a close eye on her."

"How will this start?" Olivia asked, shrugging out of his hold to pace.

Ellen didn't matter. Not right now. Only Olivia. She was jumpy—he knew how that was. Having instinct take over was a damn disorienting thing.

"Your senses will sharpen. Like that night at the truck stop." He followed, just steps behind her. "Louder, clearer, distracting. Reactive."

She glanced at him, frowning. "More so?"

The dig at their earlier conversation left him reeling. He liked her reactive. He liked the sounds she made when she was under him. He bit off a growl.

His wolf couldn't wait to meet her wolf. How could he keep tabs on the animal when the animal was in charge? Could his wolf claim her when he was doing his best not to? There was no one to ask—Finn's mate was human. He could have asked Hollis, but his answer would be theoretical.

"You okay?" Finn asked, stretching.

Mal nodded.

Finn glanced at Olivia, then back at him. "I don't think I could watch Jessa go through it."

"You won't make her a wolf?" Olivia asked.

Finn frowned. "We've never talked about it. Things have been so fast between us, we tend to focus on each day instead of the future."

"After the baby's here she'll want to be a wolf." Olivia peered into the dark. "She'll want to be with you when the moon is full—when her babies need protecting. I would."

Finn nodded. "If that's what she wants, I will."

Olivia smiled at Finn. "You always give her what she wants?"

Finn's eyebrow quirked up. "Yes. If I can."

"Huh." Olivia glared at Mal and went back to pacing.

He'd never been truly mad at Olivia before. But now he swallowed down hot, angry words. "Jessa is his mate," he muttered.

"How does that work?" Olivia asked, rubbing her arms. "Not mating, I get that. How did she become your mate?"

Mal saw the smile on Finn's face and groaned.

"I wanted her, she wanted me. My wolf would not let her go." Finn shrugged. "A life bond. A wolf mates once."

Olivia stopped, staring at Finn. "Oh."

"She is mine forever. I am hers. By choice." He shrugged.

Mal wasn't prepared for the anguish on Olivia's face. Anguish, sadness, loss. What was she thinking? What was tearing her insides apart? And how the hell could he make it better?

The distant howl of a wolf made Olivia jump.

"It's the refuge wolves," Finn explained. "Saying hello."

"Wait—we can talk to them?" she asked. "Can our wolves talk to each other?"

"Sort of," Mal offered. "Not with words." His skin tugged, tightening, preparing. He waited, watching Olivia.

Her eyes were pressed shut, her face tightening.

"Don't fight it," he whispered, stroking her back. "Let it happen."

She groaned, falling to the ground at his feet. He crouched, unable to leave her side.

"You're playing with fire, Mal." Finn's voice was hard. "Give her some space."

Mal glared at him. "I can handle a few bites."

Olivia curled into herself, her muscles rolling under the surface of her soft skin. He winced through the pop of each vertebra, the pop of tendon and bone as her shoulder blades moved forward and her rib cage expanded. Her hands contorted, her feet elongated, and her ears split. She cried out when her flesh gave way, the momentary separation of skin the final stage. Cinnamon-colored fur covered her from tail to paw to the tip of her nose. She sat up, panting, shaking her head—dazed. Her coat was lighter underneath, with brown and red tips. Her build was daintier than the rest of them, but she was still larger than the average timber wolf.

Finn smiled. "Well done, Olivia."

Mal sat there, staring at her. Hazel eyes met his. She was gorgeous, even as a wolf. "You look good, Olivia." The urge to touch her was overwhelming. But when he reached out his hand, she growled at him.

He nodded, smiling at her. "You're a wolf. And you know it." He stood, his wolf eager for the shift. It rolled over him, the discomfort lessened by years of shifting. With each snap and tug, his wolf took more control. When the wolf was in his place, he jumped up—unsteady on his legs. Until he was nose to nose with Olivia, his wolf was anxious and excited. For the first time since he'd been turned, his exhilaration had nothing to do with the hunt or a fight—and everything to do with being with her.

She sniffed him, letting him circle her once, watching his every move. When he stood before her, her eyes locked with his. He was in serious trouble. His wolf didn't give a shit about anything but her. She whimpered once, and he was there, letting her run her nose down his neck, rubbing his head against hers. He groaned, relishing in the feel of her soft fur rubbing along his side. Her nose nuzzled his ear, and Mal's wolf reciprocated.

Finn barked, pulling them apart.

Olivia froze, her ears oscillating wildly while she nervously assessed her surroundings. Processing the thousand tiny sounds that were impossible to pick out in human form could be overwhelming. Little things like the distant snap of a twig, the flap of an owl high overhead, or the snort of a distant elk would be deafening to her.

But Mal's wolf was blind to everything but her wolf. The sound of her thundering heart, the uncertain shifting from paw to paw, and her sweet scent flooded him. His wolf groaned in the back of his throat, drawing Olivia's attention. She moved close, tucking her head under his and huddling close.

Finn, a massive brown wolf, approached, nudging her shoulder with his nose. He barked, his tongue lolling out of the side of his mouth, and then he pawed the ground and took off at a run.

Olivia looked at him, then after Finn, swishing her tail before she ran after their Alpha.

Mal stared after them, trying not to let his misplaced

jealousy of Finn tarnish his relief. He'd known Olivia would make the shift well. Now his only worry was preventing her wolf and his from sealing the bond between them.

...

Being a wolf was amazing. Things she didn't know before made sense. Her wolf was all energy and enthusiasm, scenting out rabbits and a woodpecker. When Finn or Mal ran, she was faster than them, loving the wind in her fur and the boundless joy that a full-out sprint gave her.

New sounds crowded in on her, but Finn and Mal were there—showing her there was nothing to fear. Her wolf was free. She was free—and protected.

And every time Mal brushed up against her, her wolf responded. She nipped his ear, nuzzled his throat, rolled on her back in submission. Olivia was fully aware that this was wanton behavior, even for a wolf. But she couldn't seem to rein her wolf in. And, honestly, she was having too much fun to really try.

They ran and ran, covering miles of land. They worked a herd of elk into a frenzy, drank from a mountain stream, and climbed high enough into the mountains to see Finn's cabin down below. New scents came crashing in, but Mal and Finn didn't slow, so she stayed with them.

Until Mal came to a dead stop. His growl was fierce, the fur on his shoulders and neck bristling.

She wavered between Finn and Mal, scenting the air.

Three.

Two carried Finn's scent, a scent that linked them all.

One wasn't. The air didn't ripple. No anger or fear, just uncertainty—unlike Mal. She circled back to him, frustrated when he tried to push her behind him. Finn's reprimand-growl didn't make sense. But when three wolves joined them, she understood. Ellen was with them, and she was just as ready to fight. Her teeth were bared, her ears pitched toward Mal, as she crouched in the snow.

Her posture made Olivia's wolf bristle. Her blood roared and her muscles tightened. She wanted to fight this wolf, to show her her place and defend Mal.

Finn's howl was a warning Olivia couldn't ignore. Neither Mal nor Ellen budged.

Getting Mal out of there was the only way to stop a fight.

She closed the distance between them, leaning heavily into his side. Her wolf groaned softly, before rubbing her head under his jaw.

His growling stopped.

She kept it up, running her nose down one side of his jaw and up the other. He groaned as she buried her snout beneath his ear. She pushed him back, putting all her weight against his chest. He went, one step at a time, until there was enough distance she could relax. Mal's dark brown eyes glowed in the moonlight, fixed on her. She whimpered then ran away from the pack. Mal followed.

Whatever aggression Mal felt, Olivia redirected him. After leading him on a chase, she hid, scampering away when he found her. He tackled her, rolling them in the snow that still covered the higher elevation. She felt so peaceful, so at ease, it seemed wrong. Not to her wolf. Her wolf was thrilled. She assured Olivia that this was the way it was supposed to be when they found their mate. And now that they had Mal, she would never be alone.

Mal was her mate.

Mal.

Olivia agreed. She wanted him. Sullen, hotheaded, territorial, and wonderful. He was hers and only hers, and she'd let him know it.

But the non-impassioned, non-wolf side of her worried

about Mal. Did he know she was his mate?

His wolf did. But, apparently, Mal was just as close-mouthed with his wolf as he was with the rest of the world. If her wolf wasn't so happy, Olivia might have been discouraged. Instead, she raced Mal down the mountain until they toppled into a heap once more.

He seemed to like lying on her, as if he was holding her in place. She didn't mind in the least. They were still curled up, nuzzling, when the sky started to lighten. She yawned, stretched, and followed Mal back to the hollow where they'd started.

Her wolf was sad to see Mal shift, preferring his wolf. But Olivia stared at him, so hungry for the feel of the man she couldn't wait to be with him. Mal. Her mate. Her man. Her wolf.

Through the unexpected pain, she heard Mal whisper, "Don't fight it." It was hard to relax, hard to let go. She wanted to be silent and strong, but her wolf didn't want to shift. Shedding her claws, the rip of fur giving way to skin, the pop of each arm into its socket—everything felt bruised and sore. Movement was impossible, so she lay in the dirt, gasping. "*That* was horrible." Her voice was hoarse.

It was easier the instant he touched her shoulder. "You were amazing."

She looked at him, blinking against the rising sun. "I was?"

He nodded, the ferocity of his gaze chasing away her aches and pains. Her hand sought his, letting him pull her to her feet. She wavered, but he was there. Seeing him now, she knew the wolf was right.

"Tired?" he asked.

She shook her head. Sleep was the last thing on her mind. All she could think about was what he'd said before her shift and how he'd treated her as a wolf. He'd had no problem letting her know she was his then. She saw no point in letting him throw those walls back up now.

"Mal." Her hand tangled in his thick dark brown hair, pulling his head down to hers.

He groaned, pressing a hard kiss to her lips.

"That will wait." Finn came striding out of the woods, his voice hard and angry. "Mal, I want to speak with you in my office. Five minutes."

It was enough to cool her hunger, a little.

Mal scowled after Finn, then scooped her up, hanging her over his shoulder so she was eye-to-butt with him. "I'm familiar with this view."

"Enjoy it," he said, playfully swatting her rear.

She hung there, relieved when he went through the back door. Jessa was in the kitchen. She giggled but didn't stop them.

"Mal," she squealed, the sound of the pack's voices carrying down the hall. Finn and Jessa seeing her naked was one thing. But the rest of the pack? No, thank you.

He carried her into their room and tossed her onto the bed. She wasn't sure what she expected to see on his face. Hunger, frustration, even anger—he didn't like being told what to do. Seeing the shift of uncertainty and worry was unexpected.

He disappeared into the bathroom before she could say a word. She lay there, listening to the shower, wishing Finn hadn't found them. Now that he had, there was no guarantee Mal would come back ready to pick up where they'd left things off.

She sat up, wrapping herself in the quilt at the end of the bed.

Finn hadn't been happy. She only hoped he and Mal could find a peaceful way of working through this. Whatever this was.

She sat on the floor in front of the fire, running her fingers through her snarled hair. A twig was stuck, making her concentrate on the tangle until it was free.

"Get it?" Mal's voice startled her.

She smiled, turning to face him. But whatever comeback she had was forgotten. His shaggy hair was wet, his snug fitting jeans and skin-tight gray T-shirt almost as big a turn-on as seeing him naked. His feet were bare and sexy. Not that she'd ever considered feet sexy before. "I think so," she murmured.

"I'll be back." He swallowed, his attention riveted on her bare shoulder.

"I'll be here." She only hoped he'd hurry.

She waited ten minutes before taking a long, hot shower. When he wasn't there when she finished, she dressed in some of Jessa's sweats and a large flannel shirt and headed to the kitchen. Her stomach was empty and growling—far too embarrassing to be sexy.

"How was it?" Jessa was feeding something orange to a blue-eyed baby boy. It was in his hair and all over the bib he was wearing.

"Fun." She smiled at the baby. "You must be Oscar." She stooped, smiling as he slapped both his palms against the tray of the high chair.

Jessa laughed. "The one and only."

"He's adorable." Olivia spied the stack of empty baby-food jars. "He's quite the eater."

"He's always like this after the full moon." She wiped his face with a wet-wipe.

"He…he shifts?" Olivia asked.

"Yes." Jessa nodded. "But this is the first time he didn't sleep through it all. He shredded a pillow and chased Hollis around the bedroom."

"Hollis doesn't go run?"

"Hollis can't shift. He has a heart murmur." She shrugged.

"Instead, he gets horrible flu-like symptoms for a few days."

"I think I'd rather shift," Olivia said, spying a gorgeous green apple. "May I?"

"Olivia, please. This is your home now. Help yourself." Jessa pulled Oscar from the high chair, laughing at the sounds he made.

Oliva watched her carry the baby to a large mat on the floor. "I can help." She hopped up, taking Oscar from Jessa.

"I'm so big, everything's harder to do." Jessa smiled. "Thank you."

Olivia nodded. Oscar had bright-blue eyes, like his father. And when he stared at her, another bond was formed. Just when she thought she was getting the hang of things, she was blind-sided. Like now, holding Oscar. This little boy was important, like his father and his mother. He was hers, too. And she, her wolf, would do whatever they must to keep this little boy safe and happy.

Chapter Fifteen

"Hollis believes her knowledge of the Others is an asset." Finn's posture was rigid, his tone commanding. He was in Alpha mode, and he sure as hell wanted Mal to know it.

"What do you believe?" There was no point arguing with Finn. He didn't want to argue. He did want to understand. Letting an Other in didn't make sense.

Finn's brows rose. "She knows things we don't."

"And she's sharing this information with you?" Mal asked, flopping into one of the leather chairs in the office.

Finn sighed. "Slowly."

"What's in it for her? Don't give me some touchy-feely crap, or I will lose my shit." He stared at the man he'd once considered his best friend, waiting.

"I need you to trust me." Finn's patience was fading.

Mal opened his mouth then closed it.

"You think I'm an idiot. That I'm putting the pack in danger. I get it." Finn frowned.

"I don't think. I know." He shook his head. "Cyrus has someone here."

Finn froze, his hands fisting at his sides.

"You let her in," Mal growled.

"I need time," Finn bit back. "You need to chill the fuck out."

Mal's snort was dismissive.

"Killing Ellen is the only solution?" Finn asked.

"I'll feel a whole lot better." Mal ran a hand over his face. "Otherwise, lock her up." As soon as the words were out, he regretted it. He'd lived in a cage, chained to a wall, tortured for amusement. They were better than that.

"You honestly think I'd risk Jessa and Oscar?"

Mal studied him for a long time. "I don't know what to think."

"You have Olivia now. It's the same for Jessa and me. And Oscar." He broke off, shaking his head. "Putting their safety first isn't a choice, Mal. It's a necessity—the only thing that matters."

"But keeping a goddamn Other in the house is, Finn."

"It is. And you'll have to accept it."

"Is that all?" Mal pushed out of the chair, too tired to fight, too pissed not to.

"No." Finn's eyes pierced his. "Your wolves have already chosen."

Fucking wolf. Mal glared at Finn. He didn't need this shoved down his throat. He knew what was best for Olivia—not Finn. He'd been the one that kept her safe, that fought for her. Impatient or not, what the wolf wanted could wait.

"Don't pull the same shit I did, fighting the inevitable. You changed her for a reason."

"So she wouldn't *die*," he argued. "She's been caged, mauled by a bear, and bitten by me. Now I'm supposed to see her hurt again?"

Finn shook his head, but there was no judgement there, only understanding. It irritated the shit out of him. He didn't want one more connection with his Alpha. It was hard enough as it was—he didn't want to share this. It was too new. Too special. But Finn's next question cut him to the core. "You can give her up?"

Mal stared at him. Because giving her up would hurt a hell of a lot more than making her his mate.

Finn held his hands up. "Jessa made me whole. How's that for touchy-feely crap?"

Mal shook his head. "Bad."

Finn grinned. "Just tell her the truth, make her understand what's going to happen if she decides to go through with it. Nothing pisses Jessa off more than my trying to make decisions for her. My mark hurt Jessa—and gutted me. But it bonded us together. And it's—*good*." He shrugged. "Chances are you'd go through her pain, her bite, the same as she'll experience yours. Talk to her."

Talk to her. Because he had such a way with words. How was anything he said going to make this easier?

Finn cleared his throat. "Hollis hypothesizes that using a condom would prevent the bond—if that's what you're trying to delay."

"Hypothesizes?" Mal snorted. "That a condom will prevent pregnancy *and* werewolf bonding. Didn't see that on the box anywhere." Not that it changed anything. It wasn't about sex, it was about claiming her—hurting her. "Are we done?"

"No. Consider the distraction this provides. You fighting your wolf? I know how that is. It can be dangerous for you, her, and the pack." Finn's eyes bored into his.

Mal nodded, digesting Finn's words and the wolf's excitement.

"Is there something you want to tell me?"

Finn was his oldest friend. Yes, things had been hard since the change, but Finn was still Finn. Mal had never kept secrets from his friend. Keeping them from his Alpha was damn near impossible. He sighed. "Olivia has a brother. He's supplying something to the Others, something he screwed up. They took Olivia to get even."

Finn frowned. "What is he supplying?"

"Dolls?" Mal ran a hand over his face, making no effort to hide his disbelief. "She said he mentioned some sort of high-dollar collectible thing."

"They talked? She's met Cyrus?"

"He sort of forced them into an awkward dinner." And the thought of her sitting across from Cyrus, those damn soulless eyes looking her over, unhinged something deep inside of Mal. He was done talking. Since he'd found her, he'd barely left her side. Now thoughts of Cyrus crowded in—he needed to get back to Olivia.

"Dolls?" Finn repeated, his skepticism mirroring Mal's.

He shrugged, heading toward the door. "Ask her."

Finn yawned. "We'll talk later."

Mal nodded, heading out of the room and down the hall to his room. Olivia wasn't there. He pushed into the bathroom, the door hitting the wall. No Olivia. His chest hurt. There was no fucking way Cyrus had taken her—his brain knew that. But his wolf had allowed fear to creep in, and they were slipping into full-blown panic mode. He closed his eyes, concentrated on his breathing, and waited for his heart rate to slow. She was here, somewhere. Finn was right, he needed to relax. But the wolf fought back, and he fought dirty.

Find Olivia. Then relax.

She wasn't safe, in their room. But she was here, safe.

Where was Ellen?

The wolf won. Mal's heart kicked up, alarm flooding his blood. He stood in the hall outside their room, seeking her scent. He almost ran down the hall to the kitchen.

"This is so good." Olivia licked her fingers, perched on the edge of a stool without a care in the world.

He could breathe again.

"You seemed to like the apple so I figured you'd like the pie." Anders was leaning against the counter, smiling at Olivia.

He wanted to knock the smile off Anders's face, but Olivia distracted him.

"Mmm," Olivia agreed. Her *Mmm* did things to Mal.

Anders chuckled. "You got some there." He waved a finger at her nose.

Mal held his breath, hoping Anders didn't make the serious mistake of touching her. Then he sighed. *I have totally lost control.*

"It's going to be the last one for a while. My ankles swell if I'm on my feet too long," Jessa said, seated in a rocker before the fire, Oscar asleep in her arms.

Oscar had grown.

"You tell me how to make it, I'm game." Olivia took another bite and moaned, demanding his attention. "This is *so* good."

"You said that already," Mal snapped, entirely focused on the silver prongs of that fork sliding between her lips. She had to stop making that sound. Now.

"Mal, give me a hand?" Jessa asked him. "He sleeps, I sleep." She smiled down at Oscar.

Mal glared at Anders and went to help Jessa. She seemed more fragile than ever, too little to be so top-heavy. For the first time, he understood Finn's worry. Jessa was important to the pack, but she was everything to Finn. As her mate, he'd do whatever he could to keep her alive and healthy, even let one of the Others in with the pack. Not that Mal believed Ellen could do that. She was more likely to kill them all in their sleep. But if that was the plan, why hadn't she done that already?

"You okay?" Jessa asked, squeezing his arm.

Mal nodded, trying to shove thoughts of Ellen aside. Finn told him the bitch was off-limits. He had to listen.

"Thank you." Jessa laughed. "I like her, Mal. A lot."

"Think you can make it to your room?" Mal asked, eyeing her stomach.

She frowned. "I could always roll my way to my room."

He chuckled.

"You sure you want to leave her alone with Anders?" Jessa asked, smiling.

Mal scowled.

"I was teasing, Mal." She sighed. "I'm going to bed, without help." She waved at him and carried Oscar down the hall. He stared after her, watching over his Alpha's mate despite her teasing dismissal.

"Mal," Olivia called. He turned to find her smiling at him. "You have to have some pie."

He walked across the room, trying not to glare at Anders. She was fine, enjoying her pie, talking to Jessa. And Anders. Damn Anders. He didn't want pie.

"You look a little tense," Anders said, grinning.

Olivia glanced at him. "Are you tense?"

He sighed.

Anders grin grew. "Doubt he'll say as much. He's not one for a lot of chit-chat."

"I've noticed," Olivia agreed. She scooped up a piece of pie and offered Mal a bite. "Here." She was staring at his mouth, the fork shaking in her hand.

He grinned, grabbing her wrist and eating the bite. "It is good," he said.

Olivia wriggled her hand free. "Hungry?" she asked.

"Yes." He stared at her, knowing he was playing with fire but unable to stop. No matter how hard he wanted to talk his wolf down, to buy more time, he seemed set on a one-way track.

Destination Olivia.

She paused, her hazel gaze focused on him. "Wh-what do you want?"

He arched a brow, a slow, lazy smile taking hold. She asked for it.

"On that note, I think I'll take the rest of the pie to the guys in the lab." Anders chuckled, carrying the pie out with him.

Mal ignored him, enjoying the flush of Olivia's cheeks and the pounding of her heart. That she wanted him, wanted to be his mate, took his fucking breath away. Pathetic, but true.

"The whole pie?" Finn asked in the hall as Anders brushed past him.

"It's not for me," Anders argued, never slowing. "Getting a little hot in the kitchen. Fair warning. Besides, Jessa's heading to bed already."

"She read my mind." Finn's words carried, the sound of a door closing echoing down the hall.

They were alone. Finally. He didn't know if this was a good thing or a bad thing. But having those big hazel eyes look at him, full of all the things she shouldn't feel for him, could only be good.

"Olivia." He took the fork from her hand. "We need to talk."

She frowned, shaking her head. "Are you sure? You're tense. I mean, we could eat pie and go to bed. Anders said there's a cherry pie in the refrigerator. Now that the whole full moon thing is over, there's nothing urgent. Except I'm hungry. Really hungry." She paused, studying him. "Or is there? Is that it? Is something else going to happen?"

He stared at her, stroking her long auburn hair from her shoulder. He ran his knuckles along her jaw. So soft. A whisper was all he could manage. "Only if you want it to."

...

A flare of nerves settled in the pit of Olivia's stomach. He was worried. Angry. Frustrated. Impatient. All normal for Mal. But not worry. If Mal was worried, she should worry. "What is it?" she whispered back.

He didn't say anything. Those big brown eyes stayed fixed on her, intense and troubled.

"You're sort of freaking me out, Mal." Her voice wavered.

He ran a hand along the back of his neck, stared up at the ceiling, and rolled his head. When he spoke, his voice was gruff and low. "Finn has a scar on his stomach, a puncture wound from the bone that infected him. Jessa has the same scar." He paused. "Because she's his mate."

A bond Olivia was in awe of. There was no denying Finn's total adoration and devotion to Jessa, or Jessa's love and respect for him.

"She *felt* it happen, the wound—lived through it." He cleared his throat. "It's how we—a wolf—bonds."

Olivia went completely still. His words, their meaning, left her reeling.

"Now, no matter what, they're stuck together. No leaving, no moving on. Even when he's an ass and she knows she could do better. There's no one else. Not ever." He glanced at her, then away, his jaw clenched tight.

She couldn't look away. "Are you warning me?"

His gaze returned to her, the slight flare of his nostrils answer enough.

He *was* warning her. "Why?" *Don't hope. Don't hope.*

"So you understand..." The anguish in his voice squeezed her heart. "We can't do this. I can't hurt you."

Her pulse was racing then. "Losing you is the only way that could happen. I want this."

His gaze didn't waver.

"You, Mal. Us." She wanted to touch him, to remind him of the connection they already shared.

He stared at the ceiling again, his jaw muscle ticking in agitation. "It's not that easy."

"You don't *want* me as your mate?" It was hard to get the question out.

He looked at her then. "I do."

She'd expected resistance, a fight, something. She was speechless—and confused.

"Finn—" He broke off, the uneven rise and fall of his chest giving away his internal struggle. "His first shift was bad. All his wolf wanted was to kill. I held on to a tree limb, trying to pull myself up while he tore through my Achilles tendon and severed the muscle from bone. Anders, Dante, then Hollis. I bled out. I'd never known that sort of pain." He shook his head. "And woke up to an ugly world."

She could piece together images, pulling from the snippets she and Mal had shared during the bite. So much fear and pain, confusion and terror, left her shivering. Finn was their friend, and the monster he'd become would've felt more nightmare than real.

"I know how to live in that world." He ground out the words. "I know pain. You shouldn't."

"Mal?"

His hands gripped her shoulders. "Then you show up. And every fucking step of the way you make me want *more*."

"More?" she asked. "Of me?"

"Tell me to stop, Olivia. If you don't tell me, I can't."

She shook her head.

His hands tangled in her hair, tugging her head back as his lips parted hers and he pressed her against the wall. Wicked, teasing, and stroking, his tongue stole her breath and left her on unsteady legs. It was good, molten and alive—he made her feel alive.

She tugged his shirt free from the waist of his jeans, her fingertips sliding across the thick muscles of his broad back. Her nails scored his skin as his teeth nipped her earlobe. He arched into her touch, his hands clasping her hips and lifting her against him.

Instinct took over, guiding her hands and mouth. Wrapping her legs around his waist made him groan. Sucking the skin at the base of his neck made him shudder. And kissing him, his breath and tongue teasing her into a frenzy, left them both panting.

They were moving, then, bouncing off the couch, crashing into the coffee table, finally stumbling down the hall to their room. She felt his smile against her mouth and bit his bottom lip. He groaned, kicking the door shut behind them. His hands were in her hair, bowing her head back. "Dammit," he whispered against her neck.

His hunger was empowering, stirring her confidence—her wolf's confidence—and making her bold. She yanked his shirt up and off, running her hands down his chest. She watched his stomach muscles quiver at the stroke of her finger—tracing the dark line of hair down his rock-hard abs to the button of his jeans. He was all sculpted muscle, reacting to *her*. She inspected every edge and angle, bending her head to kiss his skin, marveling that this big, powerful man wanted her.

"Olivia," he ground out, leaning forward while she clung to him.

The mattress sank beneath her, his weight heavy and delicious. Nothing compared to having him crushed close to her, nothing. Learning his body, hearing his muffled moan, his growl—he consumed her. The urge to touch him, to taste every inch of exposed skin, made everything else fade away.

His hands slid along her sides, forcing her arms up and her shirt off. His gaze brushed the line of her shoulder, dip of her collarbone, and valley between her breasts. Her pants slid down her hips, tugged free by the man above her. Watching his reaction to her was mesmerizing. He was just as lost in her as she was in him. Maybe.

He slid to her side, leaning across her to kiss her stomach. His tongue dipped into her belly button and licked its way to her hip. Teeth nipped, lips sucked, and his hand brushed between her legs. She opened for him, her hunger more powerful than embarrassment or hesitation. It was a physical craving.

He traced the scar on her thigh and the uneven ridge from the bear. His kiss was soft and sweet. The scar ended above her knee and began again at her ankle. When Mal had bitten her, he'd been careful to let go of her thigh. But when the bear turned desperate, he'd dragged her by the ankle, leaving starburst puncture marks with radiating lines. Seeing her body so mangled wasn't easy. The scars looked old and faded, but they were still new to her. And yet, Mal showered every imperfection with tenderness.

She propped herself on her elbows so she could see him.

When their eyes locked, tenderness gave way to lust. He kissed his way up her leg, sucked the sensitive skin behind her knee, and her hands fisting in the comforter. Her inner thigh quivered as his teeth rasped her skin. His hands slid up, stroking her inner thighs, higher and higher until she was holding her breath.

He smiled before turning his attention to the throbbing bundle of nerves between her legs. Working his tongue against her, he had her whimpering. Over and over, his slow, lingering strokes made her body shake. "You taste so fucking good," he growled. Two fingers slid deep, dragging a moan from the back of her throat. "And you feel even better." His words had her tightening around him. His broken curse only made her hotter. Tongue and fingers, one stroked, then the other.

Without thought, she rocked against him.

She fell back on the mattress, her hands tangling in his thick hair. All she wanted was this, the building pulse that set her on fire and drove her out of her mind. He did this to her. He'd always do this to her.

Forever.

A climax tore through her, so hard and fast all she could do was hold on. His tongue didn't slow, the push of his fingers kept pace, until she'd melted into the comforter. It was magic, his breath on her skin sending sharp aftershocks shooting down her nerves.

When she opened her eyes, Mal sat between her knees breathing hard and fast.

"Mal." She didn't know how to ask for what she wanted. But he knew.

He rolled a condom on his impressive erection and braced himself over her. He rested his forehead against hers, his brown eyes searching, and kissed her. The stubble of his chin, the nip of his teeth, and the stroke of his tongue led her back into sensation.

He gripped her hips, holding her still. "Look at me."

She did. In his eyes, she was beautiful. Wanted. Cherished. And with one thrust, he'd buried himself deep and made the world fall away. His groan echoed hers. He was big, stretching her tight and full. His gaze met hers, easing her, stirring her. Discomfort melted away, leaving something hot and demanding in its place.

She wanted him to claim her, to leave his mark on her and seal their bond. Loving Mal was easy. Accepting he loved her the same was not. But here, now, it was hard to deny it. Her wolf reveled in it.

A bond. Physical and beyond.

He thrust into her slowly, his brown eyes burning into hers. Maybe it was the slide of his buttocks against her thighs or the bite of his fingers gripping her hips to hold her close. Or his scent. Or the brush of his chest against her aching nipples. Maybe it was all of it together. Her senses focused, every touch and sigh rolling over her already inflamed body.

Her nails bit into his back as his hands lifted her hips. Deeper now, tearing a growl from deep in his chest. She couldn't breathe at all.

He moved deliberately, each stroke controlled—a battle he was losing. He was being careful with her, and it was costing him. "Olivia?" It was a whisper.

"I'm not fragile, Mal," she gasped. "You won't break me." She stroked his cheek.

Her body was his, there was no denying that. She wanted him to fall apart with her, to lose himself in her with no restraint or regrets. She arched into him, so tight around him, and marveled at the onslaught of new sensations his response stirred. His jaw locked, all of him shook, and he growled, "Fuck, I won't hurt you."

He was raw and hungry for her, and it was beautiful. Jaw clenched. Cheeks flushed. Nostrils flared. And those dark brown eyes crashing into her.

The hitch in his breath surprised her. She reached up, twining her fingers in his hair to pull him to her. His lips were heaven. Feather-light kisses rained down on her lips and neck before he latched onto her throbbing nipple. The teasing of his tongue had her bucking against him. Hard and soft. Gentle and rough. His lovemaking was no different than he was.

He sucked one nipple into his mouth, his thumb and forefinger plucking and teasing the other. It was all she needed.

Chapter Sixteen

Mal couldn't hold back any longer. Watching Olivia's body bow up to meet him, gripped tight in her orgasm, was the sexiest thing he'd ever seen. Her breasts shuddered. Her nipples were hard and demanding his mouth. When her hands clutched his ass, holding him in place deep inside her, something shifted.

She was his. His wolf claimed her. Her wolf claimed him. Hollis was wrong about the condom—damn wrong. Whatever uncertainty he'd felt vanished in that moment, and with it came a peace deep in his bones. The link he shared with the pack was there, but what they shared—he and Olivia—was more. What they shared was everything. He stared at her, mesmerized by the truth.

The need to seal their bond was real.

Her hazel eyes closed as her climax lingered, as her body convulsed around him, tight and hot. He didn't stand a chance. He pumped into her, each stroke pushing him closer to the edge. She wrapped a leg around his waist and sent him free falling. He roared through his release, his blood and body throbbing with pleasure—and possession.

When he collapsed on her, her arms held him close. Olivia's scent. Olivia's skin. Olivia's heartbeat thundering beneath his ear. He pressed his eyes shut, fighting the dread of what would happen now.

"Mal?" she whispered.

He looked up at her.

She studied him, her fingers sliding through his hair and a smile on her lips. That smile was his. For him.

He rested on his elbow, stroking her cheek. He hadn't been easy with her, the way he should have been. Once he was buried inside her, he'd been too far gone to slow down. "You okay?"

That damn smile grew bigger.

He grinned, stroking his thumb along her temple and brow. The tip of her nose. The curve of her lips and shell of her ear. He explored her without the fog of desire clouding his gaze. She was incredible. "So soft," he whispered, running his fingers along her throat.

Her hand ran along his neck and shoulder. "All hard angles." Her fingers brushed his lips so he kissed them. "Except here." She sighed, shaking her head. "You were right."

"I can't wait to hear this." He grinned.

She blushed. "Mirrors weren't necessary."

The burn of want flared instantly. If she wanted mirrors, he'd get her mirrors. She was enough. Lying here watching her was enough. Sexy as hell. All woman. His. If he wanted to touch her, he could. So he did. The back of his knuckles skimmed the round fullness of her breast. A shudder racked her, making her breasts quiver. "Damn," he groaned. He could touch her all night; his wolf demanded it, and Mal didn't see any point arguing.

"I'm thirsty." Olivia frowned. "Really thirsty. Is that normal?"

He laughed. "Nothing about you is normal."

Her frown grew. "Is that a compliment?"

He kissed her, his tongue tracing the seam of her lips. He groaned then rolled off her and out of the bed. "It is. I'll get you a drink."

She turned onto her side, her gaze devouring him. "Thank you. When you come back, can you stand there? Just like that?"

He swallowed. "I'll try." But if she kept looking at him that way, it wouldn't last for long. He was already aching to be inside her again.

Her gaze settled on his rising erection. She licked her lower lip. "Hurry, Mal."

He headed into the bathroom. Once the used condom was disposed of, he washed his hands and face and filled a glass for Olivia. A white-hot pain stabbed through his upper thigh. It was hard and fast, almost bringing him to his knees. He slammed the cup onto the counter, gripping the counter. But the pain receded just as quickly as it started. He ran his hand over his thigh, feeling a new scar, and stared at his reflection.

Teeth marks.

He ran into the bedroom. "Olivia?"

She was sitting up on the bed, rubbing her ankle and calf. Her nose wrinkled. "I'm not saying it's comfortable, but I don't see what all the fuss is about."

Mal pushed her hand aside, inspecting her foot. It wasn't as obvious—his scar blended in with the damage the bear had done. Still, it was there. *He* was there. On her skin.

He cradled her face in his hands, studying her. She was his.

"Maybe it's because I'm a wolf?" she asked. "It's not so—"

He pushed her back onto the bed, his lips pressed to

hers, his hand kneading his mark on her skin. He'd tried not to worry, tried not to think about the pain she'd go through, to ease his guilt. Jessa had suffered when she and Finn had mated. So this, knowing he hadn't hurt her again, was the greatest gift. "I didn't want to hurt you."

"Mal," she murmured between kisses. "No"—her hands tangled in his hair—"more hurting"—she pulled him close—"tonight." Her tongue traced his neck, her hands stroking the length of his back.

He nodded. No more hurting, period. He didn't know what the fuck to do about Ellen or Chase or Cyrus, but he'd figure it out. As long as Olivia was safe and happy, he was good.

"Stop thinking," she said, rolling over him. She straddled him, placing one of his hands on her breast. He brushed the tip, stroking and rubbing until it pebbled beneath his fingers. "Only you and me." She smiled down at him, arching into his hand.

Her hand clasped him, stroking him from base to tip. He growled, watching her watching him. She was fascinated by his body. He was fascinated by everything about her. His fingers traced along her sides, gripping her hips. She arched forward, her head lolling back and her breasts jutting forward.

"Condom," he groaned.

She shuddered, her desire-hazed gaze meeting his. "Condom?"

"I'm not ready to share you." His hands slid back up, cupping her breasts. "Not yet."

She ground herself against him, her wet heat a dangerous temptation. "Where?"

He pulled open the bedside table. He wasn't sure where they came from, though his conversation with Finn made him suspect Hollis. Whoever it was, Mal was eternally grateful for the bulk supply at their disposal.

She took the packet from him, tearing the corner with her teeth. He helped her, showing her how to put it on and getting a raging hard-on in the process. She smiled as his dick pulsed beneath her touch.

"You want me?" She seemed surprised.

He wasn't a talker. He didn't emote. Words got in his way. But she had to know. "I wouldn't have made you mine if I didn't."

The joy on her face took his breath away.

She arched over him, her breasts swaying forward, inviting his touch. He rose, nipping one tip. Until she tilted her hips and sunk onto him.

"Damn, fuck," he bit out, his hands gripping her hips. It was so good. So tight. So fucking deep. Staring up at her, watching her passion, Mal let her take control.

She didn't hold back. Her hands gripped his shoulders as she pushed onto him, riding him, grinding against him and moaning his name. He wanted to wait, to make her come at least once, but she was too incredible. He sat up, nuzzling the valley between her breasts, sucking the skin hungrily as his release crashed into him. The power of it racked his body, emptying him inside of her.

His hands gripped her hips, rubbing her against him, pushing her until her body contracted around him. She buried her face against his neck, crying out as she shattered.

He held her to his chest and fell back on the bed, gasping.

•••

"I'm starving," Olivia said, pushing the comforter back. She glanced at the clock on the side table. "It's almost six."

Mal grunted and rolled over, spooning her back.

"In the afternoon." She giggled. "Mal?"

He grunted again.

Her stomach growled.

He sighed.

"I can't help it. We've worn me out. Otherwise I'd stay here and jump you a few more times." She wriggled her butt.

"Sleep first." His voice was gruff.

She grinned. Neither of them had slept much—she hadn't let them. Once she'd had him, she couldn't get enough of him. Her wolf wasn't much help, either. Even sore and tired, she ached for Mal. "Tired?" she asked, stroking the arm around her waist.

"Yes." His hold tightened.

"You sleep. I'll eat." She tried to move his arm. "I'll come back."

He was immovable.

"Please?" Her stomach grumbled, loudly, for good measure.

He sighed again. "We'll eat." He released her slowly and he tossed back the covers. "Then sleep."

She glanced back at him. "Too tired to make love to me but not too tired to eat?"

His eyes opened. "I never said I was too tired." He pressed the stiff evidence of his desire into her hip.

She sat up, stretching.

His fingertips traced her spine. She shuddered when his lips pressed open-mouthed kisses against her side.

"I thought we were going to eat," she mumbled, already sinking back into a state of hypersensitivity. His touch had an immediate effect on her. And she liked it.

"We are," he said. "Just looking at my handiwork."

She stared down at the discolored patches on her skin. "Aren't you a little old for hickies?"

He shook his head. "Nope."

She stood, tugging on Jessa's cast off yoga pants and sweater.

"You're wearing too many clothes," he said, still sprawled on the bed.

"For eating? With the pack?" she asked, hands on hips. "Come on, Mal. You need sustenance if we're going to keep this up."

His brows rose.

She grinned. "I'm hoping we are."

He was up and dressed before she'd finished braiding her hair. But when they headed toward the kitchen, he gripped her hand in his—tight.

"What is it?" she asked, his unease contagious.

"Easier," he managed.

She wasn't sure what he meant, but she squeezed his hand. Touching him made everything right with the world. While she didn't have the same anxiety about their new status and the pack's reaction, Mal grew more agitated with each step.

Dante saw them first. "She's up." He seemed surprised. "That's different."

"Not that we wanted you passed out in pain," Anders added. "We just thought that's how it happened."

"I'm relieved you were wrong," she agreed.

"Because of me," Jessa said, pushing herself out of the chair she was in. "I'm so glad it was just me."

"She's a wolf." Ellen's voice caused an instant reaction in Mal. Olivia could almost hear his teeth grinding. "Jessa is not," Ellen finished.

Finn was helping Jessa up, too preoccupied to realize Ellen was in imminent danger of having her throat ripped out. "After ten years, you'd think we wouldn't still be learning new things daily." Finn shook his head. "I'm glad you're okay, Olivia."

"Me, too." She tugged Mal's arm, willing him to snap out of it.

Mal stared down at her, the desire to kill and protect

burning in his dark eyes.

She slipped her arms around his waist and pressed her head against his shoulder. If she said something, his discomfort would be obvious to everyone, and Ellen would have a field day.

His sigh was deep, but his arm draped across her shoulders. "Plans?" he asked.

Finn glanced between the two of them then shook his head. "Talk."

Mal nodded.

"Food first, please?" Olivia asked. She could plan and strategize, talk about full moons and risky pregnancies—whatever needed doing, she was up to it. Her energy level was high and her outlook on life had never been so bright. She, they, could handle whatever came their way—she knew it. And it was amazing. But she also really needed food. "I can cook."

"Of course you can." Ellen made no attempt to lower her voice.

Mal growled. "Jessa. Let me kill her."

Jessa frowned.

Finn's garbled curse was hard. "Shit, Mal."

Ellen was staring at Mal, her small smile hard and taunting. As much as Olivia wanted to put the woman in her place, Finn was keeping her around. And that, for now, was the only reason Olivia needed to leave her be. For now.

Mal, on the other hand, was losing it.

"Mal." Olivia placed a hand on his chest. She lowered her voice, standing on tiptoe. "She's trying to get to you. Look at her. Watch her. She wants to fight you." If they hadn't been mates, she might have been threatened by the other woman. She was beautiful and exotic, radiating a lethal confidence that both impressed and repelled Olivia.

Mal leveled a lethal glare at the woman. "Why?" he

ground out.

"To divide the pack?" Olivia looked at him. "Drive you crazy? Because she's an evil bitch? I don't know."

Mal's gaze fell to hers, a stunned smile on his lips. "You said 'bitch.'"

She shook her head. She didn't curse, ever. "I did not."

"Yes, you did." He chuckled.

God, she loved his smile. If this was what happened when she used bad words, she'd have to rethink it. "I didn't. But I really don't like her."

"Me, neither." He kissed the tip of her nose. "But you did say it."

"Whatever." She sighed, tugging him into the kitchen with her. "Who's hungry?"

"There's chili on the stove and cornbread muffins. Or there's some beef stew in the fridge." Anders followed them, lifting the lid on the pot. "About ready."

Olivia smiled. "That smells amazing."

Mal's arm snaked around her waist, pulling her back against his chest.

"Want some?" Anders asked.

"Yes. Where are the bowls?" she asked, trying to move Mal's arm. It didn't budge. "Mal."

"Anders knows where the bowls are," Mal said.

Anders chuckled, pulling bowls and plates down. "I got this."

"Feeling better?" Mal asked Dante.

Dante nodded. "Once Hollis dug the silver out. Motherfuckers."

She might not be a fan of cursing, but Dante's description hit the nail on the head. If she were ever going to call someone *that*, it would be the Others. She glanced at Ellen, but the woman didn't react. If anything, she seemed to share their sentiment.

"Silver bullets." Finn shook his head. "On their own kind."

"They are not your kind." Ellen's voice was harsh.

"Don't you mean, 'we'?" Mal asked.

Olivia squeezed his arm, hoping he'd get the hint. No talking to her. No giving her ammunition to push his buttons.

Ellen glared at him.

"For you." Anders offered her a bowl of chili. "Mal."

"Thank you, Anders." Olivia took the bowl and inhaled deeply. Her stomach growled, loudly.

"I thought *I* was hungry." Dante hopped off the couch and joined them.

"Dinner's ready?" Hollis asked. "I'll tell Brown. Maybe they'll join us for dinner. I'm sure he'll want to see you Mal."

"Brown's here?" Mal asked. "How's he doing?"

Finn shook his head. "It's been hard."

"How is his daughter?" Mal asked.

Olivia watched their faces.

"She's with him," Finn said. "Just go easy on her."

Mal nodded, his jaw locking. He glanced at Ellen.

Ellen met his gaze. Her face was blank, no teasing judgement or cynical smile. She was watching, waiting, and studying them. A ripple ran down Olivia's back, drawing Mal's gaze. He nodded, risking one more glance at Ellen. Maybe she wasn't the threat. Maybe it was Brown's daughter.

Chapter Seventeen

Mal watched the girl, torn. She was more wild than woman, her light eyes the same as Cyrus's. She sat, pressed into the corner, her bowl of chili resting on her knees. While the rest of the pack talked and laughed around the large wooden table, Tess Brown tried to be invisible.

But every once in a while, she'd risk a glance up.

"Done?" Olivia asked, reaching for his bowl.

He took her hand and tugged her down into his lap. "No," he whispered against her temple. She rested her head on his shoulder, instantly relaxing against him.

"He been like this since you met?" Anders asked Olivia. "Man-handling and bossy?"

Olivia shook her head. "Protective, yes."

"Is that what we're calling it?" Dante asked.

"I'd love to do some bloodwork." Hollis sat at the far end of the table, watching them. "Until now, Finn was the only one to turn someone. I'm curious to see how her make-up will differ or mirror our own."

Olivia nodded. "I'm fine with that—"

"No," Mal interrupted. "Not yet." Not with Ellen and Tess around. He didn't know if Olivia's blood held anything that would interest Cyrus, but he sure as hell wasn't going to put a target on her back.

Hollis stared at Mal. "Why?"

Mal shrugged, looking first at Ellen then Tess. "I can think of a couple of reasons."

Finn cleared his throat. "We have things to talk about."

"We?" Anders asked, tossing his napkin onto his plate.

"The pack," Finn clarified.

Dante rested his elbows on the table. "As long as it gets me out of clean-up duty." He stood.

"I'll take care of it," Olivia offered, sliding from Mal's lap before he could stop her.

"You're part of the pack Olivia." Finn's announcement caused a slight reaction in the room, something Mal watched with interest.

Jessa, naturally, beamed at her mate.

Anders, Dante, and Hollis accepted Finn's announcement with grudging acceptance. She was an outsider, Mal got that. But she had a right to be there—and information they'd find interesting.

Ellen stared at her hands, but there was a smile on her lips.

Tess glanced at Finn, confused.

"I'll get Gentry and Brown to help me," Jessa said. "Maybe Tess, too." She glanced at the girl.

Tess smiled at Jessa, making something sharp and jagged settle in Mal's stomach. He glanced at Ellen again, but she was ignoring him.

Dammit.

He didn't want to talk to Ellen. She set his teeth on edge, made him hungry for a fight. Asking her questions, acknowledging she might be able to help him in any way, didn't sit right. But neither did not knowing who the enemy was.

Hell, he refused to leave Jessa alone until both Brown and Gentry were with her. Tess's response to her father was equally confusing. She treated him no differently than the rest of them, shying away from him, avoiding eye contact. If it was an act, she was good.

"Mal?" Olivia's fingers threaded through his.

He led her to Finn's office, pulling the door shut behind them.

"We might have an opportunity to catch Cyrus." Finn's statement caused absolute silence.

"We've spent the last ten years avoiding him." Dante shook his head. "Now we're going on the offensive? We don't know how many Others there are—where they all are."

"We don't need to," Finn argued. "If he's out of the picture, they have no Alpha."

"They have you," Mal argued.

Finn shook his head. "I'm not aiming to increase my pack. Besides, killing Cyrus might undo all of this."

"You weren't made by Cyrus." Hollis crossed his arms over his chest, rubbing his chin. "His pack might revert. But you exist. We exist. I don't think that will happen. You would be their Alpha."

"Back up." Anders held up his hand. "Alpha or no, I'm all for killing the son of a bitch. How are we catching him?"

Finn looked at Olivia then. "We have a way to track him—to find out where he's going and lie in wait. Olivia's brother is working with Cyrus."

All eyes turned to Olivia, and Mal's wolf bristled. He placed his hands on her shoulders, instantly on the defensive.

"Chill, Mal." Anders grinned. "She's yours, but she's pack now. No one's going to turn on her."

"Besides, if we had to pick between you and her, I'd go

with her. She's sure as hell easier to look at than you are," Dante added.

Olivia covered his hand. "I think he's hot."

The rest of them laughed. Hell, even Hollis smiled.

"We'll have to agree to disagree." Dante winked at her. "So your brother knows something?"

"Yes." Olivia nodded. "My family's company is in import and export—high-end, expensive. Mostly rare collectibles, pieces with history."

Mal squeezed her shoulder. "Her brother screwed up whatever shipment Cyrus was waiting on. They came after Olivia as collateral."

Mal grinned at the number of insults and expletives that filled the air.

"What the hell does a werewolf collect?" Anders asked.

"Dolls?" Olivia said.

The room fell silent again.

"Bullshit," Dante said, sitting back.

"We can all agree on that." Finn paced.

"My brother isn't a good person." Olivia's voice wavered. "I know that now. He kept me out of the business. He kept me out of the way."

"Bad or not, I think he was trying to protect you from the cluster he's made of his life." Mal looked at Finn. "What do we know about Cyrus's businesses?"

Finn shook his head. "Not much. He's good at covering his tracks with front men. On paper, he doesn't exist."

It hurt him to say it, but he knew there was no choice. "Would *she* know?" Mal asked.

"She who?" Dante asked.

"Ellen?" Hollis understood. He nodded. "Probably. But that doesn't mean she'll tell us."

"Can I ask how she got here?" Olivia asked. "I know I'm new, and there's a lot I'm behind on. I don't know how this works, exactly."

Finn smiled. "You can ask anything, Olivia. I'm sure you have questions."

She always had questions.

Her, "Mal's answered a lot," turned all eyes to him. "I'm just curious about Ellen's presence here. And the risks of Jessa's pregnancy."

"Cyrus took Jessa to get to me. But when they found out she was pregnant, the plan to kill her changed. Ellen has shared that the Others can't reproduce. No live child has been born in decades. And those Cyrus has turned are dying about seven years after the bite." Finn ran a hand over the back of his neck. "We know that's not the case with us. Oscar is alive. We were infected ten years ago. And while we can control our shifts and our bloodlust, the Others can't."

But Finn's words troubled Mal. He'd turned Olivia, not Finn. Would that somehow put her in danger?

"Ellen took care of Jessa, protected her." Finn looked at Mal, clearing his throat before he went on. "The Others had locked Jessa in a building and set it on fire. I left you so I could get to her. Ellen was there—she'd been beaten and left to burn with Jessa."

Mal's heart was thumping, but there was no anger. Finn had left him to protect his mate. If it had been Olivia, he'd have done the same thing. He nodded, finally able to let go.

"Jessa made us bring her." Finn shrugged. "And so I did."

"And she's helping?" Mal asked.

"She wants Jessa and the baby to live." Finn shook his head. "I don't get it, but it's true."

"It's about the survival of the species," Hollis said. "She is proud of what she is."

"Oscar's mom—you worry that what happened to her will happen to Jessa?" Olivia asked.

Finn nodded.

"Ellen can change that?" Mal asked.

"She's trying." Hollis bright green gaze met his. "This is important to her in a way that I can't understand. But I don't know if her help will extend beyond Jessa and the baby."

"If we can get some insight from Ellen, we might be able to stop running." Finn's smile was hard.

"I can try to call Chase." Olivia's voice wavered. "If it will help catch Cyrus."

Mal shook his head. "As far as he's concerned, you're dead. He wouldn't believe it was you without seeing you. All things considering, I'm not willing to put your life in his hands. Brother or not."

"So, we ask Ellen?" Anders asked. "And go after Cyrus?"

"We're going to trust what she says?" Dante's gaze bounced to each of them.

"It's a no-go without further information." Finn smiled. "Too much to risk."

Mal was tired of having his world turned upside down. He was tired of worrying about the safety of the pack—and now Olivia. He wanted a future with her and, when the time was right, a family. If there was a way to ambush Cyrus, to cut the head off the monster that was the Others, he'd do it. Even if it meant playing nice with a bitch he wasn't sure he could trust.

...

Olivia paced, her wolf on high alert. The guys sat around a coffee table, excitedly talking about the potential takedown. But she couldn't shake a sense of impending doom.

"Hey." Mal's voice was low when he came up to her, his hands resting on her shoulders. "Tell me."

She looked up at him, her mind spinning and circling back. "If Ellen tells us what we need to know, it's not just about catching Cyrus."

His brow furrowed. "What do you mean?"

"I'll know what Chase has done—is doing. I'll know what he's guilty of." She bit her lip to stop its wobble. "I know he's a bad guy but…" She faltered, and he nodded, encouraging her to continue. "I always wanted to give him the benefit of the doubt." She rested her head on his chest.

He held her close. "You don't know what hold Cyrus might have over him, Olivia. He's dangerous, you know that."

"Don't make excuses for him," she murmured, loving him even more for trying.

Once Finn had left to get Ellen, Olivia knew there was no escaping the truth. Not that she wanted to. Her life now was here, with her pack and Mal. If someone was a threat, even someone that was her blood, she and her wolf wouldn't hesitate to destroy it.

"Let's wait and see what she has to say. If she says anything." His heartbeat was slow and even beneath her ear.

She nodded, leaning into him. What she wouldn't give to be back in bed with him, discovering new things that shattered her body into tiny pieces of joy—versus learning things that would shatter her heart.

She tried not to tense when Finn came through the door. Maybe Ellen had refused his offer. But Ellen followed, her dark eyes sweeping the room. She stood in front of the fire, her long arms crossed, posture irritated. She didn't want to be there. Olivia knew exactly how that felt.

"We have questions," Finn said.

Her nod was stiff.

"About Cyrus and his business dealings." Finn glanced at Olivia.

"About the business dealing Cyrus has with her brother?" Ellen asked, her dark gaze meeting Olivia's.

Mal stiffened, but Olivia gripped his arm. "Yes, please," Olivia managed.

Ellen's brows rose. "Some things are best left alone."

"Best for who?" Olivia asked.

Ellen's eyes narrowed. "You think knowing his business will provide a weakness? Something you can exploit?" She shook her head, looking at each one of them. "You know nothing."

"We don't want your opinion." Mal's voice was hard. "Just information."

Ellen's smile was glacial. "Why should I give it to you?"

"Because you want Cyrus dead." Hollis spoke then. "Maybe more than we do."

Ellen's hands fisted. "You cannot beat him."

Olivia understood her then. Ellen was terrified. "You're safe here," she said.

Ellen's smile was snide. "You know nothing," she repeated softly. "Your brother. He deals in exotic import, yes?"

Olivia nodded.

"Like his father before him?" Her brow rose. "Jefferson Chase. A shrewd businessman. He promised what he could deliver. Nothing like his son."

Olivia swallowed. Her father?

"Cyrus gives men what they want. Unnatural things—those no one speaks of publicly. And then he traps them and bends them to his will." Her eyes were hard. "Your father, your brother, help supply Cyrus with a high-demand product."

"Dolls?" Mal's dismissive snort was jarring.

"A sort of doll. Girls. Untouched, innocent, and naive." Ellen's voice was thick.

"Are you fucking kidding me?" Anders stood.

"No," Ellen responded.

Dante shook his head. "What the hell does he need—"

"Business." Ellen faced the fire, holding her hands out. "Only the truly rare. It keeps the profit up and risk down. Faraway, forgotten countries are best. Or here, if a customer is willing to pay." She looked at Finn. "Brown's daughter, Tess. She was a special request."

Olivia's wolf growled, wanting to tear Cyrus into little pieces. And Chase? Her brother? She was shivering, flinching away from Mal's touch. "*How* does this happen?"

Ellen looked at her. "Cyrus meets with Mr. Chase. And Byron—Cyrus goes nowhere without him. No notes, no emails, no phone calls, no trace. He gives Chase his order and delivery date."

"Big guy?" Finn asked, exchanging a look with Mal.

"Big and angry." Ellen nodded. "The last shipment was wrong, missing one. A virgin. You are—were—a virgin so Cyrus wanted you."

How the hell would they know that? She didn't run around in an "I'm a virgin" T-shirt. Unless? "Chase told them?" Because they had no secrets between them—at least, she had no secrets from him. He was her brother, the one person she'd trusted completely. Her stomach dropped. She wasn't going to cry. She wasn't going to fall apart. Or scream. She let Mal pull her against him then, clinging to him.

Ellen nodded. "To save his own life."

"All right, enough." Finn was shaking. "Mal. You and Olivia can go."

"No, we will not go." Olivia pushed out of Mal's hold. "You can't tell me this and expect me to walk away. My family is responsible." She pressed a hand to her chest. Everything she'd thought she knew was a lie. "My brother—we have to stop this from happening. We have to. I was lucky—Mal was there." She looked at Ellen, trying to wrap her mind around it. "After, when it's over, the girls go back to Cyrus?" Poor Tess. She'd been through so much.

Ellen nodded. "To him. Some he keeps. Some he gives to the pack. He finds uses for them."

"Olivia's right." Anders's anger rolled off him. "We can't

let this go. I have three sisters, Finn."

"Where do they meet?" Finn asked Ellen.

"Each meeting is somewhere different," she answered. "Three times a year, no more. No more than ten girls each time. After the last order, I don't know if he'll trust Chase again. If the fool is still alive."

"Why is he necessary?" Dante asked. "Why not do it without the middle man?"

"Cyrus is untraceable. Chase gets the girls and Byron handles payment and delivery." Ellen was watching them closely. "He needs Chase—and hates that he needs him."

"How would he get them without Chase?" Finn asked.

"Eventually the fool's partner will take over. The woman, his office manager." She glanced at Olivia. "With the red hair?"

"Miss Rangell?" Olivia asked, nausea washing over. Chase had been infatuated with her—said she was hot. No matter how many times Olivia told him that wasn't a requirement for the sort of work she'd be doing, Chase hired her anyway. "She sends fruit baskets at the holidays, picks up Chase's dry cleaning, handles accounts payable."

"She keeps Chase in line." Ellen shrugged. "He knows what Cyrus is. It scares him. She calms him down."

"Is she a wolf?" Finn asked.

"No, but Cyrus likes her." Ellen shook her head. "Cyrus prefers humans. Easier to dispose of."

A dull ache started at the base of Olivia's neck. Miss Rangell was working for the Others? She kept Chase calm and in line. Had kept—past tense if he was dead. Chase. How could he do this? How was her brother capable of such things?

"So, we go after Miss Rangell?" Dante asked.

They all looked at Finn, waiting for his answer. His nod was slow. "We're not doing this half-assed," he promised. "It'll take time and planning. I'm not losing anyone."

"Chase is a better target, if he is alive." Ellen looked at Finn. "Cyrus scares him. He is weak. If he feels threatened, he would betray Cyrus."

Like he betrayed her. To save himself.

Ellen stared at her for a long time, and then beyond her to Mal. Finally, she left the room without another word.

Mal's arms slid around her waist, pulling her back against him. "Let me hold you, please," he whispered in her ear. She shuddered and turned, pressing her nose to his chest and breathing him deep. She needed the comfort only he could give her.

"We're believing her?" Anders asked.

"There's nothing to gain by lying about this." Hollis stood. "We should be grateful she said as much as she did."

Olivia pressed her eyes shut. It would be easier to dismiss Ellen's story. But she couldn't. The cage and the terror—how many girls had been kept there? What had happened to them? How many more would follow if they didn't do something about it?

"Damn hard to feel grateful right about now." Anders anger was tangible.

"She told us a hell of a lot more than we bargained for." Dante sounded sad.

"A lot to think about," Finn mumbled. "Not a word to Brown, understood?"

She couldn't concentrate on what they said, couldn't get beyond what she'd learned. It wasn't just Chase that betrayed her. Her entire life was based on a lie. An evil, horrible lie. Mal hadn't dragged her into this life—her father had, when she was a little girl.

Chapter Eighteen

Mal closed the bedroom door behind them and led her to the bathroom. She sat on the edge of the tub, dazed and pale, but didn't say a word. He turned on the faucet, making the water nice and hot before kneeling in front of her. Damn, he hated to see her like this.

Fuck Ellen and her pearls of wisdom.

No, he should have pulled Olivia out of there before the shit hit the fan. It was his job to take care of her, not lead her in front of the firing squad. Not that he'd had the slightest idea what Ellen was going to say. How could he?

But now it was out there. Whatever memories Olivia had were forever tarnished. How could she think fondly of her past, of vacations or gifts, without it being tainted by what her father was capable of?

As for Chase…his wolf would only be happy when he was in pieces. He'd been willing to give her up, to trade her to Cyrus? But she didn't need his anger. She needed his support. He could swallow the rage for now. He'd had years of practice.

"Olivia," he whispered, rubbing one hand between

his. Her fingertips were ice cold and tense. He watched her eyes drift close, but she stayed withdrawn, and it killed him. "Olivia," he repeated. Slowly, her fingers warmed, and her hands clutched his. "I'm sorry."

Her hazel gaze shook him to the core. "You have nothing to be sorry for," she said. "I wanted to know the truth."

He cradled her face. "The truth according to Ellen."

Her hands covered his. "I believe her, Mal.I wish I didn't, but I do. And so do you."

He didn't argue—she was right. Everything Ellen said made sense—horrible, awful sense. The problem was nothing could be said or done to make it right. Olivia knew this; the torment on her face told him so. "Tell me how to make this better."

"You can't." Her lower lip wobbled. "I just want to do something. To find them, save them. We have to stop it from happening again—to anyone."

He nodded. "We'll figure it out, Olivia."

"Promise me?" she asked.

"I promise I will do everything I can to stop it—to stop him." And he meant it.

She nodded, shivering.

"Shock," he said, pulling her to her feet. "Water's hot." He nodded at the nearly full tub. "It'll help you warm up."

"Join me?" she asked, letting him pull her shirt up and over her head. She pulled the tie of her sweatpants, letting the soft fabric pool at her feet. He loved that there was no modesty between them.

"Not a good idea," he confessed.

"It's a very good idea," she argued. "Make me feel good, Mal." She took his hand, pressing it to her bare breast. Resistance was impossible. His thumb stroked the tip, rolling the nub until it pebbled hard. His pulse kicked into overdrive, sending his blood southward with evident results. "That's what the bath is for." Because baths and condoms weren't a good idea.

With a little frown, she stepped into the bath and sank into the clear water with a sigh.

"Hungry?" he asked.

She shook her head.

"Thirsty?" he asked.

She looked at him. "No."

He nodded, sitting on the floor and resting his chin on the lip of the bathtub.

She slid her fingers through his hair, drops of water running along his jawline and back into the tub. "Talk to me."

"About?" Because talking came so naturally to him.

"You." Her fingers slid through his hair again. "You know I'm the daughter of an organized criminal, whose whole life was a lie." Her attempt at a joke made her sniff and blink rapidly.

"Not anymore, Olivia," he promised. "No lies here. That I promise."

She sniffed, giving a slight nod. "I'm going to hold you to that."

Damn, what he would give to kill Cyrus right now and drag his body to her—so she could rest easier. Her voice wavered as she went on. "I know you're a big manly wolf I've attached myself to for all eternity. I'm not complaining. I'm just curious about your day job and your parents and where you grew up. You know, normal stuff."

All things she should have known by now. "My dad raised me. He died a few years back—heart attack. Mom left before I was old enough to remember her."

"Only child?" she asked, moving around so her face was close to his.

"Why mess with perfection?"

She smiled.

"Jobs." He stared at her. "My dad worked for Dean, Finn's dad. He was a damn good mechanic. Finn's dad valued my father, helped me get into the right schools. Finn and I grew up together. He was my best friend. But once I figured out Dean was paying for everything, I acted like a shit and ran off, ashamed of my dad for taking a handout. I bummed around, using what my father had taught me to pay the bills. Finn tracked me down. Our reunion vacation turned me into a wolf, and I took off again." He shook his head. "Finn and I didn't talk for a long time. I tend to move around a lot. I wouldn't want to put a target on the people I worked for."

"No one special in your past?"

Mal cleared his throat. He'd locked memories of Jude deep inside, to keep himself sane. It had gotten easier in time, but he knew he'd never fully recover from what happened. He could lie to Olivia, pretend she'd never existed, but he didn't want secrets between them. "Once."

"I didn't mean to pry, Mal. It's none of my business." Her fingers stroked along the side of his face.

Only Olivia would say something like that and mean it. "Her name was Jude, and we were engaged. I thought I'd be able to make it work, even as a wolf. But the Others found her." He shrugged, his brown gaze searching hers.

"Did she know?" Olivia's voice was soft.

"That I was a late-night-movie monster?" He shook his head. "I never wanted her to."

She nodded. "I'm so sorry Mal." She slid closer, kissing his forehead. "I'm so sorry."

He was, too—for Jude. He'd wanted Jude, wanted the family that came with her. She'd been funny and sweet, bringing joy to his life again. But his wolf had known. His wolf had tried to leave, running farther and farther from their apartment every time they shifted. The wolf had been waiting for its mate. And now they'd found her.

"I wish I'd taken you up on your offer." He held her hand up, kissing each fingertip. "Me, you, and a beach in the middle of nowhere."

She smiled. "Maybe we can convince Finn we need a getaway. He could buy our own little island, set up a new refuge just for the pack. Surround it with all sorts of defenses and wolf-eating sharks."

He laughed. "Wolf-eating? Different than man-eating?"

She grinned, shrugging. "Fine, Others-eating. Maybe Hollis could scent train them or something?"

"If that was a thing, Hollis could do it." He adored this woman.

She nodded. "We should talk to him."

"Sounds good." He sat up, reaching for the shampoo. "Lean back." He poured the gel into his hand and ran it through her hair. "You? After you got your graduate degree, what did you want to do?"

"Work in a museum. Growing up, it felt wrong to see these pieces of history sold off. I always thought history was exciting, and artifacts were something meant to be shared with everyone, for anyone to learn from." She sighed, closing her eyes. "It all seems so far away now."

He rinsed her hair, wringing out any remaining shampoo suds.

"Mal." She grabbed his hands. "Your turn." She tugged.

He shrugged out of his clothes and climbed in, facing away from her. Her breasts pressed against his back, silky soft. Her legs fitted against his sides, cradling him against her. He closed his eyes, relishing each caress as she washed his hair, using her nails on his scalp until he was groaning. She laughed, massaging the muscles of his neck and shoulders before biting the nape of his neck.

He was pretty damn relaxed by the time the washcloth was gone and her hand started stroking his ever-ready erection. If she wanted him, he wasn't going to argue. But he wasn't going to take any chances, either. He gripped her wrist, eased her hand away, and stood. "Bed."

She nodded, taking his hand and letting him rub her down with the thick towel. But she was impatient, tugging the towel from his hands and launching herself at him before he'd fully dried off.

He carried her back to the bedroom and laid her on the edge of the bed, standing between her thighs as he rolled a condom on, then lifted her hips. She was panting beneath him, hands gripping his forearms as she arched up to meet him.

He slid deep, growling at the heat that welcomed him home.

•••

Olivia closed her eyes, focusing on the slide and tug of Mal inside of her. The friction was magic, raking her from head to toe, teasing her with flares of pleasure, flooding her with hunger.

She slid her hands over his, then up her sides and over her head, stretched out across the mattress. He pounded into her, the bed shuddering beneath her, making her rock. Her breasts bounced in time, another jolt to the senses. His fingers tightening on her hips ratcheted up the swell of heat and want tightening her stomach and melting her insides.

She looked at him, then, in tune with her body. And his.

His arms and neck were clenched as he battled his release for her. He was so beautiful, so powerful, the relentless thrust of him—again and again—making her weightless. His muffled groan made her tremble.

"I love you, Mal," she whispered.

He came instantly, his chest and stomach, arms and hips clenching. He pulsed inside her, his release driving her own. She arched into him, the slow burn blazing over her and setting each nerve on fire. She cried out, her hands gripping the edge of the bed as pure bliss took over.

He fell forward, his lips seeking hers. His kiss was heaven.

Mal. Hers.

She wrapped her arms around him, needing him—needing comfort. He was all she had left now, the only real and solid thing in her life, and it thrilled her. And it crushed her.

The sting in her eyes was unexpected. Worse was the sob that slipped from her lips. She'd been so strong. Now she was going to fall apart?

Mal braced himself over her, the sadness on his face crumbling her resistance.

She covered her face and sobbed.

Mal was off her in an instant.

"No," she said, reaching for him. "No."

He tugged her into his lap and wrapped her tightly in his arms. "Cry. I've got you." At least he shared her grief. Knowing that helped. He smoothed her tangled hair from her temple, burying his nose and breathing her in. She'd done the same, pressed her face into his chest—seeking his scent and the relief it offered. "I won't let go." He rocked her, leaning against the headboard and pulled the quilts up and over them.

She had nothing to cry about. Her heartache and tears were for the victims of this new life she lived. Evil had always existed, on the nightly news or the latest election cycle, but it hadn't touched her. She'd lived in a bubble—a privileged, sheltered bubble—with no true understanding of what darkness existed.

Mal. Finn. The pack.

Ellen and Tess.

These people had always been there. While she'd been bouncing from graduate school to graduate school, they'd been fighting monsters. She'd been studying history, stressing over her GPA and whether Chase was taking care of himself since he was on his own.

Chase. Bile flooded her mouth. She'd never hated someone before—she'd never had the need. But hate was just the beginning. He disgusted her. He'd known what he was doing. She'd been a bargaining chip to him, something to use when it would best suit him.

And their father. She couldn't think about him.

"I need to believe my mother was clueless, Mal." Her words were broken and raw. "I need to have someone left in my past."

"She didn't know," Mal assured her. "I've seen her, in your memories. Her eyes weren't haunted, Olivia. She didn't know. And she loved you completely. Like I do."

He loved her. "You love me."

His nod was tight—and amazing.

She clung to Mal, her arms so tight she worried she'd hurt him. But he didn't argue. His arms were fixed, holding her close. He loved her. His heartbeat was rapid because he ached for her. Hurt with her. Understood her. Loved her. When the tears finally started to ease, her head was pounding and her arms, still vice-like around Mal, were shaking.

"I've got you," he said again, his lips brushing her temple.

She looked up at him, studying the stubble-covered line of his jaw, his thick neck and strong shoulders. "I know." She eased her hold on him.

He stared down at her, his frown and the furrow between his brows both deep. "It's not over yet."

She pressed her fingers between his brows, smoothing the lines away with a smile. "It's hard to accept. Chase, I mean. But there are no more surprises. I know now what makes things go bump in the night, and that not all monsters are monsters. You and I are proof of that." She ran her hand across his chest.

Mal was rigid, his eyes darkening.

"What's wrong?" she whispered.

"I want to kill him," he ground out. "He gave you to them. And I can't let him live for that. Even if he is your brother."

She swallowed.

"Once he gives us what we need—" He broke off, his gaze boring into hers.

She drew in a deep breath. "One step at a time, right?" she reminded him. Rage rolled off him, simmering just beneath the surface. "First, we plan."

Mal's nod was tight.

"But now we sleep?" she asked, bone-weary.

He kissed her, soft and sweet, then clicked off the bedside lamp. She lay with his heart beneath her ear, unable to stop the images in her brain. Her own heart felt bruised after so many painful truths.

And Mal's? Jude. He'd loved someone enough to marry her, and he'd lost her to the Others. If Mal had uncontrolled rage, he had every right to it. What they'd done to him, body and spirit, was unforgivable. She wanted vengeance for him.

"You're not sleeping." His voice was gruff.

"Neither are you," she said, running her fingers down his arm. "Why not?"

"Ellen." He sighed. "Her eyes."

Olivia looked at him, able to see him just as clearly now as when the lights were on. Some wolf things were cool. "What about them?"

"All of Cyrus's victims have the same eyes—devoid of color, pale. Ellen's are not." Mal's voice was low.

"If Cyrus didn't turn her, is she an Other?" Olivia murmured.

"I'm not sure." He rolled over her. "But since we can't sleep, I say we wear each other out until we can."

His lips found hers. He tasted too good to refuse. His teeth nipped, his tongue dipping into her mouth. Her hands ran over his back, tracing the dozens of scars that covered the skin. Cyrus did this to him. Fury rolled over her. She had no choice but to channel all her rage, all her frustration, into loving Mal.

Chapter Nineteen

Mal paced Finn's office, listening to every detail. Again.

"We take them out and take their place," Anders repeated. "Easy."

"He'll get suspicious." Dante shook his head. "If he panics, he can bring a shit-storm of Others down on us."

Mal glared at Dante.

"I get it." Dante held up his hands. "But Finn's right on this one. Why take unnecessary risks?"

"We know his routine," Anders argued. "What risks? I'm thinking there's never going to be a perfect time to kidnap the son of a bitch." Anders glanced at Olivia. "Sorry."

Olivia nodded, her eyes red-rimmed and shadowed.

No matter how many times he told her none of this was her fault, she took her brother's sins onto her shoulders. Her dreams were haunted by Cyrus, the only place he couldn't physically protect her. And her days were full of plotting ways to bring down her brother. Gentry and Brown had reported everything they'd learned the last few weeks of watching his activities.

Chase had bodyguards. Some wolves, some not.

If Miss Rangell wasn't with him, a guard was. The redhead was intent on assuming Chase's place, the large rock on her left hand announcing to the world—and the pack's surveillance cameras—that she would soon be Mrs. Chase. And once that happened, Mal suspected Olivia's brother would meet with a sudden, untimely death. If Ellen was right, Teresa Rangell was the brains of the operation. Clearly, she was done standing in Chase's shadow.

While the pack was unified in their goal, Finn's focus wasn't as razor-sharp as Mal hoped. Finn's preoccupation with Jessa's pregnancy was understandable, but also infuriating. Time was slipping away, time that Olivia seemed to be tracking by the second. He hated seeing her this way, hated being helpless—especially now that they had intel they could use.

"We wait?" Anders asked, frowning at Mal. "Again?"

"Unless you come up with something foolproof, we have no choice." Dante rolled his neck. "I'm starving."

"Me, too," Olivia said, pushing up out of the chair.

Mal fought the urge to keep her close. If she ate, it was good. She smiled at him, stood on tiptoes to press a kiss to his cheek, and left with Dante.

"She stressing out?" Anders asked.

Mal nodded, sliding one photo aside. Images of Chase covered the long table. Chase going to the gym, going to the warehouse, going out with Miss Rangell, going to his favorite club—without Miss Rangell. No Cyrus. No Byron the butcher. It was for the best. If Mal had seen the giant sadist, he's not sure he'd be able to keep his shit together.

He still woke up in cold sweat with the feel of Byron's teeth on his throat. Nothing could erase the pain he'd felt. Or the fury. Byron had been the one to string him up, forcing Jessa to watch.

"We could do this," Anders said, glancing at the door.

"You know we could."

Mal nodded. He wanted to.

"We wait too long, and we're condemning more girls to this shit. I can't shake it, Mal." He shook his head. "Tess—think she'll ever get over it? Lead a normal life? I can't pretend I don't know this. I can't keep doing nothing."

Mal agreed, 100 percent. "We go."

Anders stared at him. "No shit?"

"No shit." Mal nodded. "I'm on perimeter tonight." He slid more images aside, studying Olivia's brother with his guards. No matter how much he wanted to take the fucker out, he had to do this right. "These aren't wolves." He tapped the image. "They should be with him tonight. We go in as clients, get what we need, and leave."

"Easy," Anders nodded.

"No. Clients go through Cyrus," Ellen said, walking to the table. "He'll know."

Mal stared at her.

She pushed through the pictures. "But if you show him you're rich, get him drunk, pretend you're interested, suddenly he is your best friend." She looked Mal in the eye.

"How do you know this?" Anders asked.

"I found a way to stay useful." Her smile was hard. "It's easy to be quiet and listen. Cyrus complained about Chase, how he likes to talk and be important." She rifled through the photos. "This one drives him to the club?" she asked, tapping the man in one picture.

Anders nodded.

"Because this one's job is to keep him happy, to let him… let off steam? And clean up messes. If Chase leaves with a woman, he hides it. If Chase drinks too much, talks too much, he takes care of any problems. He is dangerous, but he works alone."

"Wolf?" Mal asked.

She nodded.

"Fucking great," Anders growled.

"Not so easy," she agreed. "Nothing important is."

Anders nodded. "Damn straight. But it'd be nice to catch a break."

"She just gave us one," Mal argued. He glanced at the dates on the pictures. "Tuesday and Thursdays are club days."

Anders shook his head. "It's Sunday."

"Finn?" Ellen asked. "Your Alpha won't be pleased."

Mal shook his head. "A club is public. The guard is a wolf. Too many variables."

Ellen's eyes narrowed. "Your mate?"

Mal frowned. "Doesn't need to know."

"Secrets are dangerous." She sighed. "But I will not waste my words warning you." She left the office as silently as she'd entered.

"Think she'll spill to Finn?" Anders asked.

Mal shook his head. "She wouldn't have told us if she didn't want this done."

"Unless it's a trap," Anders muttered.

But Ellen's eyes were proof enough. Ellen had been kept by the Others, but she wasn't part of their pack. One blue eye, one green eye—all the Others Mal had ever encountered had the same pale, almost colorless, eyes. Like their bastard Alpha: Cyrus. Whatever questions he had about the woman, her origins, and her loyalty, he had one answer. They shared a common enemy, and she wanted vengeance almost as much as he did.

...

Olivia took a bite of her apple, watching Oscar wriggle and kick on the floor. He squealed with glee, batting at one of the toys that hung off his play gym.

"Who's the strongest little guy?" she asked, wiggling his foot.

Olivia had taken one look at Jessa and told her to go to bed. She didn't know much about pregnancy or childbirth, but Jessa looked close to popping. Her poor feet and hands were swelling, too, something Hollis has sighed over before agreeing with Olivia's nap suggestion.

"You're going to be a big brother soon, Oscar," she said, smiling down at him.

He smiled back, making a long gurgling noise.

"You don't say?" She lay on her side. "What else is happening down here?"

Oscar turned his head toward her, those big, blue eyes fathomless. He blinked, inspecting her features carefully.

"Your dad looks at me like that sometimes." Olivia giggled. "I'm pretty sure he thinks Uncle Mal has made a colossal mistake."

Oscar gurgled again.

"No, no, I'm pretty certain." She stroked Oscar's little cheek. "But thanks for trying to make me feel better."

"How is a one-sided conversation supposed to make you feel better?" Hollis asked, striding into the room. Hollis always seemed like he was late on the way to somewhere important, even when he was just getting a cup of coffee.

"We're just hanging out," Olivia offered.

Hollis glanced at her. "You and Oscar?"

She glanced behind her. "Tess was here a minute ago." No matter how hard Olivia tried to engage the woman in small talk, Tess didn't budge. She listened to everything being said around her, never interacting or responding. Most of them acted like she wasn't there. But Olivia and Jessa kept at it while Ellen watched her with narrowed eyes.

"She does that," Hollis said.

"What?"

"Moves on silent feet." He came around the couch to sit, carrying his mug with him. "Ellen has the same knack."

"I trip over my own feet," Olivia said.

"You look tired." Hollis peered at her, his gaze thorough. "Not sleeping?"

She shook her head. "Dreams."

He nodded. "Vivid?"

"So real," she agreed.

"What about, if I may ask?" He sipped his coffee.

"A white wolf—Cyrus, I guess." She shrugged, making a silly face at Oscar. Oscar's giggle was enough reward.

"Often?" he asked.

She nodded. "It starts the same. I'm running from him. I realize I'm a wolf and turn back to fight him, but he's gone. Other times he charges me. The ground, the snow, is covered in blood."

"Sounds distressing." Hollis set his cup down.

"Yes," she agreed.

"Are you always alone?" he prodded.

She shook her head. "Sometimes there's someone else with me, in a cave. I'm protecting the entrance. I have no idea who or what is inside, but I can't let anyone in."

Hollis sat back.

"Mal is with me sometimes. But sometimes he chases after the white wolf and leaves me alone with the rest of them." She made a funny noise, scrunching up her face at Oscar.

"Rest of them?" he asked.

"A large pack. They all have the same eyes." She smiled as Oscar yawned. "Tired little thing."

"He'll be starving tomorrow. The full moon. Should be interesting." He shook his head.

"Why?" she asked, sitting up. "Something different?"

"A lunar eclipse," Hollis said.

Olivia hadn't been aware of Ellen, leaning against the

doorframe until she said, "The first of the blood moon. It will look red, ringed—quite a sight."

"First?" Olivia asked.

"A lunar tetrad." Ellen sat on the arm of the couch. "Four lunar eclipses in a row. There are legends linking a lunar eclipse and the wolf. Some foolish, some not."

Oscar squeaked, his mouth pulling down at the corners.

"Oh, Oscar, don't do that," Olivia cooed, scooping him up. "No tears little guy." She patted his little back, oddly giddy at holding him so close.

"You'll be a good mother," Ellen said, nodding. "This pack will grow strong."

She'd never expected a compliment from the woman—even though she and Mal weren't ready for a child, it was nice to hear. Olivia glanced down the hall, toward Jessa's room. "You're not worried about Jessa? Or the baby?"

Ellen shook her head. "No. There is no danger between mates. It will be better for you, as a wolf. But I believe Jessa will be fine." She paused. "These dreams you have, do you ever fight the white wolf?"

Olivia glanced at Hollis, uneasy. "No."

"Why not?"

"A voice tells me I'm not ready." She shrugged. "And I wake up."

"You are ready Olivia. Oscar, Jessa, and the baby need you to protect them." Ellen's eyes locked with hers. "Your wolf can do it, but you must believe in yourself, in your wolf."

"How do you know?" Hollis asked.

"Her wolf is still uncertain." Ellen stood. "You need to learn to shift at will. Come, I will show you. It will help."

Olivia glanced at Oscar, sleeping in her arms.

"I'll take him," Hollis offered, holding out his hands. "You don't have to do this, Olivia."

Ellen snorted, dismissing Hollis. "Her wolf wants her to."

Olivia tried to shut out the noise and listen, really listen. "She does." Olivia handed Hollis the baby and followed Ellen outside.

Ellen glanced at her. "You think too much."

Olivia laughed. "I've been accused of talking too much."

"That, too." Ellen smiled. "Your wolf needs attention, room to bond with you. Instinct rules the wolf."

"I—"

"You don't trust your instincts," Ellen finished. "But you must."

Olivia sucked in a deep breath.

"She is always with you. The only thing you can count on, Olivia." Ellen stripped, talking the whole time. "You must respect her and what she needs. What she is capable of."

Olivia tried not to stare at the woman. She was incredibly fit, her form feminine and strong and lovely. But every inch of her, save her face, was covered in scars.

"What is she capable of?" Olivia asked, suddenly nervous.

Ellen smiled. "Anything. Once you defeat him, the dream will go away. Now, shift."

Olivia watched the woman shift, mesmerized by how easy she made it look. It was quick, almost fluid. She shrugged out of her clothes and focused all her energy on one thing. Not the shift, or her fear, but her wolf. Her wolf was ecstatic.

Chapter Twenty

Mal passed through the kitchen, but there was no sign of Olivia. She wasn't in their room, with Jessa, in the yard, or reading in her favored armchair by the fire. She was devouring books on wolf lore faster than Hollis could find them. Considering how extensive Hollis's library was, he assumed she'd have plenty of reading to do. Why wasn't she there?

His agitation was misplaced. He was the one who got caught up in plotting, leaving her to her own devices. But so far, her devices had been reading or playing with Oscar or trying, unsuccessfully, to get Tess to engage in some sort of conversation. She seemed more than willing to continue her one-sided conversations with the woman—Mal admired her tenacity. But Tess was alone, dozing in front of the fire under one of Oscar's blankets, and Olivia was nowhere to be seen.

No Olivia.

His hands fisted.

Hollis glanced up from his book. "She's gone running."

Mal paused. "Who?"

Hollis cocked an eyebrow. "Olivia? Who else would you

be looking for? She went running—with Ellen."

Mal ran a hand over his face, biting back the litany of obscenities that clogged his throat. "You didn't think I might want to know this earlier?"

Hollis shrugged. "She's a grown woman, Mal. Ellen offered to teach her how to shift—"

"She did what?" Mal snapped. Did she want to fight him? Because for every *useful* thing Ellen did, she did three things to piss him off. And most of them pertained to Olivia. "When?"

"I'm not sure," Hollis said, turning his attention back to his book

"Try," Mal said, slamming his hand down on the pages.

Irritated, Hollis stood, hands on hips. "You're tense. Why? Because your mate has gone on a run as a wolf? She *is* a wolf and needs to learn what that means, even if you aren't there to help her every step of the way." He leveled a hard look at Mal. "She's independent and strong, qualities I'm sure you noticed?" He shook his head. "Acting like an overbearing asshole all the time is getting old. She wanted to go with Ellen. She wanted to learn from her."

Mal's anger crowded in on him, red tinging his vision and heating his blood. He brushed past Hollis and onto the porch, scenting the air.

Damn her.

Damn Ellen.

And fucking Hollis.

Where the hell had was the rage coming from? He wanted Olivia to connect with her wolf. Nothing was as freeing as those moments he and his wolf worked together, without thought or awareness. He wanted that for Olivia. And teaching her was beyond his comfort zone. Still, a little notice would have been nice.

Not that she needs permission.

Fucking Ellen.

He stared out at the towering pines and the massive peaks of the Grand Tetons beyond, reining in his temper. The cold air burned his lungs, stealing some of the fire in his blood. He gripped the wooden porch railing, searching for some sign of Olivia…and Ellen.

A snapped branch. A scar in the moss and earth of the forest floor. There was a path if he chose to follow them.

Overbearing asshole.

He could wait. Ellen might not be his favorite person, but he no longer considered her a threat to the pack. His sanity was another matter.

He stormed back inside, stomping across the living room and toward the gym.

"Not going after them?" Hollis called after him.

"Fuck you," he snapped, loudly, then slammed the door to the gym.

By the time he was done exercising, he was drenched and weak-limbed. He'd pushed himself hard, sweating out the stress and anger. Every voice, every closing door, every sound in the goddamned lodge made him tense, hoping she was back.

He glanced at the clock on the way back to his room, his anger returning with a vengeance. Where the hell was she?

He was in the shower when he heard the howl—long and husky and close—calling to him as if she was calling his name. He tried to ignore it. He was pissed, and she should apologize for making him worry.

His wolf pushed back. *Go to her.*

He rinsed the soap from his face, ignoring the pull and tug of his skin as she howled again.

Now. It was a growl. A threat.

Mal sighed, resting his forehead on the tile in the stall, his body aching to shift.

"Fuck it," he groaned, turning off the shower and climbing out. He was on all fours before he'd had a chance to dry off. His claws tore through, clicking on the granite floors. The wolf was ecstatic, impatient for the realignment of bone and tendons, muscles and fur. Mal was panting as the wolf trotted out of the bathroom and down the hall.

Ellen stood just inside the front door, wearing a tattered shirt and a smug smile. "You're a stubborn fool," she said as he brushed by her.

He growled.

She laughed.

He'd have been more than happy to take a bite out of her, to teach her to mind her own business. But his wolf didn't care about Ellen or staying angry with Olivia. He tore through the door and into the yard, the call of his mate demanding his presence.

Olivia waited. Her hazel eyes fixed on him, steady and warm. With a lazy stretch and long whimper, she rubbed along his side. She groaned deep in her throat and circled him, sniffing his shoulder and neck and ear.

Mal watched her, giving up the fight. She was so goddamn happy, ears perked up, tail curled. His wolf would do whatever she wanted. Her scent was all wolf and Olivia—now one.

His resistance crumpled, returning the full-body rub with a moan. His head slid under her jaw and nipping her ear playfully. It was more than a greeting this time. A new tension rippled along both wolves. His wolf's instincts had been to defend and fight, to hunt and kill. But a new and distinct drive was coursing through his blood.

Her wolf whimpered, trotting several feet away and glancing over her shoulder at him. She wanted him to follow her. So he did.

When she ran, he ran. She led him all over the refuge, the wolf's curiosity demanding she sniff every damn pile of leaves or hole in the ground. Her enthusiasm was contagious, making his wolf just as inquisitive. They tore up the mountain, terrifying a heard of elk in the process. But when they reached the top, her wolf stopped to stare out over the valley below. The nearly full moon was massive in the sky. She threw back her head and howled.

Mal joined her.

Far below, the refuge wolves echoed their cry, sending a shiver down her back.

He nudged her with his nose, and she faced him.

She shifted, startling him. She'd been practicing, he could tell. Watching her long arm and sleekly muscled thigh return was oddly sensual. The line of her hip and dip of her waist… and her breasts. She sat at his side, breathing hard but smiling. "Hi," she whispered.

Her hands sunk into his fur as she buried her face against his neck. He sat, wolf and man, letting her fingers slide through his thick fur. It was heaven. When she rubbed his ears, he groaned, leaning into her hand. He stared into her eyes. "You are so beautiful, Mal," she murmured. "So, so beautiful."

She rested her head against his. "I wanted to share this with you." She continued to comb his fur, leaving pure pleasure in its place. "My wolf wanted to share this with your wolf."

His wolf groaned, content.

• • •

Olivia was exhausted. She'd shifted several times, and each time it was easier. They'd covered so much ground that she'd had to shift to make the run back to the refuge. Never in her life had she been this exhausted. Maybe she'd sleep tonight without dreams. Today had been good—spending time with her wolf had been amazing. But that didn't mean she wanted to test out her newfound bond by taking on their mortal enemy, even if it was only a dream.

Mal's wolf rubbed against her wolf, demanding her attention. She licked his ear and nuzzled his neck. It didn't matter if she was on the verge of collapsing in the dirt, her wolf never tired of his. The only problem with this was the very real hunger between them. The air hummed with it, their scents giving off a blatant invitation.

The wolves wanted to bond.

Mal shifted as soon as the lodge was in sight.

She whimpered, disappointed and relieved all at once.

"We can't," he murmured, staring at her. "Wolves don't use condoms, and I'm not sharing you." He reached for her, hesitating.

Her wolf sat still, waiting and watching, curious yet defensive.

He ran a hand over her head. Warm. Firm. He sighed, cradling her head in his hands. "I like having you to myself." He smiled.

She rubbed her head against his, groaning at his scent and touch. They couldn't mate as wolves, so she was done with being a wolf. She danced away from him, lingering in the shade of the trees to change. Her bones ached, and her skin felt raw and chafed, but she'd done it. She stumbled out on trembling legs. "My wolf wants to mate," she said, somewhat breathlessly.

Mal caught her in his arms. "Your wolf?"

She nodded. "She's very bossy about some things. Namely, the need to have you in every possible way."

Mal's arms tightened around her. "I like your wolf."

"Dinner is getting cold," Finn called from the porch.

Mal groaned, resting his forehead on hers.

"Dinner sounds pretty good, too." At the mention of food, Olivia was instantly starving.

Mal chuckled. "All the changing takes a lot of calories."

"After we eat, I'm so going to rock your world." She smiled up at him.

"In every possible way?" he asked.

She paused, hunger for food warring with her hunger for Mal. The ridge of his jaw was hard, clenched. He did that when he was buried inside of her. She shivered, her voice husky, "How many ways are there?"

His thumb traced her lower lip. "You're going to make me walk in there with a hard-on."

"It's huge." Her fingers closed around him, loving his shudder at her touch. "You should be proud."

His muffled curse was sexy. "Not so sure Finn will appreciate it. Or Jessa."

Olivia let go of him, his words forming something hard and jagged in the pit of her stomach. Jessa wasn't the only woman inside. Ellen. Tess. Neither was a threat, but her wolf didn't care. She hadn't expected the surge of jealousy that ripped through her. She stiffened, the instinct real—if misplaced.

"Olivia?" he asked, tilting her face back. "What's wrong?"

She shook her head, refusing to admit to such an adolescent reaction. They were all adults. All the women here had seen a naked man before.

Her wolf refused to be pacified. *Not our man.*

Mal's eyes narrowed. "You're mad?"

She shook her head. "Can we go in the back?"

"You think I'd let the guys see you like this?" he growled. "You're mine. No fucking way."

She stared up at him, relieved.

"I'm a possessive son of a bitch. It's who I am." He frowned. "It won't change."

"I don't mind." She stood on tiptoe to kiss him, keeping her own insecurities to herself. She followed him into the house, crouching behind him as they made their way to their room. "Shower?" she asked.

He shook his head. "Faster we eat, faster we get to fu—"

"Mal." She cut him off, instantly on fire for him.

He grinned. "You like it when I talk dirty, Olivia?"

She stared at him, then nodded. "I guess I do."

He pressed his eyes shut. "You're killing me."

She giggled, tugging on the clothes she'd left in the yard hours earlier. "Hurry."

He watched her, holding the door open once she was dressed. "After you."

"You need clothes," she pointed out, waiting outside their room just long enough to get dressed—before she tugged him toward the kitchen.

Anders and Dante were dishing out a massive pot roast, the conversation centering around the latest litter of wolf pups she and Ellen had found next to a downed motion detector on the far side of the refuge.

"Storm knocked it out," Dante said. "I'll go fix it tomorrow."

"Not tonight?" Mal asked, glancing at him, then Olivia.

"You want me to go tonight?" Dante asked. "Can you pass the rolls, Olivia?"

"Yes," Mal answered.

Maybe it was Tess's instant tensing? Or a sound she'd made? Whatever the reason, Olivia was startled by the furious expression on Tess's face. There was no sign of the fragile victim Olivia had come to accept. No, this woman was full of fury. And then it was gone. In a span of seconds, Tess's face went slack again, her eyes glazing over once more.

"Rolls?" Dante asked.

She turned to the table, risking another glance at Tess. She stared vacantly ahead, poking the food on her plate. Maybe she'd imagined the change. But her wolf disagreed, Ellen's advice repeating. "Trust your instincts."

"How many pups were in the litter?" Hollis asked.

"Four," Ellen answered. "Olivia found the den. Her wolf is quite capable."

Hollis sent Mal a look.

Mal scowled back.

"You are displeased?" Ellen's voice was sharp, making Olivia wince. She'd understood Mal's reticence to accept the woman into the pack when they thought she was an Other. But she wasn't. And even though neither of them knew who she belonged to or where she came from, Ellen had done nothing to make Mal distrust her. Today, she'd given Olivia a sense of camaraderie with her wolf, something she was beyond grateful for.

"Olivia's had a lot to deal with." Mal shrugged. "It's been less than a month—I don't see the need to push her." Her heart ached at his words. She couldn't blame him for being overprotective. How many times had he rescued her since they'd met? How many times had she relied on him for survival?

But Olivia didn't need rescuing. She was strong. She wanted him to be proud of it.

"Her wolf is pushing. She needs freedom to reach her full potential. So she can protect the pack when you're gone." Her words were factual.

Mal's eyes narrowed, his lips pressed flat. Ellen's comment infuriated him. She knew he'd never leave her—he'd promised. But she did want to do her part when it came to protecting the pack.

"And you're going to teach her?" he barked.

"I cannot teach her to have instincts. But she has to learn to use them, to trust them. You need to let her do that," Ellen bit back.

Mal sighed, loudly. "I know what she needs."

"Do you?" Ellen's tone remained impartial, almost cold.

Olivia was right there, but neither of them seemed the least bit curious about what she had to say about what she needed. Yes, she was new and learning, but she wasn't incompetent. They shouldn't fight over her because they shouldn't be making decisions for her. Olivia stood, her temper flaring. "Thanks for dinner guys." She smiled at Anders and Dante. "I'm beat so—"

"See you in the morning." Jessa smiled.

She rinsed and loaded her dishes in the dishwasher and smiled her good-nights, grabbing a book off the side table and heading to her room. Being a wolf meant she didn't need lights, so she left them off as she went in and ran a bath. When steam flooded the room and the water was high, she slipped into the bath and rested her head against the edge. If she could have five minutes of Ellen-Mal-wolf-free thoughts, maybe she could calm down.

She soaked a washcloth and draped it over her face, letting the warmth ease her tension.

"I get jealous." Mal's voice made her jump.

She dragged the washcloth from her face, watching him.

"Up until now, it's been you and me. We're part of a pack, but I still want it to be just us." He shook his head.

"It is." She smoothed her hair from her forehead. "Me and you. My wolf and your wolf. I know you better than I know anyone. Ever. I know you better than I know her."

"Ellen?" he asked, frowning.

She smiled. He was adorable when he felt vulnerable. "No, Mal. Her, my wolf. You have a bond with yours. I'm still forming one with mine."

He nodded. "Okay."

"At this point, I'm pretty sure she likes your wolf best, then you, *then* me."

"I don't see a problem," he said, leaning against the doorframe.

She threw the washcloth at him. "Running with Ellen let me tap into my wolf, without her wanting you to the point of distraction. She's just as addicted to your wolf as I am to you. It's overwhelming. She sort of locks up when you're around, lets you take charge, steps aside for you."

"Addiction?" he asked. "I get the distraction thing. He wants to drag her into the woods and make a dozen litters. But he knows better."

She stared at him, his words evoking something primal and raw.

"How do we fix this?" he asked. "I don't want her, or you, taking a backseat to anyone. Especially me. Whatever you and your wolf want, I want. So be strong, Olivia. It might take some getting used to, but I can take it. I want it."

She smiled, draping one leg over the side of the tub. "In every way possible?"

He stared at her, his eyes narrowing. "Yes."

Chapter Twenty-One

Mal couldn't look away. He didn't want to. Olivia stood, her body slick with bathwater, a hundred drops sliding along every curve and valley. She had no idea what she did to him, or how essential she was to him. It was more than claiming her as his. It was the satisfaction knowing he was hers. He'd never wanted to belong to someone else, to compromise who and what he was. Olivia didn't expect that—she wanted him as is.

She stepped out of the bath, reaching for her towel. But he grabbed it before she could.

"Mal?" She hugged herself, uncertain, and so fucking beautiful it took his breath away.

He ran the towel along her shoulder then stooped to lick a drop of water from her throat. One taste wasn't enough. Neck and shoulder, silky side and stomach, the underside of her breast and the pebble-hard tip—his tongue raked each drop from her skin. He dropped to his knees, loving the grip of her hands on his shoulder, the shudder of her every breath. His lips brushed her belly, lightly sucking on the ridge of her hipbone and the swell of her buttock. When his nose nuzzled the soft hair at the juncture of her thighs, she moaned and arched into him. It was sexy as hell. She was sexy as hell.

"Tell me you want me," he said, looking up at her.

Her heavy-lidded gaze burned into his.

His fingers stroked the inside of her thigh, higher and higher. He stopped, so close he could feel her heat. "Tell me."

"I want you, Mal." Her voice shook.

His fingers parted her skin and slid deep into her heat. Her nails bit into his shoulders. When his tongue licked her tight nub, she rocked against him. Nothing tasted as sweet as Olivia. He closed his eyes, his other hand cradling her ass and holding her still against his mouth. Her hands went from bracing to kneading, his tongue merciless as it stroked and teased her into a frenzy. He loved the power he had over her. He made her shudder with his touch, his mouth. Her body craved his—a feeling he understood all too well.

She bowed frantically against him. Her fingers tangled in his hair as a long, broken moan slipped from her lips.

When she swayed on her feet, he caught her close and swung her into his arms. His hunger still raged, but he was content to hold her. He was, she wasn't.

As soon as they fell onto the bed, she rolled over him. With a wicked gleam in her eye, she slid down the length of his body and clasped his throbbing dick in her hand. He sucked in a breath, damn near swallowing his tongue when her lips closed over the tip of his erection.

"Aw, fuck," he ground out, his hands fisting in the quilts.

She moaned, the vibration running the length of him. Her lips were firm around him. The the sweep of her tongue, up and down and around. The light suck when she pulled him deep against her throat. She tugged his hand free of the comforter and placed it on the back of her head. The spill of her hair between his fingers taunted him. Alpha or no, the urge to dominate was there.

"Mal." Her voice startled him. "Show me what feels good."

She kissed the tip, easing him back into the hot wetness of her mouth. She pressed his hand against her hair again. He stared down at her, his control slipping away at the sight that greeted him. Her ass was in the air as she leaned over him. His hands slid through her hair, tangling in the amber locks to hold her steady as he pumped into her mouth. And every time he disappeared between her lips, he groaned. It was good, too good. He wasn't going to last.

Hands trembling, he let go of her hair to frantically tug open the night table drawer and pull out a condom. "Don't move," he ground out. He slid out from under her and off the bed, clasped her hips, and pulled her glorious ass to him. The stroke of his hands down her back had her arching back into him. It was too sweet an offering to pass up.

He wound one hand in her hair, tugging just enough to make her moan. The things her moan did to him. With his other hand, he traced the curve of her ass. From this angle, Mal's view left him breathless. He wanted to love her and claim her all at once. So, he did.

One thrust and he was lost in the feel of her body. She was tight, and hot, and so fucking intense he needed more. He pumped into her, watching the spasms of her skin, feeling the clenching of her inner muscles, and listening to every gasp and moan. Hunger—for him—forced him on. The way she arched back, leaning forward onto her elbows to take him deeper, had him gritting his teeth. But he couldn't wait.

He reached around, his fingers working her clit until her cries gave him permission to let go. There was no holding back. One thrust, then another, hard, and he emptied himself into her.

They fell to the side, his arms holding her tight against

him.

She was gasping, one hand reaching back to rest on his arm. "The things you do to me."

He kissed the nape of her neck, smiling at her full-body tremor.

Her passion-glazed eyes glanced back over her shoulder. "Don't ever stop."

The longing in her voice made him groan, his dick stirring against her.

She smiled. "Exactly."

Rolling her over separated them, but he wanted to see her face—see what she was thinking. He ran his fingers along the side of her face, stroked feather-light across her eyelids and brows, the tip of her nose, her lips and chin. If he could etch her into his memory like this, he would—flushed from loving him. Happy from loving him.

Her hand cradled his cheek. "You're a mystery."

"Nope," he argued.

"Then tell me what you're thinking."

"I'm happy."

"Good." Her hazel eyes gazed into his. "You have soulful eyes. They tell me what you won't."

"Oh?" he asked, waiting.

She nodded. "You worry about the Others. You worry about the pack. You want to be strong for them, to protect them."

He shook his head. "I am strong. I—we will protect them. You and me and the rest of the pack."

She smiled. "We."

He nodded. "I don't worry about that, or them. The only thing that scares me is losing you."

She frowned, her hazel eyes searching his.

"I don't deserve you, but I can't let you go." He studied her face. "I want to know every part of you. To make you happy, inside and out."

Her smile was pure joy. "Wow."

He shook his head.

"No, really, Mal." She placed his hand over her heart. It was racing. "There's no reason to be scared."

He wrapped her up in his arms then, pulling her against his chest. He wanted to believe her. They were surrounded by the best security money could buy, and a big-ass pack of overprotective wolves to boot. But his fear wasn't rational. He didn't know what the fuck to do about it, except hold on to her.

He did, until she was sound asleep and pliant in his arms.

Even then, he held on, running long, slow strokes the length of her spine.

He should tell her about their plan. It was concrete. With Anders's help, it would be an easy in and out—all about the intel. He might be tempted to let out a little aggression on Chase, but he wouldn't. This wasn't about teaching Chase he was a stupid motherfucker. This was about something bigger.

Every time he thought about Olivia in that cage, he wanted to fight. His time in that fucking basement had taught him to live in his head—a dangerous habit now. It was pointless to think about what might have happened if he hadn't been there. She'd been so weak—too weak and human to defend herself. And if they'd managed to heal her, what then? Would she'd have been sold off to the highest bidder? Sure, she'd have settled Chase's debt to Cyrus, but what sort of life would she have had?

Olivia rolled over in her sleep, a soft growl grounding him in the present.

She was here, safe and sound in his bed and his heart. He'd make sure she had her vengeance—God knew she deserved it.

She rolled again, growing more agitated.

He laid his hand on her shoulder, watching the rapid shift of emotions on her face. Her dreams weren't peaceful, but she'd have to face them alone. "Kick their ass, Olivia. Let your wolf have some fun," he whispered, wishing he were there to see it happen.

•••

She was following someone. Tracking something. There were prints in the snow. Her wolf scented the air, searching, reaching until she found the den. It was silent, but she knew what was inside. Oscar and the baby. And Jessa, too.

She glanced at the fallen tree that shielded the entrance, made sure there was no trace of her pack to reveal their hiding place, then ran—not wanting to bring attention to the den. She ran until she came to a clearing.

The hair on the back of her neck bristled at the howl that split the air. The white wolf was in front of her—teeth bared, blood staining his chest and nose, and near-colorless eyes fixed on her. There was blood on the snow. So much blood. There were more wolves behind Cyrus, many more. They watched her from the dark of the tree line, silent and ready.

If she fought, she'd have to win.

If she lost, the pack would be on her.

She charged at the white wolf, baring her teeth and tackling him. There was shock in his eyes, giving her the advantage. Instinct took over, lethal and swift. Before the wolf could regain his footing, she'd ripped his throat out. She stood over the body, pulsing with adrenaline. She threw her head back and howled over and over.

Her eyes popped open. She felt so awake and exhilarated she almost woke Mal. But the sight of him sound asleep and snoring on the pillow next to her made her pause.

Everything in her life was irrevocably changed. And,

bizarre or not, she was happy for the first time in...maybe ever. Knowing her father was a mastermind criminal muted whatever positive childhood memories she had. And her brother's willingness to sacrifice her for himself wasn't exactly pleasant, either.

Unlike Mal.

Her life with him was more than she'd ever dreamed of. He filled the void inside, where something had been missing her whole life. She felt more grounded. She could do anything.

Including fight the big bad wolf in her dreams. Adrenaline still flowed in her veins—and it felt good.

Her wolf agreed. Olivia lay back, listening closely to her wolf's banter. The wolf was proud of her for standing her ground and confronting—and defeating—their enemy. If push came to shove, her wolf promised there was nothing they wouldn't do to protect those they loved.

The adoration she had for Mal and his wolf was unwavering and fierce. That was the way to feel about a life mate. Mal and the wolves, his and hers, were still concerned about Ellen. And Tess...was she a threat to the pack? Olivia couldn't see how the woman was capable of anything diabolical. And yet, she did make her uneasy. Instinct told her something was off.

As happy as her wolf was, she was also sad. Mal was keeping a secret—a big one. He and Anders were going after Chase. His wolf wanted them to go, too, but Mal had shut him down. Shut him down and told him to keep it from her.

Coldness settled in the pit of Olivia's stomach.

He's trying to protect us. Her wolf was willing to defend him even when he was wrong. And he was. Dead wrong.

Finn, their alpha, had told them to wait. She was new at this wolf thing, but the chain of command was hard to miss. If Finn gave an order, she'd follow. Mal didn't seem to have that problem. How could he do this? And why? Being a pack meant working together, not going rogue. That was the exact opposite of the whole pack mentality. But the angrier she got, the more defensive her wolf became.

She frowned at Mal, who was still peacefully snoring. He was going to split hairs over Finn's orders, find a way to make this okay. It would be different if he talked to her about it. But, no, he was making decisions on his own which impacted all of them.

And he was going to leave her.

She waited for Mal to roll over then slid from the bed. Her arms shook as she tugged on more of Jessa's hand-me-downs. Gray sweatpants and a gray sweatshirt to suit her gray mood. She brushed her teeth and hair and crept from the room, wincing as the door squeaked on its hinges. There was no winning an argument with Mal. Her wolf was too besotted with him. And so was she. But Anders was a different matter. She wouldn't get all weak-kneed with him, so he was going to get an earful from her.

She walked into the kitchen, ready for a fight, and came to a complete stop. Jessa was hunched over, her face creased and her lips pressed tightly together. She was in pain.

"Jessa?" Olivia asked.

The woman straightened immediately, pressing her hand to her back. "Everything is aching today." Her attempt at a smile was pathetic.

"Maybe a little more than aching?" Olivia asked, truly concerned. Her wolf went on full alert, ready to do whatever Mrs. Alpha needed.

Jessa was pale, slightly ashen around her eyes and nose. "I'm fine," she said, waving her hand in dismissal. "Finn wanted you to join them in his office when you woke up. Mal coming?"

Olivia sighed, shaking her head. "Still sleeping."

"Which is harder? Having a mate or being a wolf?" Jessa studied her.

"A mate." No comparison.

"Really?" Jessa smiled. "What's it like? Being a wolf?"

"I like it. Is it something you're considering?" she asked. "After?"

"If I make it through this?" She answered Olivia's unanswered question. "Yes. Definitely." She pointed at the counter. "There are muffins and cinnamon rolls. If Anders ever finds a mate, he'll impress the hell out of her with his cooking."

Olivia laughed, taking a muffin and a cinnamon roll and heading toward Finn's office. She could hear the arguing before she'd opened the door. She stood there, glancing back and forth at Ellen and Anders, who looked ready to face off.

"What did I miss?" Mal asked, his voice soft against her ear.

She jumped, dropping her muffin on the wood floor.

"Sorry." He grinned at her and stooped to pick up the muffin, devouring it in three bites.

She glared at him before brushing past him into the office.

"Olivia." Dante nodded at her.

"Good morning," she said. "Maybe? I'm getting the impression something's up?"

"No." Finn sighed, looking at Mal. His eyes narrowed. "You know how I feel about lying, Mal." He rolled his neck. "As you're all aware, I've fucked up plenty. First infecting you, Oscar. Jessa. This baby. And I've owned it every damn time. I would *never* put you in harm's way. What are you thinking?"

Mal stiffened.

"Putting yourself in danger, real danger, is selfish. And you know it." Finn's gaze shifted to Anders. "We are a pack. What one does affects the others."

Her heart ached as Finn voiced what she'd been thinking.

Mal's voice was low. "We have an opportunity to get information—"

"Information? Is that all you're after?" Finn cut him off. "Look me in the eye and tell me you're not going to pick a fight. That if you see Byron or Cyrus, you'll be able to walk away."

Olivia looked at her mate, the struggle on his face making her heart hurt.

"You and Anders?" Finn shook his head. "No lookout? No backup?"

"We can do this," Anders argued. "Ellen told us—"

"Stop." Finn held his hand up. "We need to get one thing straight. I am Alpha. If I say we're waiting on something, we fucking wait."

Mal stared up at the ceiling, the muscles in his neck and arms clenched tight. If she weren't mad at him, she'd go to him. But she was. Her wolf might want to nuzzle in and offer comfort, but she wanted to…to yell at him. He *knew* what could happen to him if he and Anders failed. Death wasn't the worst thing the Others could do. Coldness seeped into her bones, smothering some of her fury.

"*I* talked to Ellen this morning, and I agree that there is an opportunity here." Finn sighed. "Dante, Brown, and Gentry are ready to go." He paused. "Dante will make contact with Chase. I need you to go, take point, and have their backs—in case something goes wrong. Not that I expect it to go wrong. This should be easy, right?" He looked at Mal. "Can you do that? Or are you too close to this."

Mal blew out a long, slow breath, his posture easing.

"Anders?" Finn asked.

Anders nodded. "Definitely."

"Mal?" Finn asked.

"I'm in." Mal nodded. "We should have talked to you. It was a dick move."

"It was," Finn agreed. "But it won't happen again?"

"No. It won't." Mal's promise rang hollow in her ears.

Finn might be satisfied with that, but she wasn't. He'd said he needed it to be the two of them, that he'd never leave her, and he wanted her to be strong. His plan to go after Chase with Anders while leaving her safely with the rest of the pack was not only a lie, but an insult.

I never lie. Those words had made it easier to trust him, to let him in and believe she could do this whole new werewolf-life thing. And later, when she'd learned the whole horrible truth about his family, he'd promised never to lie to her.

Her heart twisted sharply, the urge to cry and lash out warring for control. Forgiving him wasn't an option yet, no matter what her wolf—or his—wanted.

Not that he'd asked for her forgiveness, or acknowledged he'd done anything wrong. Instead of wasting all this pent-up frustration, she might as well find a way to let it out.

"And me? What am I doing?" She looked at Finn.

But his gaze bounced to Mal before he said, "You sit this one out."

She did her best not to glare at Mal or Finn, or throw her cinnamon roll. He—they—expected her to sit by and do nothing? No matter what they said, she wasn't part of the pack—not yet. Why else would Finn keep her here? Or was it for Mal, some sort of ridiculous "protecting the mates" thing? Whatever the reason, it hurt, and deeply wounded her wolf's pride. She stared at her cinnamon roll. "We're done here?" she asked, her voice hard. Space—she desperately needed space. Now.

"Yes." Finn's answer felt final.

"Great," she said, turning on her heel and carrying her breakfast back into the kitchen. She wanted to run, to shift, or bite someone. Biting someone sounded extremely gratifying. Instead, she threw her cinnamon roll into the sink—hard.

The normalcy of Jessa winding up Oscar's swing, talking softly to the smiling baby, grew stifling. Tess's silence was deafening. How could she sit there, flipping through a nature magazine, tracing the pictures with her fingers, when the house was buzzing with energy? The pack was excited about their hunt.

A hunt she wasn't *allowed* to join.

"You okay, Olivia?" Jessa's brow creased.

"While they're off on an important mission, we women get to defend the fort." Olivia tried to tease, but her tone was hard and flat.

Jessa straightened, that odd tightening on her face again. "I'm happy for the company."

Olivia swallowed her temper. None of this was Jessa's fault. Considering the amount of stress the woman was dealing with, Olivia could keep her cool. Jessa was doing her best to act like she was fine, but Olivia suspected it was a brave front. And if Jessa could be brave, so could she. She sucked in a long, slow breath and tried to speak without sounding like she wanted to hurt someone. "Maybe you can give me a few cooking lessons—you know, to pass the time?"

Jessa nodded, smiling. "Oh good. I'm craving some chocolate mousse, and I have a pretty simple recipe."

She forced a smile. "Sounds yummy." It did. And, as she always was after earth-shattering sex with Mal, she was hungry. Making mousse would take care of that. But not her anger. If she was going to bond with her wolf, to hunt and fight and—if necessary—kill, maybe staying home to make chocolate mousse wasn't the best idea.

Chapter Twenty-Two

"Got my big guns and my little guns," Gentry said, all smiles. "And a few knives, too."

"Knives?" Anders asked, grinning.

"A man can never have too much silver around them sons of bitches." Gentry nodded.

"Then watch where you're sticking them." Anders clapped Gentry on the shoulder. "Our wolves aren't too fond of the silver stuff, either."

"Intel, Gentry, intel." Brown expression remained stony, as always. "If done right, you won't need weapons of any sort. I've got three shooters, all men I trust with my life, waiting to meet you when you land in Chicago."

"Well, that sounds like no fun at all." Gentry frowned.

Mal watched the exchange, wishing he could get as amped up as the rest of them. Instead, he was painfully aware of how absent Olivia was. She'd left the room without a backward glance and hadn't been back since. Because he was a stupid shit.

"Get your head straight, Mal," Dante murmured.

Mal nodded. Olivia was pissed. She had every right to be. But there was nothing he could do about it now. Now, he had to focus.

"About two hours from Jackson Hole to Chicago. No more than four hours there, then straight back." He looked at Dante. "You can't get a meeting or, if we're really damn lucky, information on shipments, you walk. Understood? I don't want this to turn into a fight." Finn leveled a hard look at each one of them before continuing. "Mal, you and Brown's recruits will take exits. You're here," Brown said, pointing at the rear door. "Two will cover the front. The other stationed here." he pointed at a tower with a wider range. "In case. Gentry, Anders, and Dante are all going in."

"They've seen Dante," Mal argued.

"In Alaska," Finn said. "If there's one thing we know about Cyrus it's that he keeps his pack regional. The chances of one of them recognizing Dante are slight."

"I fucking hope so," Dante mumbled. "But if not, I don't mind taking a few of them down with me."

Finn sighed.

"He must think you're a big spender," Ellen said as she sat on the corner of the desk. "He will want to impress you."

Dante nodded again. "Wanna come along as arm candy?"

"No," she answered.

"They'd know her," Mal said. "It's not safe."

"You care?" she pushed.

"About jeopardizing the mission? Yes." Mal snapped. He wasn't really pissed at Ellen. She'd told Hollis. And Hollis, being who he was, had told Finn. In the end, this was better… except for Olivia's reaction.

Focus.

"You have"—Finn glanced at his watch—"ten minutes before takeoff." He glanced at Mal. "This can't be about revenge."

He nodded. Finn was giving him an opportunity to repair the damage he'd done. He'd shaken the trust his Alpha had in him. He owed Finn—and Olivia. His mate. The person he loved most. He'd lied to her. No matter how good his intentions were, it had been a jackass move and he knew it. Which meant he had ten minutes to say good-bye. He carried his bag outside to the waiting truck, tossed it into the back, and stared at the lodge.

"Wasting time," Brown said, nodding toward the house. "Bad idea."

Mal headed toward the front door, fully aware that they were all watching him. This was new for them. Hell, it was new for him. He wasn't one for giving a shit about what other people thought. He still wasn't. With one exception.

He pushed through the front door and went into the kitchen. Olivia, her hair slipping from the clip on her head, stood working amongst stacks of bowls, aggressively whisking something.

"Smooth?" she asked, peering doubtfully into the bowl.

"Yes," Jessa said. "It's all in the wrist."

"Apparently, my wrist is faulty," Olivia mumbled, blowing a stray hair from her face.

He could watch her all day.

"What does light and peaked look like?" she asked, glancing at Jessa. But she saw him, and everything about her changed. For one brief moment, she looked so goddamn happy his heart almost thudded out of his chest. But then her anger returned, and she tore her gaze from his.

"You know, I'm not really sure," Jessa said, yawning, cradling Oscar in her arms. "Oscar's finally out, so let me put him down, and I'll come help you."

Olivia continued to ignore him. "You rest. I'll keep trying."

"Need help?" Mal asked Jessa.

Jessa looked pointedly at Olivia. "*I* am fine. Just tired."

She stared at him. "You be careful. I get what you are doing, but it doesn't stop me from worrying about you guys."

Mal nodded. "In and out."

Jessa sighed. "See you soon."

Tess unfolded herself from the corner of the couch, nervously glancing his way before hurrying out of the room.

And still Olivia ignored him.

He crossed the room, his irritation mounting, and pinned her against the kitchen counter with nowhere to go. "I'm sorry."

She didn't look at him.

"I didn't think things through."

"You thought it through with Anders." Her eyes blazed. "You had a plan. You knew exactly what—"

"I messed up," he ground out.

"You *lied*, Mal." Her voice broke. "You promised." She shook her head. "What do I believe now? How do I trust this?"

His frustration bubbled over. "I'm leaving."

"I *know*." She pressed a hand to her chest.

"Dammit," he pulled her against him. He'd done this to her. "I'll be back. Soon."

"I don't like this part," she muttered.

"What?" He didn't like the sadness in her voice.

"Being hurt by you." Her words sliced through him.

He pressed his forehead against hers, reeling. No matter what he said, it wouldn't undo the pain he'd caused them both.

"Don't kill him," she whispered. "Chase."

He tilted her head back. "No one's getting killed." Her hazel gaze searched his, making the ache in his chest ten times worse. She doubted him now—because of what he'd done. He could see it, could feel it. So he added, "But if it comes down to them or us..."

She nodded. "He's a 'them.' I know." She blinked away

the tears in her eyes.

"Olivia..." What could he say?

"Go." She tried to shrug out of his hold, to put space between them, but he couldn't bear it. "You've got stuff to do." Her eyes flashed.

"Kiss me?" he pleaded, leaning forward.

The brush of her lips against his wasn't going to cut it. Only cupping her face, savoring the softness of her mouth, sliding his tongue inside would satisfy. The kiss went on until her posture eased and her hands gripped his shirt, holding on to him—he needed her to hold on to him.

The rev of the engine was hard to miss. Someone laid on the truck horn.

She broke away from him. "They're waiting for you."

He nodded, staring long and hard at her before leaving the room and slamming out the front door.

"Better?" Anders asked as Mal climbed into the truck.

He pulled the door shut, peering out the window at the empty front porch. No, it wasn't fucking better. Knowing what he'd done to her? Fuck no. His chest hurt. But worrying about Olivia wouldn't do any of them any good. He shoved it all down and tuned into the conversation taking place.

"You want a knife?" Gentry asked. "In case Chase is a threat?"

Mal shook his head. "It won't come to that." He'd given Finn his word, and he'd keep it, no matter what. "Chase isn't a fighter. If he suspects anything, he'll run."

"How do you know?" Anders asked.

"When they jumped him, Olivia tried to stop it. He ran—leaving her." He bit out the last two words, trying not to think about the state she had been in when they'd met.

"You shitting me?" Gentry called back from the driver's seat.

"No." Mal's hands fisted at his side. She was one of them

now, the surge of anger and hostility filling the cab of the black SUV confirming it. "She wants him to live."

"He's still her brother." Dante nodded. "But damn, that's got to be a hard pill to swallow, knowing everything."

"He's sort of the bad guy here," Anders reminded them.

"No," Mal argued. "Chase is a waste of humanity, but he's not the prize. Cyrus is. We find out where to find him, how to hunt him—we have an edge. We have surprise." He didn't want a pack war any more that Finn did. They might be stronger than the Others, but their numbers couldn't compare. There was no guarantee Chase would know something to help them with Cyrus, but if they could help those girls—expose the trafficking ring—that was more than enough.

Dante nodded. "Not that I'm opposed to seeing this Chase kid bleed a little."

Mal grinned; he couldn't help it. "Agreed."

•••

Jessa was in labor. Mal had been driving away when her first cry reached Olivia. For the past thirty minutes, Jessa's ragged moans and screams spilled down the hallway. Olivia was helpless—and useless. Hollis and Ellen were with Jessa. Finn was with her.

At Finn's request, Brown was in the control room, tracking Mal's group while staying close to Tess—Brown was never far from his daughter.

Tess hadn't moved. She sat, staring down the hall, at Jessa's room.

"She'll be okay," Olivia said to her. She talked to the woman all the time, unable to pretend she wasn't there. She was a living, breathing person, even if she didn't necessarily act like it. "She's strong. Ellen and Hollis know what they're doing." Maybe Hollis didn't, but Ellen did. At least she acted like it.

An especially loud cry echoed down the hall. Olivia winced, gripping the kitchen towel in both hands. Poor Jessa. Poor Finn. She hurt for them.

Pain was a part of a normal childbirth. This wasn't normal. She wished Mal were here. Even with her mad at him, he'd ease the anxiety in her gut.

Oscar was playing on his mat on the floor, content and clueless. She joined him, needing a happy distraction. "How's your day going? You look pleased with yourself." She held one of his little fists in each of her hands. "Yep, you're getting stronger every day."

Oscar cooed, loudly, startling himself.

"That was all you, big guy." She laughed. How could holding something so small make everything feel better? She lifted Oscar and sat back, bracing him on her knees. He pushed his legs straight and flailed his arms in excitement. "I know. You are adorable."

Oscar squealed, his smile full or bubbles and gurgles.

She shook her head. "You don't say?" She ran her hand over his head, smoothing the blond curls. "Want to read a book? I have this amazing one that counts to five." She picked up the padded red, white, and black illustrated book, and Oscar's gaze focused. "Riveting stuff, right?"

She flipped the pages, watching his animated expressions as his bright blue eyes narrowed then drooped. She hadn't realized she'd drifted off until a shrill beep flooded the room. Her arms tightened around Oscar's sleeping form, senses immediately on alert.

It beeped again.

"Fire alarm?" she asked, holding Oscar close as she stood.

Jessa's door opened, and Hollis emerged. "What's up?"

"I don't know." She bounced Oscar on her hip. "Oscar and I were chilling out with Tess— "

Tess was gone. Olivia spun, searching the corners for the woman's favorite spots. No sign of her.

The alarm beeped, setting her nerves on edge.

"Brown?" Hollis asked.

She shook her head, foreboding crushing in on her. "Still in the control room?" Something was wrong. Her wolf was pushing, eager to come out.

Another beep.

Hollis ran down the other hall, past the gym to the control room. Olivia waited, staring after him. When Hollis came back, her fears were confirmed. "No Brown."

"Jessa?" Olivia asked.

"She's close." He ran a hand over his face.

"I'll find him. Tess was freaking out over Jessa. He's probably calming her down." It was a logical explanation. But her wolf didn't believe a word of it. "Or maybe she got scared and ran, and Brown followed her." Another possibility her wolf dismissed.

Finn came stomping down the hall, wild-eyed and tense. "What's happening?"

"Tess is gone. Brown isn't in the control room," she said calmly.

Finn stiffened, bracing. "Call Mal back," he told Hollis.

"Wait," Olivia said, knowing how important their mission was. "Give me five minutes to find them."

Finn's eyes narrowed. "What does your wolf say, Olivia?"

She frowned. "Something's not right."

Finn nodded. "Call them back." Hollis headed again to the control room.

"Let me do something, Finn. You kept me here for a reason. Don't tell me it was to babysit while the others are protecting the pack." She swallowed. "I need to *do* something."

Finn rolled his neck. "Track them—at a distance. I mean it, Olivia, stay upwind and out of sight. When you find them, head straight back to report."

She nodded, her wolf thrilled.

"At a distance. If something is wrong, you get back here." Finn's brows rose high. "No taking chances, you hear me?"

"I hear you." She nodded. "Oscar?"

Finn took the baby. "Be safe Olivia, or Mal will rip my goddamn head off." He headed back down the hall to Jessa.

She ran from the house. Her skin was aching, the pull and push of bones and muscles making her itch. Whatever was happening, her wolf demanded control. Olivia breathed through it, relaxing her mind and body. It hurt, but not the way she imagined it would. She had to push to find the relief on the other side. When her claws sliced through her knuckles and her skin gave way to fur, the shift was over.

Her wolf was running, pausing to sniff and search. Her ears perked up, shifting through the sounds of the forest for something else—some sign of Brown or Tess. But she was too agitated, her senses all over the place.

She let instinct take over. Through the forest. Over two mountains. Up high, in the snow.

Her wolf found Brown's scent. Sour. Stressed. Musky. He was running hard.

Tess's scent joined his now.

Olivia slowed, not wanting to intrude on father and daughter. At the same time, she couldn't leave without knowing they were okay. Why had he left his post? Why had they run off—now, when Jessa was so vulnerable.

She passed through a ravine, ears alert, and paused.

Brown sat in the snow several feet from Tess. Tess's wolf sat, uneasy, at his side. Olivia's wolf moved into the trees, watching.

Her heart ached for Brown. He'd never give up on his daughter. He didn't care that she was a wolf, or that her human form was utterly broken. The man was loyal and patient.

Whatever had brought her out here, he seemed content to wait until she decided it was time to return to the lodge. He loved his daughter.

An image of her father popped up. He'd had the biggest laugh. People loved him; he had a sort of magnetic pull that made them want his approval. She'd always had it. Chase always tried. It was hard to reconcile that man, her father, with what she now knew of him. For all his charm and affluence, she would trade her memories of him for one moment with a father like Brown. To sit in silence, knowing he was there for her—no judgment, just love. Did Tess know how lucky she was? Did she know she had a second chance here, a chance at a good life?

Brown looked at his daughter, speaking to her softly—too soft for Olivia to hear.

Tess's wolf's ears dropped, her tail wagged, but she didn't move.

Brown smiled.

Olivia's wolf tensed. A new scent. New but familiar. And terrifying. And a ripple in the air so strong, her wolf pressed down under the trees. Memories and fear crowded in on her. Of punching Chase, being stabbed, and getting thrown in the back of a van. This scent belonged to the creature responsible for that. Which was nothing when compared with what he'd done to Mal—tearing his throat out. Skinning him.

Fury choked out fear. Her wolf coiled, aching to pounce—to attack. Byron was here, somewhere.

Tess perked up, her eyes focusing on a distant point. She stood, ears pivoting, then looked directly at Olivia.

She knew? She knew they were coming. And she'd led Brown here.

Two more distinct scents reached her. Scents she didn't recognize rapidly approached, coming through the ravine at her back. Others.

Something cold and hard was pressed against her head. "Shift or he bleeds out on the snow."

Olivia's wolf fought her, wanting to run or howl. She glared up at the man, ignoring the gun he pressed against her skull.

"Now," he repeated, smiling.

She did, and her wolf fought her the entire time. Her lungs ached, gasping for air when he grabbed her by the hair and yanked her to her feet. Her wolf fought to be free, aching to protect her—and go for the jugular.

"Damn shame," the man said. "Boss claimed you."

Olivia was still recovering from the shift and couldn't speak. Cyrus had claimed her?

"Come on," the other one said, far less interested in her. "The sooner we get this over with, the better. Even if we don't get the other female, we have her."

Olivia tripped over her own feet, the man's hold punishing her scalp and dragging her behind him. Why were they here? What did they want?

"Shit." Brown stood, his hand going to his waist.

"Nope." The man holding Olivia pointed the gun at her.

"You were supposed to come alone," the other man said to Tess.

Tess cowered, her eyes shifting to the ground.

"They're coming," Olivia said, looking at Brown. "Finn. His pack."

"No one's coming." The man yanked her hair for good measure.

The other one sighed. "You mark her, he's gonna be pissed."

The man smiled at her. "He won't care."

"He will." It was Byron—big, tall, and emerging from the trees like nothing out of the ordinary was taking place. "Mr. Brown, you were not supposed to be here. I apologize for this.

Give it to me, Jake."

Jake handed Byron the gun.

"Silencer," Byron added.

Jake frowned. "Why do we—"

"No backup," Byron ground out. "You shoot, you announce our presence."

Jake rifled through his backpack, handing the silencer to Bryon.

Panic clamped down on Olivia's throat. Byron wouldn't need a silencer if he wasn't going to use the gun. The air grew charged, crackling with anticipation.

Tess whimpered then, stepping between the two men. She glanced back at Brown, her whimpering more desperate.

"He can't follow us." Byron's voice was sharp. He fired once, and Brown crumpled to the ground. "You've outlived your usefulness." He fired again, and Tess collapsed, flopping to the snow. His gaze shifted to her. "We have you. Once we have the Alpha's mate and his pups, Cyrus will see how much he underestimated us. We get them all, and he'll welcome us back."

Had Tess brought them here to lead them to the compound—for Jessa and the children? Olivia stared, horrified, as the snow beneath her bare feet turned a brilliant red.

Chapter Twenty-Three

"Something tripped the alarm." Hollis's voice crackled in Mal's earpiece.

"Turn around," he barked.

Gentry did, not bothering to slow his speed.

"Brown's take?" Mal asked.

"We don't know where he is," Hollis answered. "Or Tess. Jessa's in labor," he continued. "So Olivia's gone after them."

"Did Tess know Jessa was in labor?" Mal's gut tightened. Tess was the plant. Not Ellen. Tess—too wounded to be suspect. *Fucking idiot.*

Hollis paused. "Yes."

"Headed back," Mal said. "Put down the blast doors, seal everything up. This is not a fucking drill. They know where we are, and they are coming."

There was silence.

"Tess?" Hollis's surprise was almost funny. Almost.

"Now, Hollis," Mal snapped. "We're fucking idiots."

"Floor it," Dante bit out.

"You really think they're coming?" Anders asked.

"They want the baby. Hell, Jessa, the baby, Oscar, and Ellen, too. Jessa's in labor—they're vulnerable." Mal shook his head, his stomach turning to lead. "If Cyrus is as obsessed with breeding the pack as Ellen says he is…"

"Jessa's like a magic decoder ring," Anders finished. "Shit. Drive man. Drive."

Mal shut the world out. His wolf wanted blood, and Mal wasn't going to hold him back. As soon as the SUV slammed to a stop, he jumped out. "Big guns. Lots of silver," he yelled at Gentry. "Be ready."

He started running, shifting as he went. His wolf sped up, flying across the ground. Anders and Dante were close behind, feeling the need to hunt.

His wolf scented Olivia immediately, drawing her in as he tore across the ground. There was no time to waste—

A gun shot—muffled but distinct—echoed in the trees. Then another.

He almost stumbled, his heart coming to an abrupt halt. It wasn't Olivia. He'd know if it were. She was strong and alive and full of fight. She needed him, and he wasn't going to let her down. His wolf focused on fury. His vision faded to red, the thud of his heart pulsing heavily in his ears, his nose sorting through the earth and must of the forest. Focus, not fear, would keep him moving—and strong.

The scent of the Others forced a shudder down his spine.

One Other in particular. Byron the butcher. His wolf snapped his jaws, craving the fight. Not yet, not yet. He slowed, exchanged a look with Anders and Dante, and headed through the ravine. They moved on silent feet, alert and ready. His wolf did his best to sneak up, find an angle, look for a weakness—but all he could think about was getting to Olivia.

Blood, so much blood. His nostrils burned from the metallic tang in the air.

Byron liked to make his victims bleed.

His wolf tensed, ready to spring, but Mal reined him in again. A quick glance told him Byron wasn't alone.

He didn't recognize them—two nameless Other drones doing Cyrus's bidding.

Olivia. Naked. Shivering. Her hair gripped tight by one of the men. Mal's wolf would take great pleasure in removing that hand.

Anders nudged his haunch, forcing Mal to focus.

Byron held a gun in his hand. And, fuck, Brown lay on the ground in a pool of blood. Tess lay beside him.

"She said they were coming," the one holding Olivia said.

"Of course she did. Let go of her before you damage her." Byron smiled at Olivia. "What else can she say?"

"That you're going to die." She spoke slowly, clearly. She was beautiful and fierce, staring Byron down. Pride rolled over him. This was his mate. Why hadn't he recognized what she was capable of instead of trying to shelter her?

Byron's eyes narrowed. "Are you going to kill me, little wolf?"

It took everything Mal had not to charge. The fucking smirk on Byron's face was all too familiar. Every time he'd filleted his back, he'd looked like that—smug, taunting, and fearless.

"You have a gun," Olivia argued. "Hardly a fair fight."

"Hardly a fair fight?" Byron laughed, tossing the gun onto the ground. "Now it is? You like to fight, little wolf?"

Olivia scowled at him. "I can fight."

Byron sighed. "I'd enjoy your fight. If Cyrus didn't want you for himself, I'd take you. Again and again." He leaned forward, stroking her cheek, then her collarbone. "But an Alpha has certain rights." His gaze fell to her breasts, leaving no room for misinterpretation.

Mal saw red. His wolf's control was gone. He leaped through the air, closing the distance between him and Byron in a matter of steps. He saw the surprise in Byron's eyes, then the anticipation. As much as he wanted to go for the bastard's jugular, he needed Olivia safe.

But she had other ideas. She shifted, chasing the dumbass that had tried to hold her captive.

His wolf was amused. Olivia could handle things. He needed to let her.

The wolf cared about one thing: killing Byron. There were no silver blades or collars to weaken him this time. He couldn't wait to show the son of a bitch a thing or two about karma. He stepped back, wanting him to shift. Byron nodded, the condescending smile on his face adding fire to Mal's already blazing rage.

He could attack him mid-shift, when he was weak and vulnerable. It was what the Others would have done to him. Had done. No matter how much he wanted vengeance, he would never stoop that low.

He waited, unimpressed by the defensive display Byron's gray wolf put on. He could bare his teeth and growl all day long—Mal was in no hurry. He'd been waiting for this for so long.

Byron went for his leg, flipping him onto his back and biting into the meat connecting his hip and thigh. Mal curled, biting into Byron's nose and holding tight. Even after Byron released him, Mal held on, crushing bone.

He heard the gunshot, felt the sting of the bullet, and his back leg gave out. The thick, white heat of silver buried itself on his hip. He let go.

Motherfucking Others. Fucking cowards didn't respect a challenge—didn't respect shit. Byron circled him, sinking his teeth into his injured leg and tugging. It was a dick move, but it wasn't going to slow him down.

Mal shook off the stupor of the silver, shut out the pain, and attacked. He ripped one of Byron's ears free, the spurt of blood invigorating. For every bite Byron made, Mal bit harder. He tore at his fur, clawed through the skin of his stomach, and tore through the muscles of his neck. He knew he'd win this fight. He had no choice.

Byron rolled, trying to knock him lose. Mal let go long enough to clamp onto his throat. His teeth sunk deep, his jaws locking in place. After the hell Byron had put him through, Mal enjoyed toying with him.

But he saw Olivia. She nudged Brown with her nose, her long broken whimper grounding him. Sadness clamped onto his heart. No vengeance could heal today. This was over now. He bit hard, snapping Byron's neck and letting the wolf fall. He watched the gray wolf return to its human form. He was dead. The bastard was no longer a threat.

"Brown's not dead," Anders said. "They shot him clean through the shoulder." He patted Mal's shoulder.

"We need to get back," Dante said. "If the rest of them are coming, we need to be there."

Olivia was struggling to stand, her hand pressed to a gash in her thigh. He ran to her side, trying not to bristle when she stepped away. "They're not. Getting Jessa and the babies was Byron's way of redeeming himself to Cyrus." She rubbed her forehead with the back of her forearm. "This was Byron's plan. The Others don't know where he is."

Relief rolled over him, over all of them. The air seemed cleaner, lighter. Olivia was safe. So was the pack. Brown was alive. And fucking Byron was dead. All in all, a good day. Until he realized Anders and Dante were doing their best not to notice how naked Olivia was. Considering how gorgeous she was, it was damn impossible to do. Or maybe he was still being too overprotective. Either way, there was nothing he could do about it. With the burn of silver in his leg, there was no shifting.

"How's your leg?" she asked, hesitating briefly before

running her hand along his shoulder.

He groaned, pushing his head against her side and neck. He rubbed and rubbed, burying his nose against her chest and leaning into her.

She held his head in her hands and stared into his eyes. Her pain gutted him.

He had a hundred things to say to her and no way to say it. He nudged her with his nose, steering her toward the path home.

"We're not leaving Tess here," she protested. "I'll carry her if I have to."

That's when Mal realized Tess was still a wolf. Which meant she was healing. And, good or bad, she was still alive.

•••

Olivia sat in stony silence at the dinner table. While the rest of the pack was celebrating the birth of Jessa and Finn's baby girl, Olivia was consumed with guilt. Mal sat across from her, his eyes never leaving her face. Did he know she was close to losing it? She'd killed someone. How did they do this? Cope with it?

Yes, the man had shot Mal—and she'd seen vivid red—but she had taken a life. In that moment, it had been the only thing to do. If she hadn't, Mal would be dead.

Her gaze met his.

Mal.

Who'd left her and lied to her and made her feel whole. Saving him was all that mattered.

She was crying. At the table. In front of everyone.

"Olivia?" Anders patted on her back. "You okay?"

She sniffed, nodding.

"Does she look okay?" Ellen asked.

"No?" Dante asked.

"Killing someone is hard," Ellen answered. "Especially the first time."

"Y-yes." Olivia sniffed. The first time? She wasn't sure she could do that again. But remembering that man pointing his gun at Mal… Yes, she'd do it again. "It is. But I'm fine."

"She was amazing," Dante said, smiling at her. "As soon as that gun went off, she was on him. Saved Mal's ass."

"I'm fine," she repeated.

"Leave her alone." Mal's growl silenced the room.

And it infuriated her. "I don't need you to talk for me."

Mal's eyes narrowed.

But she wasn't done. "Or make decisions for me. Or lie to me. Or…or leave me when you swore, you promised, you never would. I'm fine."

All eyes were on them, the energy in the room charged. They were waiting. For what?

"Olivia." Mal's voice was low—awkward and tight. "Let's go talk—"

"Somewhere private?" She shook her head. "I don't think being alone with you is a good idea."

Anders chuckle turned into a smothered cough.

"You're mad?"

She stared at him, stunned. "That is one of the many emotions I'm experiencing."

Mal's nostrils flared. "My day hasn't been a fucking picnic, either."

"No?" Her voice shook.

"No. Once I knew you were in danger, I couldn't get back here fast enough." He pushed out of his chair and stalked around the table. "I didn't give a shit about anything but you. And it scared the shit out of me. Be pissed. Yell at me. Do whatever you need to do. But don't expect me to let you out of my sight again." He leaned forward, his hands gripping the chair. "I can't go through that again."

She hadn't expected that. Not from Mal. Not here, surrounded by the entire pack. The dam broke, tearing a ragged sob from her throat.

One minute she was sitting in her chair, and the next Mal had scooped her up and was carrying her to their room. And even though she was still mad at him, it felt so good to be in his arms. He kicked the door shut behind them and sat her on the edge of the bed.

"I wasn't done," she hiccupped.

"You weren't eating." He stared down at her. "Talk to me."

"Where do I start? I'm a wreck. My head won't stop spinning." She rubbed her face with her hands. "I didn't *do* anything. I should have done something." She'd dreamed of being some avenging angel, swooping in and protecting her pack. Instead, she'd been dragged around by her hair.

"You saved my life."

"We're even," she murmured.

He knelt in front of her. "Like hell we are." Mal stared at her, his gaze sweeping over her face. "You saved me long before today. It was back in that cage, in that nightmare. I had a new reason to live—a reason that was good."

She stared at him, her heart pounding in her chest.

"You showed me how to trust. How to believe. How to love." He shook his head. "And I still screw it up."

"By lying," she whispered. Even now, after everything, it was there—too raw to ignore.

His head fell forward with a groan. "I can't take it back. If I could, I swear I would. It will never happen again—ever. I can't stand you looking at me like this. Like I've disappointed you."

Pain edged his words, and regret. She tilted his head up, craving his gaze on her. His brown eyes were haunted—desperate.

He tilted her face up, toward him. "I'm not going to figure this out overnight. I need you to show me how to do this. I need you in my life to remind me of the good. To keep me from living in the dark."

She wanted to believe him. "Then why do you keep trying to shelter me from things? This is my life now, too. I'm not some weak, incapable creature."

He groaned. "You're not weak. You're stronger than me. You look monsters in the eye and stand your ground." One warm hand cradled her cheek. "And it scares the shit out of me. Not because you can't take care of yourself, but that you can. That you won't need me anymore." He broke off, swallowing. "I will always try to protect you, Olivia. Always. Not because I doubt you, but because I'd rather filter out whatever bad I can before it gets to you."

Her wolf was satisfied. Olivia wanted to be, too. "Don't lie to me again, Mal. There have been too many lies in my life. I don't want them between us." She crossed her arms over her chest.

He nodded once. "All I could think about is you in that cage, what might have happened if I hadn't been there," he whispered, leaning forward. "I didn't want to leave you. I'll never want to. But I told you I'd do what I could to make sure no one else ends up there. If I have to leave, next time you'll go with me. No more lies, okay?" He clenched his jaw, his voice raw. "Forgive me."

She had no choice. "I do."

He melted into her, sliding his arms around her waist and pulling her flush against his chest. "You were fucking amazing today."

She stroked the side of his face. "Today was hard. But I'll do whatever I have to to keep from losing you."

"Never going to happen," he said, leaning forward. "I'll never let you go." He kissed her softly. "Never. You hear me?"

She nodded. “I hear you.”

He ran his fingers through her hair. “I love you, Olivia. I know this life isn’t what you imagined living, but I’ll do my best to make you happy.”

She ran her nose along his and up along his brow. “In every way possible?” she asked, her lips soft on his.

“Every fucking way,” he said against her mouth.

Epilogue

"How's the kid?" Mal rubbed the towel over his head, drying his hair.

"*She* is great. Jessa is, too. I think she and Finn are having the talk." She took the towel from him, running the thick fabric over his broad shoulders and down his back.

He chuckled. "Considering they have a kid, I think it might be a little late for the talk."

"I meant the turning Jessa into a wolf talk." Her lips replaced the towel, pressing feather-light kisses over each scar.

"Bother you?" The vulnerability in his dark eyes was worse than the scars.

"Only knowing what you went through." She moved to stand in front of him, sliding her arms around his neck and smiling up at him.

"Took three Others down, who-the-hell-knows how many more to go. It doesn't make what happened better or erase what they're doing, but we're going to stop them. It's a start." His fingers traced the side of her neck. "Your skin is so soft."

She arched into his touch.

His hand paused. "Jessa wants to be a wolf?"

She giggled. "You just caught that?"

"You distract the hell out of me." His eyes bored into hers. "Why would she want that?"

She shook her head. "Because she wants to be a part of Finn's world. Every part of his world." Her fingers slid through Mal's thick, damp hair. "And their children. It's got to be hard not to be there for them, too." It was beyond imagining. "It would be unbearable not being a wolf, not running with you. I wouldn't want to."

"So, you're happy?" There was that vulnerability again.

"Yes." Her grin widened. "I love that my wolf is faster than yours. And that I'm learning to be as stealthy as Ellen—"

"No one is as stealthy as Ellen." She didn't miss the hint of frustration in his tone. Ellen was still a mystery—but at least she wasn't their enemy. In the weeks since Byron's failed kidnapping attempt, she and Ellen had developed a friendship. Sort of. "Glad she's on our side."

She nodded. "Glad she's going with you guys to Chicago." She wanted to go, too, but Finn wouldn't let her. Chase was a bad-guy, and stupid, but he was still her brother. He held the key to ending Cyrus's trafficking, something none of Finn's pack was prepared to sweep aside. She couldn't jeopardize that. Mal had offered to stay with her, but she'd insisted he go. Mal needed to go—for those girls and their families.

Gentry and Brown fed tips to every military and police connection they had. Knowing the docks were being watched for any sign of Cyrus's shipments was a huge comfort. So was Ellen's willingness, albeit reluctant, to help them. Mal was right on that front, as well. Ellen wasn't an Other. But why she'd stayed with them remained a mystery to them all.

"Hey." The word was low, gruff, and delicious, pulling her

back into the present.

She was in her mate's arms. And he wanted, and deserved, all of her attention.

"I am faster than you." She tugged his head down to hers, pressing a kiss to his lips.

"You are," he said, his lips brushing hers as he added. "Faster. Softer." His hand gripped her breast.

The rigid length of his arousal pressed against her hip. "You win in the rock-hard category." As his hand slid under her hair to cup her head, she arched against him.

"Your fault." He sucked her lower lip into his mouth.

Her breath hitched. She loved what she did to him. And, oh, the things he did to her. No matter how many days they spent tangled up in each other, it was never enough. One look, a single touch, and her body throbbed to life. She craved him like her lungs craved air.

"My fault?" she whispered as his lips moved to her neck. "Are you complaining?"

"Hell no," he mumbled. His teeth nipped her neck. "No complaints." His lips brushed hers. "You're mine. That's all I need."

She smiled against his mouth, her fingers twining in his thick, dark hair. "You're talking too much."

He lifted his head, chuckling. "You have something else in mind?"

She nodded, tugging the towel from his waist and pressing herself against him. "I do."

He growled, his hands sliding up and under her shirt. "I like the way your mind works."

About the Author

Sasha grew up surrounded by books. Her passions have always been storytelling, romance, history, and travel. Her first play was written for her Girl Scout troop. She's been writing ever since. She loves getting lost in the worlds and characters she creates; even if she frequently forgets to run the dishwasher or wash socks when she's doing so. Luckily, her four brilliant children and hero-inspiring hubby are super understanding and supportive.

Discover the Blood Moon Brotherhood series

FALLING FOR THE BILLIONAIRE WOLF AND HIS BABY

PROTECTING THE WOLF'S MATE

Also by Sasha A. Summers

ACCIDENTALLY FAMILY

Discover more paranormal romance from Entangled...

The Werewolf Wears Prada

a San Francisco Wolf Pack novel by Kristin Miller

Melina Rosenthal worships at the altar of all things fashion. Her dream is to work for the crème de la crème fashion magazine, *Eclipse*, and she'll do pretty much anything to get there. Even fixing up the image of a gorgeous, sexy public figure who's all playboy, all the time. Even if he's the guy who broke her heart a year ago. And even if Melina has no idea that Hayden Dean is actually a werewolf...

Playing the Witch's Game

a Keepers of the Veil novel by Zoe Forward

Pleiades witch Jennifer Marcos is certain that the host of *Extreme Survivor* is her soulmate. All she has to do is find a fake boyfriend, get on the show, and *voila*! She'll have her destiny. Unfortunately, she has to rely on ex-Russian spy Nikolai Jovec's six-foot-something of gorgeous, infuriating hotness. To make matters worse, the electric attraction between Jen and Nikolai is hotter than ever. But the only way Nikolai can protect Jen is by hiding the identity of her true Destined...*him.*

The Alpha's Temporary Mate

a Fated Match novel by Victoria Davies

Witch and matchmaker, Chloe Donovan, takes pride in helping her clients find their happy endings. But when werewolf alpha and millionaire playboy Kieran Clearwater stalks into her office, she may have finally met the one man she can't help. For Kieran, love is a weakness he can't afford, but he coerces Chloe to be his fake girlfriend. While these two burn hot when they're together, behind-the-scenes politics work to rip them apart.

Baby's Got Bite

a Take it Like a Vamp novel by Candace Havens

What could go wrong after hooking up with a super-sexy bad boy at her best friend's wedding? Ten weeks later, a pregnant Bennett Langdon has her answer. Linc Monahan isn't supposed to be able to father a child with a human. He has to find some way to tell Bennett that not only do werewolves exist, but she's about to have a baby with one. Then word of their surprise conception gets out. Now Bennett and Linc aren't just fighting each other… they're fighting for their lives.